I0588296

WICKED fortune

NEW YORK TIMES BESTSELLING AUTHOR
J. KENNER

All rights reserved.

No part of this publication may be sold, copied, distributed, reproduced or transmitted in any form or by any means, mechanical or digital, including photocopying and recording or by any information storage and retrieval system without the prior written permission of both the publisher, Oliver Heber Books and the author, Julie Kenner except in the case of brief quotations embodied in critical articles and reviews.

PUBLISHER'S NOTE: This is a work of fiction. Names, characters, places, and incidents either are the product of the author's imagination or are used fictitiously. Any resemblance to actual persons, living or dead, business establishments, events, or locales is entirely coincidental.

Wicked Fortune Copyright 2025 © Julie Kenner

Release Me excerpt Copyright 2013 © Julie Kenner

Cover design by T.M. Franklin

Cover art by depositphotos.com, ©epic22, ©stokkete

Published by Oliver-Heber Books

0 9 8 7 6 5 4 3 2 1

AUTHOR'S NOTE

This book takes place in Los Angeles, and as I sit here proofing the final pre-publication document, the fires are still raging through that city I once called my own. I spent several happy years practicing law in SoCal and was thrilled to call myself an Angeleno. I love LA. Always have and always will, and my heart goes out to everyone who has suffered through the horror of those fires.

ONE

The dream is always the same.

My parents have gone out, and I'm trapped in my own living room, held tight in the prison of the monster's arms, my back pressed against his chest.

I whimper, but I don't yell. I know the rules. The monster reminds me of them every time he comes. I'm eight and I know how to follow rules. I'm a good girl. I do what I'm told.

But I don't want to do this at all.

I whimper again, and the arm around me tightens. My captor whispers words in his monster language, but I squeeze my eyes closed and try not to hear or feel or even exist.

It doesn't work.

I don't want to be here. Downstairs. This close to the monster.

I don't want to be in the house at all.

Mommy says there aren't really monsters. That there's nothing bad hiding in my room or lurking under my bed.

She's right about my room. But not about the monsters.

I open my eyes, and hot tears snake down my cheeks. "I want to go," I whisper.

Except I don't. I say it only in my head, because I'm not supposed to talk. He told me the rules. And when a monster gives you rules, you have to follow them.

I start to squeeze my eyes shut, and that's when I see *him*.

My eyes go wide as I gape at the man. He's dressed all in black, his body flattened into the shadows on the staircase. I don't know him. I don't even know the monster holding me. Not really. I only know Celia, my babysitter, who invited the monster into the house. Who brought him last time, too, and the time before that. She says it's only a game, but I don't like how he touches me. I don't want to play that game again.

But this time, the Stair Man is here, and he's looking toward me, and I don't know what to do. I want to call out. Maybe the Stair Man will help me. But before I can yell, he puts a finger to his lips, and little tickles of hope dance in my belly.

I don't let myself believe, though.

It happens fast, as things sometimes do in nightmares and memories. One minute the monster has me in his grip. The next, I'm clinging to the Stair Man as he uses bad words and a voice like a knife to tell Celia and the monster to get out. To go. And to never, ever come back.

The words are like music, and my body wants to burst from the warm wash of joy that spills through me when the icy terror finally slithers away.

Tears clog my throat as the Stair Man carries me up the winding staircase. "He won't be back. Not ever." The Stair Man's voice isn't sharp now. It's as soft as Mr. Quack, the yellow stuffed toy I've had for as long as I can remember.

I cling to him, and that's when the tears finally flow. Fear. Relief. A whole wash of emotion that feels too big for my small body.

The Stair Man makes shushing noises as he tucks me into bed with Mr. Quack, then whispers that it will be okay.

I believe him. Then he turns out my light and leaves, but I'm still not scared. He's there, somewhere in the house. He saved me from the monster. He'll stay to watch over me until my parents come home.

I roll over and try to sleep, but I can't. My body aches. My breasts are swollen. I feel a needy pressure between my legs. I'm Aurora and I did sleep after all. I slept for years. I had to. How else could I catch up to the Stair Man?

I'm no longer in my little girl nightie. Now, I'm all grown up in a lacy camisole with matching panties. He's with me, and I realize the Stair Man isn't a Stair Man at all. He's a cat, with feline cunning and grace. With eyes that see right through me, and a tongue that works magic on every inch of my body.

I try to see his face, but I can't. Not really. No matter how hard I look, he's always in soft focus. All I can see are deep green eyes and a taunting smile.

"Please," I whisper. Those gorgeous eyes narrow, and I fear he's going to ease away from me. That he'll disappear from my bed, from the house, from this city. *From me.*

But then a flash of heat fires behind the green. I barely have time to breathe before his mouth finds mine. Before his hands are stroking me, undressing me.

His lips tease over my bare belly, sliding down until his tongue is dancing along the elastic of my panties, then lower and lower until I'm arching up. Until my hands are fisting in the sheets, and I'm trying not to scream as he brings my body to life, sending heat racing through me only to pool back between my legs until I'm shattering beneath him, crying out for him, gasping from the power of the orgasm that has almost broken me.

I reach for him, trying to pull him down. I'm weak with longing. Ridiculous with need. I feel as though I'll die if he doesn't ride me hard. If he doesn't take me over again and again and again.

But he doesn't.

He never does.

Instead, he brushes a kiss over my lips, then disappears, leaving me alone on my bed. My fingers grasp the tousled sheets. My heart pounds in my chest. And I clench my thighs together in a desperate attempt to cling to the lingering wisps of passion that twine through me.

But it's no use, and I whimper as my eyes flutter open, pulling me out of the world of dreams. I fight back a soft moan, hating that I feel the loss of him so much. This man I haven't seen for twenty years. Who I barely saw that night, hidden as he was in the shadows.

He's a man who lives only in my memory. And in my fantasies. A man I can't control. A shadow. A savior. *A fiend.*

A bastard and a thieving son-of-a-bitch.

And a jerk, to boot.

He may have saved me from the monster, but he betrayed me, too. And now—when he slides into my dreams—I hate how much I crave the fantasy. How much I crave *him*, a man whose face I've never fully seen and whose name I do not know.

Once, I'd called him the Stair Man. But that was before I learned the truth. That he'd broken in to steal from my family. A damn cat burglar.

I should hate him, but I can't. Despite knowing the truth about him, what started as a little girl's gratitude for being saved has turned into an erotic escape where I imagine his hands, his lips, his tongue.

His cock.

I still remember the feel of his chest and arms as he carried me up the stairs, then tucked me safely into bed. I recall the musky scent of cologne that tickled my nose.

At the time, it had been only a pleasant, safe aroma. Over the years, though, my innocent childhood thoughts devolved into deliciously erotic fantasies. And now that woody, citrus scent makes my nipples peak and my core tighten and tingle with longing.

Acqua di Parma Colonia. An elegant, timeless scent. And popular enough in Los Angeles that I often feel like Pavlov's dog, brought to arousal by that familiar fragrance, only to sag with disappointment when the random man who caught my attention lacks even an inkling of the presence and bearing of The Cat.

"Idiot," I mutter, as I force myself fully awake, then rub my face, as if that will scatter the unwanted memory and the dream it sired.

The dream is always the same.

But this time, it had been different. I frown, trying to grab the tail of the dream before it fades.

Jenny.

The memory of my friend hits me like a slap, and a cold chill rushes through my veins.

Jenny had been there when the dream began, whispering to me while the monster held me. Begging me to help her. But how could I when I was trapped myself? And now that she's dead, what help could I possibly be?

A wave of caustic sadness rolls through me. It's too late. I don't even know what I could have done back then. Maybe I'd missed a sign. A cry for help that she—

"Dammit, Aria!" Bree's voice beckons from the other side of my bedroom door, and I jump, now fully jarred from the dream world. "Will you turn off the stupid alarm and get out here? I'm starving!"

"Sorry! Sorry!" She's right—my phone is squalling. I roll

over and slap the screen to turn off the alarm. "Gimme five secs."

I yank on the leggings and long-sleeved tee I'd left hanging on the back of the closet, then hurry into the living area. As soon as she sees me, she cocks her head, raises her brows, and says, "Another erotic fling with Mr. Cat?"

I grimace. Sometimes having a lifelong bestie can be a real pain in the ass. "It's *The* Cat," I tell her. "And a girl doesn't dream and tell."

She just crosses her arms and lifts a brow.

"Fine," I say. "He was there, it was hot, enough said. Just put away your prurient fantasies for a sec and listen to me, okay?"

Her dark eyes widen at the edge in my voice, but she nods.

"Jenny." I cross my arms, letting the name hang there as I give her my most meaningful stare.

She exhales with a surprised little *oh* as she takes a step back, looking down as she tucks a strand of long, dark hair behind one ear. With a Jewish father and a Cherokee mother, she is both exotic and stunning. And the only reason I don't hate her for it is because she's my best friend in the world.

Or I thought she was. She should be able to read my mind, and the fact that she's not jumping on the Jenny train has me sighing with exasperation.

"*Jenny*," I repeat as Bree looks up, brushing a fingertip under each glistening eye. "She was in my dream," I add softly, undone by Bree's tears. I've always been the emotional one. Even after the hell she went through with the kidnapping and the blackmail, she's the practical, self-controlled one. Comparatively speaking, anyway.

"I'm sorry," I say. "I shouldn't have blurted it out like that."

She shakes her head. "No. It's okay. Tell me. Did you learn something? Do you know why she ...?" She trails off with a shudder, then draws a breath as if steeling herself. "Do you know why she did it?"

In lieu of an answer, I cock my head toward the kitchen. She nods, then heads into the galley-style kitchen like she owns the place. Which, actually, she does. I used to be her roommate. Now she's my landlord, having decided that moving out to live with her new husband after the wedding would be a jolly good idea.

Thankfully, she's not here to collect the rent.

I watch as she pops bagels into the toaster and starts a pot of coffee. When the bagels pop back up, she grabs two plates, two knives, and the tub of cream cheese. She slides it all onto the newly retiled kitchen bar, courtesy of yours truly's labor and Bree's credit card. Then she comes around and hops on the stool next to the one I've claimed.

"Shouldn't you be off banging your husband?" I ask. "It's only been three months. Don't tell me the honeymoon's over."

"Yes, alas, we're done with all of that." She digs into the cream cheese and starts slathering her bagel. I do the same. "Now all I do is walk around in a frumpy housecoat while he repairs appliances and scratches his balls."

"Living the good life." We share a grin. "Is it horrible that I'm insanely jealous of how happy you look?"

Bree cocks her head, giving me *that* look.

I stop her with a hand up. "Nope. Nada. Nyet. This is not Neuroses on Parade. I'm okay. Really." And that's true. Mostly. For the time being I'm doing just fine with toys in lieu of a guy. Complete control and all the attention focused on me. That's the dream, right?

And as to the small issue of my current unemployment and empty bank account ... well, that should be remedied soon.

She narrows her eyes. "Come on, Aria. This is me. Whatever it is, I can help. Do you need to skip this month's rent?"

Yeah, she knows me well. I have to smoosh down the urge to say yes so that I can shake my head. "No," I say. "I told you. It's not me who needs help. It's Jenny."

TWO

"Help?" Bree's expression tightens as she glares at me. "What the fuck, Ari? That's a horrible thing to say." Tears fill her eyes as she struggles to speak. "We sh—should have been helping her before she killed herself."

"That's my point," I say, forcing the words out past a clog of my own tears. "I don't think it was suicide."

A slideshow of emotions passes over her face. "What are you talking about?"

"She asked me to help her. Don't you get it? She didn't kill herself."

"Ari ..."

"But—"

"It was just a dream," she snaps. "You're sad and upset. I am, too. But—"

"*Dammit, no.* It was more than a dream." I'm certain of it. But I can see the doubt all over Bree's face. "Please." I taste the salt from an errant tear. "*Please.* We can't just ignore her. She needs our help."

"Ari ..."

"*Listen to me.* Jenny wouldn't kill herself. Plus, hello, she *told* me she didn't."

"In your dream." Her voice is flat. She's talking to me with the kind of voice she might use to tell a little kid that why, yes, of course fairies are real.

I'm about to say exactly that, but she cuts me off with, "Come on, Ari. You know that you—"

"I *am* a little bit psychic," I insist as I go into the kitchen, yank out the carafe, then pour our coffees, my back to her.

"Ari ... I want to believe you," she says, as I slide the coffees onto the bar. "You have to know that. I hate that something was so terrible she felt like the only way out was to kill herself. But she's gone now. And we—"

"I can prove it." I'm staring her down, and she's holding her own right back at me. Weirdly, the familiar back and forth gives me a warm feeling in my belly. This is my total BFF. There's no one else in the world I could have this argument with, because there's no one else who gets me the way she does.

Which is why I'm not even remotely surprised when she leans back in her stool, her whole body telling me that she's surrendering even before she says, "Fine. You say you can prove it? Then prove it."

"Done." I race into the bedroom, her *"What the hell?"* still echoing when I return seconds later bearing a deck of Tarot cards.

I see the grin that tugs at the corner of her mouth before she says, "Why am I not surprised?"

I shrug, fighting my own smile. She's not surprised because she's Bree and we know each other as well as we know ourselves. Not only were our mom's besties, too, but they were pregnant at the same time, and—hello freaky universe—they gave birth on the same day. To say Bree and I are close is like saying there are a lot of stars in the sky. Yeah, *duh.*

I take the Tarot cards out of the box, then hold the deck out to her. "Draw."

She takes one, then lays it on the bar. *The Hermit.*

I wave at the card, feeling more than a little smug. "See? See?"

"See what? It's an old guy with a staff."

"Forgive my poor, ignorant friend," I say, looking up toward the heavens. Then I look directly at her with a small shake of my head. "Girl, that's the Hermit. And everyone knows he bridges the gap between the known and the unknown. He's like a guide."

"Uh-huh."

"He's a messenger. Don't you get it? Jenny's asking us to look closer."

"It's a twelve-dollar deck of cards you got at the Beverly Center a few years ago."

"Twenty dollars." I hop back on my stool, then hold out the deck again. "Pick another."

"Ari—"

"*Dammit, Bree,*" I snap, surprising both of us. "Jenny wouldn't kill herself. Fuck the cards," I add, tossing them across the room, then watching them flutter down to the carpet. "We both know she'd never do that."

I can tell by her face that she wants to argue, but before I can open my mouth to parry, her shoulders drop. "Fine. You win."

I exhale in relief. "The cards know what they know."

"Not the cards," she says. "Me. It's not only that I can't imagine her killing herself, it's that I can't imagine her killing herself like that."

"Exactly," I say, but softer. Now that she agrees with me, the persuasive *oomph* has left my voice, replaced by lingering sadness for our friend, now dead for just over two weeks.

Beautiful and outgoing, Jenny was the girl who landed the lead in every single play and musical in high school. Everyone in our graduating class knew she was going to leave New York for La La Land five seconds after she tossed her cap. Bree and I always figured we'd see her on TV the very next season, because how could Hollywood ignore her?

With a sigh, Bree grabs our mugs and moves to the lumpy couch. I take my untouched bagel and follow. "We should have been better friends," Bree says the second I sit down.

"She was usually the one who blew us off," I remind her, probably to assuage my own guilt. "I swear she went to acting class more than she ever went to chemistry."

"Can you blame her?"

I trail my fingertip through the cream cheese, then shrug. "Really can't."

Bree nods. "And once that guy at Hardline started inviting her to those parties—"

"She called them meet-and-greets."

Bree shrugs. "Like I said—parties. When she started going to those it seemed like she was busy every weekend."

"I always figured it was more about the guy that invited her than the work." I suck the cream cheese off my finger, then slide my plate onto the coffee table, realizing I'm not hungry at all.

"I don't think there was a guy involved," Bree says. "She always said those parties were opportunities."

I take a sip of coffee, hoping my brain will kick into gear and what she just said will magically make sense.

Nope. "Opportunity for what?" I ask.

"Hardline's Talent Relations department throws those parties for aspiring actors," Bree explains. "I guess the parties are meant to be a kind of pre-audition. Which is why she went to everyone she could." She shrugs. "That's how Jenny explained it to me, anyway. And then Matthew pretty much said the same thing."

"Wait, wait, wait. Slow down." I shift on the couch to see her better, one foot tucked under me. "Matthew Holt? *The* Matthew Holt? He told you that? Why would he tell you that?"

Holt is the CEO of Hardline Entertainment—the company that sponsors the meet-and-greets. He also has the starring role in my various nighttime fantasies.

Or he did until Jenny died. Now, he's got a big, red, Jenny-sized question mark above his head.

Which is why he is very, very firmly in my crosshairs.

"I know him," Bree says, and I remind myself of the circles she now travels in. "You've met him, too, remember? At that party at the Starks' house?"

Bree used to work as a nanny for Damien Stark—a billion-aire force of nature—and his wife Nikki. Now she's married to Damien's son, Ashton. So she's been to a lot of parties at the Starks' Malibu estate. I, however, have only been to a few. Usually as Bree's plus-one.

"I'm sure I introduced you," she adds. "You were waiting for a drink."

I shrug, totally nonchalant. "I barely remember him." I'm trying to sound casual. The truth is, I remember only too well.

The party had been a celebration because Nikki's best friend, Jamie, and her husband, Ryan, had a new baby. I'd said my congrats, then got in the drink line.

That's when I caught the familiar scent of his cologne. I turned to look behind me, then almost melted from the force of pure, animal pleasure.

I'd seen his picture before, but the camera didn't do him justice. He seemed more god than man, with that chiseled face and perfect body. And his smile ... that smile was like the glow of a full moon. Bright. Sensual. But somehow full of secrets.

Bree had been passing by, and she paused to introduce us. He met my eyes, and my insides had melted away. It was as if I was looking at myself from some other dimension, and I saw my whole life spread out in the warmth of his embrace.

The moment had been wonderful and terrifying and very, very strange.

The second Bree moved away, I made up some excuse to get out of line, abandoning my desperate need for a drink. Then I scurried to the far side of the pool and avoided looking at him until I finally had to just leave the party.

But I looked back once before I slipped through the gate. And there he was, his eyes on mine. And I couldn't shake the feeling that he'd been watching me ever since the bar.

That should have been the end of it, but he'd lingered in my thoughts. And starred in some very, very vivid fantasies.

With a hard mental shove, I force myself back on track and turn my focus back to Bree. "Why was Holt talking to you about Jenny's parties?"

"Oh, he wasn't. I was kind of eavesdropping."

I grin. "Do tell."

She glares. "I'm trying to."

I mime zipping my lips. She smirks but continues. "This was about a year ago. I wasn't living at the Starks' place anymore, but I'd come over to babysit. The kids wanted to swim, and I didn't realize that Holt and Damien were having cigars on the patio when I agreed to the pool."

I've never been jealous of Bree's job as Damien and Nikki Stark's nanny, but for a while, she actually lived in the guest house at Stark Mansion, which was almost the same as living like a billionaire in Malibu. Now that she's married to Ash, she hangs out at the mansion all the time.

Nope. Not jealous at all.

Then again, if she hadn't taken the nanny job, she never

would have been kidnapped or blackmailed. So ... yeah ... not jealous at all.

She tilts her head, her mouth curved into a frown, as if she knows exactly what I'm thinking. Considering this is Bree—who knows me better than anyone—she probably does.

"Sorry," I say, then clear my throat. "Mind wandering. Please continue."

She does a massive eye roll but complies. "Matthew and Damien were talking business, so I was only half-listening. But then they mentioned those parties. Jenny had been to one or two back then, so I listened."

"And?" I twirl my hand when she pauses to take another sip of coffee.

"I don't remember exactly, but Damien was asking about the cost/benefit, and Matthew said the parties were worth the cost. That the value lay in community involvement, brand loyalty, and all that."

"That's it?"

"And that they usually pull a dozen or so guests for screen tests. I got the feeling the parties populated a nice roster of extras, but rarely found a star."

"Sounds like a lot of work and money for little return," I say.

"I know, right? But Matthew's worth almost as much as Damien, so I figure he knows what he's doing."

"Guess so." I frown, thinking. "I wonder how Jenny got invited. For that matter, I wonder what goes on at the parties themselves."

"Oh, I know all that," Bree says. "I remember her first one. It was right after she did that play in West Hollywood. Someone from Hardline saw her in the show and gave her an invitation."

I nod. "Oh, yeah. I do remember that."

"And she loved the parties from the get-go. Said they were a great place to meet other actors and learn about casting calls and acting coaches and all that stuff. I know she got some work as a background actor at Hardline and somewhere else. Disney, maybe? And she landed lots of auditions. And the alien guy said she might be right for some roles they were casting in London."

"Alien guy?"

Bree shrugs. "I just remember his initials. E.T."

I laugh. "Who says mnemonics don't work? Oh!" I add, remembering. "She also landed the lead in that other play. No connection to Hardline, but she met someone at one of the parties who knew the director, and she landed the part."

"It was all about the networking," Bree says.

"Except it never really went anywhere, did it?" I draw in a breath, then let it out slowly. "I mean, she really worked those parties. Talked to folks, made connections. If the world was fair, I would have thought she'd be Margot Robbie by now."

Bree frowns, then stares down into her coffee before saying, "Maybe that's why she did it. Jumped, I mean. Because she wasn't Margot."

Margot. There's a casualness to her voice, and I gape at her. "Oh. My. God. You know Margot Robbie."

A slow blush rises up her cheeks. "Matthew and Carson and I took her to brunch when we were casting *Reveries at Dusk*."

"Oh, well, of course you did." Bree's first book was optioned by Carson Donnelly, a producer/director who then took the project to Hardline. To say my life is becoming less and less like Bree's by the minute is an understatement.

Bree waves her hand as if her success is so much fluff. I'm tempted to lecture her—again—about how she needs to stop with the *it's nothing* attitude, because it is *so* not nothing. But right now it's All About Jenny time, not All About Bree.

"I think you're right in a way," Bree continues. "The slog was getting to her. She was expecting high school all over again. Instant stardom."

"I get it. She really did think she'd be Margot Robbie. And she was expecting it to happen overnight."

"That's my take," Bree says. "If she really believed it would come so easily, then maybe she snapped and—"

"No," I blurt. "No matter how much she wanted it, she didn't melt down. I already told you. Someone from one of those parties killed her."

Bree groans, then pulls her bare feet up onto the sofa and hugs her knees. "Fine. Whatever. Let's say you're right. Who? And why?"

I shrug. "Maybe something funky was going on. Drugs? Money laundering? And maybe she figured it out. That casting director doing something dirty? Or a producer? Hell, I don't know. I saw a picture of her with Matthew Holt at one of those meet-and-greets. She told me he hardly ever goes to those—the team who actually put them together thinks having him there could intimidate the guests."

Bree's brows rise. "You're saying Matthew went especially to one so he could kill Jenny? No way. Matthew's cool," she adds, offering an assessment that's a long way from my very heated thoughts about the man. "He's nice, too," she tells me. "After you get past the hard outer shell, anyway. I'll re-introduce you one of these days, and you'll see. Besides, why would he do that?"

My mind is still on the *I'll re-introduce you* part. Then I blink, as I realize I've totally lost the train of the conversation. "Why would he do what?"

She presses two fingers to her forehead, just above her nose. "Kill Jenny."

Right. I clear my throat. "Sorry. I was thinking. But that's the point. I don't know. And I want to find out. And as for him being a nice guy, how many folks did you believe were perfectly nice, only to learn the truth in the worst possible way?"

Bree should know better than anyone that people aren't always what they seem. But when I see her shudder, I immediately regret my words. "Oh, Bree, I'm so sorry. But just because you know and like him—"

"Yes. Fine. Point made." Her voice is as sharp as a blade. "He could be the devil himself and how the hell would I know?"

I wince, mentally kicking myself even harder. I know she's fragile, and I went there anyway.

But I'm right.

"All I'm saying is that maybe she slept with him thinking he'd cast her, but he's a cold, unfeeling son-of-a-bitch who tossed her aside, and she was going to go public."

"Don't bite my head off," Bree says, "but I really don't think Matthew's that guy. Besides, that dude's seen all kinds of scandal. I don't think a threat from Jenny would rattle him."

"How can you know that? The guy's a machine." Holt has his fingers in every form of media and entertainment, from local magazines to recording artists all the way to Oscar-winning films. And from what the gossip rags say, he is very hands on with all Hardline projects. "Even if he didn't kill her, I bet he knows who did. And he'd keep it quiet to save his business.

"You know I'm right," I add, meeting Bree's dark eyes. "He's a machine who has a billion-dollar industry to protect. How many machines do you know who have a conscience?"

She just shakes her head.

"The dude's got power," I say, laying out the understatement of the year. "He's the kind of guy who has to be in control, everything set up exactly his way. And I bet he's the kind of guy who has no trouble holding onto his secrets, too. The kind of guy who can put on the good face that everyone likes, but underneath, he's rotten to the core."

"Ari ..."

Her voice is chiding, and I know what she's going to say. I hold up a finger. "Don't even go there."

I watch her face, thinking that she's totally going to go there.

He's not The Cat, Ari. Not every man is The Cat. There are some men you can trust.

But she stays silent. She knows damn well that no matter what my personal issues might be, my read of Matthew Holt could very well be dead-on perfect.

Dead on.

I shiver, thinking about what I'd put in motion two days ago —and hoping I wasn't about to make a huge, giant, gargantuan mistake.

I start to speak, intending to tell her the rest of it. But at the last minute I call back my breath and curve my lips into a silent smile.

It doesn't fool her at all. That's the downside of having a bestie. It's really freaking hard to keep a secret.

"Spill it," she says, cocking her head and crossing her arms. And when I hesitate, she lifts a single eyebrow and stares me down. It's a trick we taught ourselves when we were eleven years old. We'd practiced in front of the mirror for weeks until we had it down. And we only pull out the one-brow raise when one of us means business.

"Fine," I say, trying to make my voice sound matter-of-fact. "I've got an interview for a job as Holt's personal assistant. I'm going to get that job," I add. "And I'm going to learn the truth about those parties, about Hardline, and about Matthew Holt. I'm going to find out who killed Jenny," I add. "And that's a promise."

THREE

Bree gapes at me. "He hired you as his PA?"

"Well, not yet." I offer up a casual shrug. "I happened to learn that he needs a new assistant. His old one's getting married and moving to London."

"How do you know all this?"

"I told you. Three dreams. I haven't been sitting on my ass for the last few days."

"So you snapped your fingers and got an interview? The man's like Damien. You don't simply jump to the head of the line."

I shrug.

"Seriously," she presses. "How the hell did you land an interview like that?"

"Fine, fine," I say. "Nikki got me pushed up the list." She's become a friend of mine through Bree. And Damien Stark might be a billionaire master of the universe, but he's also a surprisingly nice guy.

And, yeah, wildly intimidating.

"She just flat-out asked Matthew to give you a shot?"

I shake my head. "Nikki said it felt weird calling him

directly, but she knows the head of Human Resources at Hard-line, so she made a call. I've got an interview with Matthew on Monday."

"What did you tell her?"

"Well, duh. I told her the truth."

Bree winces.

I exhale a put-upon sigh. "I told her that I'm out of work and want something steady, and I'd love to work in entertainment, and I'd heard that Matthew Holt needs an assistant. With all the jobs I've held, I have killer skill sets."

"You do?"

She sounds genuinely confused, and I flip her the bird. "Yes," I say indignantly. "I can handle all software known to man, I can put up with asshole bosses, I order a mean lunch, I can organize the shit out of the most clueless exec, and I can handle angry ferrets like nobody's business."

"I swear, I need to buy a leash for you."

"I'll be careful. I mean, yeah, I'm going into the killer's lair, but I'm being smart about it."

Bree's expression suggests she thinks otherwise. "He's smart. He's ambitious. He's not a killer."

"Because you know him so well?"

Her brow furrows. "Sort of. I spent some time with him in Austin. He and Ash are friends, and he really helped me out. I told you all that. Plus, he's had dinner with us twice since we got back from our honeymoon. And I already told you that we've had meetings about the movie. He's solid. A player, but solid."

"Maybe. Maybe not."

"Honestly, you should write thrillers. I'm telling you, he's a good guy."

"You're saying that because of what you've seen. Of course, Holt would be on his best behavior for a friend and sometime business partner. He's doing your movie. And isn't he an investor in Ash's new venture? That souped up engine thing?"

"I think it's a little more technical than *souped up*."

I give her *the look*. "Come on, Bree. I know how Holt built his business. I've read dozens of articles about him over the last two weeks. He's ruthless."

The fact is, I've been reading about him for longer than that. After the party at the Stark estate, whenever I noticed his name on a news stand or online, I dove into the words. And yes, he is ruthless. But he's pretty damned enticing, too.

That, however, is not something I'm going to confess at the moment.

Bree rubs her temple. "Girl, you need to chill out. You don't even know the guy. You have no idea what kind of ego he has or how he runs his business or anything at all about him, really."

I shrug. I've been addicted to Hollywood gossip since I was little. I've even been an extra a few times, although I don't have any desire to truly work in the biz. Acting is ten percent real work and ninety percent waiting around. No thank you.

But peeking in on all that glamour? I'm all over that.

Plus, a deep dive into Matthew Holt specifically has shown me that he is not a man lacking in self-esteem. He's confident as fuck with an ego the size of Alaska. And from what I've read, he's so damn used to getting his own way, that he'd probably freeze up in confusion if someone said no to him.

Maybe Jenny said no.

When I suggest this, Bree scowls. "Like there wouldn't be another woman he'd be hot for. And, again, I like him. He helped me out, remember? That whole blackmail thing."

"Of course he helped you," I say. "He must see himself as the hero. And a man with an ego like his would totally believe he could get away with murder."

"You're watching all those true crime shows again, aren't you?"

"No." I'm sure she recognizes my words as a lie, but to her credit she doesn't turn on the television and check my watch history. "I figure if I'm working in his office, I can poke around. He's the kind of guy who delegates because he has to, but he'll still keep an eye on every division of his business."

"And in addition to positioning yourself in Matthew's office, you're going to try to wheedle your way into one of those parties, aren't you?" She sounds exhausted. And concerned.

"Well, yeah. Who knows what I might learn mingling with half-drunk wannabe actors? Maybe someone knew Jenny and —" I cut myself off, seeing her face. *"What?"*

She drags her fingers through her long, black hair. "I can't believe I'm saying this—but I'm hoping you're right. Not about Matthew—seriously, I like him. In fact, I'm kind of bummed he's not going with us to Monte Carlo. He's fun to hang out with."

"Oh, man. I forgot you're leaving on Tuesday."

"Grand Prix," she says. "Ash isn't driving, but he's got a car in the race, and it's the biggest showcase yet for the INX-20 motor."

"You sound like a regular car fan."

She grins. "More like an Ash fan. And *Monaco*. Hello? I mean, it's going to be fabulous."

"Not jealous." *So jealous.*

"Anyway," she continues, "I really do like the guy. I mean, he's not a warm fuzzy puppy. He's arrogant, but he's brilliant. And he definitely knows he's good looking, and—"

She cuts herself off with a wave of her hand. "Sorry. Not the point. All I'm trying to say is that even though I'm sure Matthew's hands are clean, I hope you're right that it wasn't suicide. Because we've known Jenny since third grade, and I hate the idea that she would kill herself and neither of us even had a clue she was struggling."

"Me, too."

She meets my eyes. "So I guess it must have been murder. Or an accident."

"Jenny loved that bridge," I say. "It represented Hollywood royalty to her. She picked her apartment because it had a view of the damn thing."

"I know. She said the towers made her think of castles."

The Glendale-Hyperion Bridge really is awesome. With its arches and towers, it has both a majestic and an industrial look. You can't help but notice it. I've always thought it looks lonely, but Jenny saw a raw beauty that she found inspirational. As far as she was concerned, it was the gateway to her Hollywood dreams.

"She'd never kill herself there." My voice is barely a whisper, and I wipe away fresh tears.

Bree sniffles. "I can't believe I'm leaving the country." She swallows. "Listen, it probably was suicide. But in case it really was murder ... you're not going to do anything stupid, are you?"

I shrug. "Probably."

As I'd hoped, she laughs. "Fine. Whatever. How can I help?"

I realize that at some point I'd stood up and started pacing. Now I plunk down on the coffee table in front of her. "I don't see how you can, especially if you're leaving so soon."

"You want to check out one of the parties before your interview with Holt?"

I nod. "I figure if I can get into one tonight or tomorrow, then I can ask around. Maybe she slept with the wrong guy and someone's wife was pissed. Or someone wanted her to transport drugs. Or, I don't know, something else. I won't know until I go."

"And that's all you've got?"

"At least until Monday morning when I walk into Holt's office. I'd hoped to look through her stuff, but her roommate's already mailed the boxes to her parents. Which sucks, because I figure there's probably an invite to one of the parties mixed in with her things. Which would have made things a hell of a lot easier."

"I can ask Matthew for you."

I cock my head and give her a look that I hope she translates as *What conversation have you been having?*

"Right. Suspect. Got it."

"Who else do we know who might have a party invite for this weekend?"

"No one I can—*oh*."

I sit up straighter. "What?"

She pulls a face. "No. Forget I said anything."

"Um, yeah. That's not happening. Spill it."

"Dammit. I shouldn't say anything. It's sort of a secret."

"Sort of?"

"I guess it's an open secret. But only to people who, you know, travel in certain circles." She bites her lower lip and gives me an apologetic shoulder raise.

I fight a laugh. "Marrying Ash has definitely pushed you up in the world."

She flips me the bird. "Actually, I know about it from Nikki."

I narrow my eyes. "Okay. I'll bite. What do you know?"

She draws a breath, then lets it out. "I know about the parties at Masque."

FOUR

I see Matthew Holt the moment I step over the threshold and into the overwhelming opulence that is Masque. He's on the second-floor landing, all the way on the other side of the huge entry hall. He's leaning casually against a marble pillar, just a few feet away from where one half of the majestic double staircase meets the landing.

And while it's probably my imagination, I think he's looking at me, too.

The thought sends a wash of heat rushing through me, and I'm only interrupted from my little moment of prurient pleasure by the low whistle emanating from the man on my arm.

Apparently, he's noticed Holt, too.

"Girlfriend, you weren't lying. That man is so hot he's going to melt that marble column if he stands any closer. And the suit? Ari, my love, I'll dump you as fast as a hot potato for either the man or the suit."

"Can't say I blame you." I shoot a sideways glance at Clive, who despite being as queer as they come, is totally rocking the role of my date for the evening. He's also attracting considerable attention from others who are mingling in the hall before going up those stairs to what I assume is the heart of Masque.

Men and women keep giving him the once-over, and even though I—sadly—won't be touching that, I stand up a little taller and hook my arm firmly through Clive's. At least this chiseled, buffed, and blond god in a Brioni suit and a mask is all mine for the evening. Or that's the script we're performing, anyway.

Not that I'd balk at going off-book. Considering my current —and frustrating—dry spell, if I thought there was any chance of getting Clive to shift his attention toward the double-X side of the equation, I'd suggest we check out the delights of Masque together.

At the moment, the man on my arm is looking at Holt with the same expression I'm probably wearing. Not to mention every other female and gay man in the building.

"What?" Clive asks, his eyes narrowing.

I realize I'm grinning. "You're close to drooling. Sorry, sweetie. But I'm pretty sure you're not his type."

He lets out a long, put-upon sigh. "It's a cold, cruel world. Luckily there are plenty of consolation prizes almost every-where I look."

I follow his gaze to see two guys in a far corner standing so close there's no room for religion, as my grandmother used to say.

Of course, my grandmother would be freaking the fuck out if she saw this place.

"What?" Clive asks as I stifle a giggle.

"Just thinking what a good friend you are for being my date on such short notice. That, and how awesome this place is. It's like a buffet of beauty and raging libidos. How did I not know this place existed?"

"I think that has something to do with it being a secret club."

"Yeah, well, Bree's actually been here. She broke the Girl Code by not telling me."

"And then she broke the club's code by doing the opposite."

"Technically, we followed the club rules. Besides," I add with a shrug, "I need to lock in that PA job. Holt's a known player. I figure if he sees me here—maybe more than sees—then he'll be more likely to want me close by in the office."

"You can be his beck and call girl."

I roll my eyes. "Old joke. But accurate."

Our eyes lock, and we both have to stifle a fit of giggles. Sometimes I really do wish the boy was straight.

We each grab a flute of champagne from a passing waiter and move further into the grand foyer. I know the place is patrolled by a stellar security team, but since they dress like guests, I haven't spotted one. Even so, I half expect one to sidle up to us, whisper that I'm a fraud, and kick me out. Clive, I'm sure, they'd let stay.

That, however, is just paranoia talking. I might not be able to get into an elite private sex club under normal circumstances, but tonight I'm here with VIP tickets in the form of the black masks with red trim that Bree got for Clive and me from Nikki Stark.

Until the moment she handed them over, I didn't believe the club she'd described in answer to my *What is Masque* query could possibly be real. But it is, and here we are, and damned if I don't want to forget all about the mission that brought me here and just find the hottest guy in the room and convince him that his purpose in life is to make me feel better than I've ever felt in all of my twenty-eight years.

"Slow down on the bubbly, girlfriend," Clive says, and I realize I've already drained my flute. "I may not know exactly why we're here, and I'm damn sure not going to complain," he adds, eyeing a man with a firm ass and the broadest shoulders

I've ever seen. "But if your mission is to ensure you get that PA job, I think sober might be the better choice."

I shoot him a sour glare. "You are far too pragmatic."

"Honey, that's what they all say. Come on."

"It's the parties, too. Not just the job." I don't know for certain that any of the industry meet-and-greets ever took place in one of Masque's many rooms, but Hardline sponsors the parties, and Holt owns both Hardline and Masque—Hardline openly and Masque through a twisted web of identity-hiding papers. At least, that's what Nikki told Bree. And since she's married to a Master of the Universe who's at least one step above Holt in the Hierarchy of Wealth & Power, I assume she knows what she's talking about.

Even if no meet-and-greet action happens here, at the very least some of the guests might overlap. And with a few well-placed questions, maybe Clive—in the role of aspiring actor—will learn something.

My arm is hooked through his as we move across the entry hall toward the stairs. I want to look aloof and confident so I can attract Holt's attention. But the truth is, I can't take my eyes off him. Nobody in this room even compares to the man. Not Clive. Not the broad-shouldered hottie. Not anyone.

Matthew Holt is in an entirely different league, and from the way he stands, tall and confident in a perfectly tailored Tom Ford suit, it's very clear that he knows it. The charcoal color suits him perfectly. Power and confidence and elegance all rolled together. It's subtle, not flashy, but even so, he's drawing the gaze of everyone in the room by doing nothing more than simply standing there.

I feel my nipples go hard, and I remember what happened after I left the Starks' party after my close encounter with Holt. I'd raced all the way home, then immediately called Decker, my go-to FWB. That boy must have patted himself on the back for a month after that night. But it wasn't him I was fucking. And it wasn't him who'd made me so hot.

It was Matthew Holt. The man I'm interviewing with on Monday. And who—the stars willing—I'll begin working for on Tuesday. The man whose business I'm going to be poking around in, trying to find all his dark and dirty secrets.

A guy who makes my entire body go gooey.

A man with one hell of a lot of power who just might have something to do with the death of my friend.

A man who, if the tabloids are right, has a temper as sharp and dangerous as the hard lines of his jaw.

And—most relevant for tonight—a man who owns the most elite sex club on the West Coast. That, however, isn't common knowledge. From what Bree learned from Nikki, only patrons with the highest level of "key" know that he's the man behind this infamous club tucked away inside a Beverly Hills mansion. Tonight, Clive and I are holding those top-level keys.

Too bad I still have no idea exactly what kind of door—physical or metaphorical—they open.

In other words, I don't have a clue what I'm walking into.

"—upstairs?"

I blink stupidly at Clive. "What?"

"Turn down the volume on your lady parts. I can hear them begging from here. Make the man work for it, girlfriend."

I tilt my head. "I'd flip you off, but the gesture doesn't match the dress. I'm a lady tonight."

"Uh-huh."

We share a grin.

"Come on, Lady Parker. Let's go up. And as for that dress? Honey, it's almost enough to turn me straight."

"Don't tease a thirsty woman in the desert."

"I said almost."

I laugh as his finger makes a twirling motion. I comply and do a sultry spin, noticing as I do that Holt is looking right at me.

"That look on Holt's face almost counts as first contact," Clive whispers. "He's practically panting for you."

"You better not be teasing. You know I need this job." And not just because of Jenny. He knows I'm behind on my rent. And he also knows that if I don't come up with five months of back payments pronto, the Car Gods are going to repossess my Honda. As for my credit cards … well, you're not really living until your bumping up against that limit, right?

Fuck my life.

"What's your plan?" Clive asks as we cross the room toward the stairs. Since we're in no hurry, I suggest we veer toward the bar. Perhaps alcohol will remedy that overarching flaw in my, well, plan. Or un-plan, as it were. For that matter, if Holt really is panting for me, then maybe by turning away from him and having Clive on my arm, I'll stand more of a chance of actually catching my prey. An experienced seductress, I'm not.

Unlike me, Clive seduces without even trying. I watch, both entranced and amused when a woman in a slinky, strapless dress about the size of a bandaid sidles up and strokes his arm. "I'm heading to the Rec Room," she says. "Second floor. I'd love to see you there." Her eyes dip, roaming slowly up and down his body. "All of you."

"And doesn't that sound delicious?" He takes her hand and kisses it. Then he winks. And despite the fact that this is a sex club where that kind of behavior is about as tame as a third-grader's birthday party, she actually blushes.

I tilt my head and stare him down as soon as she's out of earshot. "Did you have a sudden change in orientation?"

"Just getting her ready for the guy who's going to comfort her when I don't show up." He frowns. "Actually, maybe I can comfort him when he realizes who she's really hot for."

"You're such a bitch."

He laughs. "That's why we adore each other."

"True that."

We get our drinks, then head up the stairs. Holt is no longer standing by the column, and a little knot of disappointment twists in my gut. I catch myself looking for him the moment we hit the landing—and I tell myself I'm only looking because he's my mission.

I am, of course, lying to myself. I know because I do it all the time.

The lighting up here is even dimmer, and the area is much larger than it appears from below. In fact, the second floor extends so far back the space fades into a hazy gray broken only periodically by flickers of light when doors are opened and closed.

We've paused by the railing in the center of the landing, and from that vantage point I can see four rooms with closed doors, one of which is clearly designated as the Rec Room. But not everything is happening behind closed doors. There are chairs and sofas and chaises in the open spaces, and each and every one has been claimed by various couples—or solos or trios or more—in various states of undress and doing things that any porn producer would love to get on tape.

I'm not a prude by a long shot, but my first reaction is shock. My second is arousal. Like serious, hardcore, fuck-me-now arousal.

I realize I'm casting my gaze all around the area, but not so I can get off watching others. No. The truth hits me like a slap. *I'm searching for Matthew Holt.* And the fact that I'm not finding him has my lady parts threatening to shrivel up and die.

I lean toward Clive and whisper, "Where did he go?"

He shakes his head, then pulls me in front of him and holds me close, his hands cupping my breasts and his already-at-attention cock pressing against my lower back. I know why he moved me—because otherwise we stand out like a celibate sore thumb —but damned if all the ooey-gooey places inside me aren't begging for some action. I cast my gaze over the erotic show going on in front of us and turn my head enough to whisper, "Are you sure you don't want to change your orientation?"

"Tempting," he says. "But it's not me you want."

Then his hands slide down my sides to find my hips. He steps back, breaking contact as he turns me ever so gently until I'm facing the dark passage that leads into the bowels of the second floor. And there, stepping from the gray and into the light, is Matthew Holt.

Clive steps back, gives my ass a pat, and whispers, "You're welcome." Then he slips away to disappear into the Rec Room, leaving me staring at Holt, my nipples hard, my skin tingling, and my mind wondering how the hell I'm going to accomplish my mission when every single one of my brain cells has ceded rational thought to a deep, primal need to strip naked and surrender to the gorgeous hunk of a man who's now walking straight toward me.

FIVE

I glance down at my feet, currently rocking a pair of five-year-old Louboutins that I found at a thrift store. They may be out of season, but they make my calves look damn good.

Unfortunately, they're also hell to walk in, so I'm not moving very swiftly as I do a quick one-eighty, zigging so as to parry Holt's zag. Then I leave Holt in my wake as I take off down the hall, hoping it seems that I'm doing nothing more than working up a sensual little buzz as I scope out the action on the various couches and loungers.

I tell myself not to look back.

I remind myself that I don't want to be his destination. Not yet, anyway. While I certainly wouldn't balk at the idea of basking in his glow and upping my chance of being hired as his PA, my primary purpose in coming up here is to mingle and eavesdrop and see if I can garner even the tiniest hint of whether this mansion ever hosts the Hardline meet-and-greets. Or, better yet, follow someone down to the secret playroom where even now all the meeters and greeters are—possibly—partying.

Once I've accomplished that mission, I'll happily play

footsie with Holt. But Bree enticed me here by pointing out that since Matthew owns both Hardline and Masque, it might be one of the party locations for regular guests who've demonstrated an open frame of mind.

All of which means that right now, I'm in detective mode.

I try to saunter, as if I don't have a care in the world. And I don't look over my shoulder even once to see if he's still behind me.

I also don't mingle and eavesdrop because—let's be frank—no one is talking. And except for a few couples who extend an invitation to join, everyone is very much in their own dimly lit world on their own upholstered sex perch.

And, yes, that does represent a possible flaw in my plan to learn about the parties, but I figure I'll roll with it, and I keep on walking, exploring these new and enticing surroundings. With the soft music and sensual shadows—not to mention the whispers and groans and orgasmic gasps—I feel like I'm walking through a classy porno. Or what I imagine one would be like.

With each step, I'm becoming more aware of my own skin. Of the needy heat pooling between my thighs. Of the way my rock-hard nipples are brushing against the soft silk of my dress. And it's getting harder and harder to remember why I'm here, and not just turn around and beg Holt—or anyone—to fuck me right then and there.

I'm almost relieved when I realize that while this level may be a circle, the hall isn't. I've come to a dead end at a set of double doors. I remember the scattered glimpses I've had into some of the rooms I've passed and decide that it's time to join the party. A little break before continuing to reconnoiter.

With more than a little anticipation, I reach for the handle, but it doesn't budge. I can hear soft moans and gasps coming from within, and I feel a deep need tugging at every cell in my body.

Why, why, why is the damn door locked? And who around here has the key?

I turn, intending to hunt down the key master, and find Holt leaning casually against the railing, his suit jacket open to reveal a pale blue shirt.

"Oh." Not the most articulate, but it's the only word I can manage.

He doesn't move, but his eyes meet mine, and in that moment, it feels as if he's standing right beside me. My skin tingles from this faux proximity, and my mouth goes suddenly dry.

When he stands upright, I catch the familiar scent of his cologne, and my knees go weak. *Acqua di Parma Colonia.*

It's the same cologne The Cat wore, and like Pavlov's puppy, my body responds with a full-on wash of need, my mind twisting and turning until the sexy, traitorous thief of my fantasies and the darkly dangerous billionaire blend together to form the compilation of a man to whom I desperately want to surrender.

I turn back to the door, my heart pounding as I realize that it's not just his cologne I'm smelling. There's incense on this floor, too. A smoky scent under which I catch the unmistakable bouquet of weed.

I fight a smile, relaxing a bit as I let myself lean into the lust, somehow less naughty now that I know it's partly fueled by cannabis.

"You shouldn't be here." That deep, almost musical voice is right behind me, and I hope he doesn't notice the way I tremble from the shiver that's racing up my spine.

I turn again to face him and find him so close that I'm now staring at a spot about four inches below the knot of his tie. A half step forward, and my nose would brush silk.

I tilt my head up and hold his gaze. "On the contrary," I say with the sauciest smile I can conjure. "I feel perfectly at home."

He takes a step back, so that we're standing about a foot apart. His eyes narrow as his gaze rakes over every inch of me, and I begin to melt from the heat of that penetrating gaze.

For what feels like an eternity, he simply watches me as I try to tamp down the craving that is slowly building inside me. When he inches closer, I'm so ready for his touch that I have to work to hold my ground.

When I again catch the scent of his cologne, my body clenches with a sensual need, every cell wanting to pull me back into those delicious fantasies of The Cat. A man to whom I can surrender in my dreams, knowing that despite his dangerous edge, he would never hurt me.

But The Cat is a fantasy I've molded over the years. Matthew Holt is flesh and blood with a reputation for taking what he wants and destroying those who get in his way.

Like me.

"Ms. Parker," he finally says. "Why are you here?"

"I wasn't sure you remembered me," I say, not sure if the knife-edge I hear in his voice is real or my imagination. "We only met the once."

"I remember you," he says with deliberate firmness. "And now I'd like to know what the hell you think you're doing. I've been asking myself that since you walked through the front door with a man who clearly isn't your type. Please, do enlighten me."

"I guess you're not as smart as everyone says," I quip, but the words come out flatter than I intended, mostly because I'm a bit shook that he's noticed me at all.

"Is that how you talk to a man who holds your next potential job in his hands?"

I stand up a bit straighter, surprised. "I heard you were

doing a dozen interviews tomorrow. Have you already reviewed all the resumes and memorized the names? I thought it was the applicants who did the heavy-duty prep."

"Perhaps they do. And no. I haven't reviewed the full list."

"But you know I'm coming."

One brow rises as he says, "Are you?"

I'm suddenly grateful for the dim light, as I'm sure I've turned bright red. "Maybe that's why I came," I say, then want to slap my own face. "You know what, never mind. I'm just going to throw myself over the balcony and save us both the trouble."

He chuckles and reaches for my elbow. The shock of his touch ricochets through me, and I fear he's about to turn my embarrassing misspeak into an actual reality. "Don't jump," he says. "It's a bitch getting blood out of the grout between the marble tiles."

And just like that, I'm laughing. Still slightly embarrassed, but that's fading fast. "I wouldn't know. I'm a terrible housekeeper."

"Probably because you're out partying instead of keeping your home clean and shiny."

"Oh, I'm not partying. I'm working."

"Are you." He keeps his expression blank, but I hear the humor in his voice. "How so?"

"Research."

He releases my elbow, and I mourn the loss of contact. "I'll bite," he says, sliding his hands into his trouser pockets. "What kind of research?"

I run the tip of my finger down his tie, a remarkably bold move for only one glass of champagne. "Isn't it obvious? I'm researching you."

"I'm intrigued. And why the need to pop me under the microscope?"

"You have my resume. I figure it's only fair that I have a feel for who I might be working for, too." It's all over my voice—I've crossed the line and am now a full-fledged flirty little minx. Honestly, I have no idea what's come over me. But whatever it is, I'm enjoying it. So is Holt, if the crinkles at the corners of his eyes are any indication.

Then again, maybe he's studying me and not fighting a grin.

"What?" I demand as silence lingers, but he only shakes his head, a smug grin now tugging at that wide, glorious mouth.

Apparently he wasn't studying me. Either that or he approves of what he sees. Score one for Team Parker.

I stumble a bit as I step backward, then lean against the railing, positioning myself so I can easily see him. He's done the same, and for a moment we just stand there, both of us taking the other in.

I know he's twenty years older than me, but I don't see it when I look at him. Except for those sexy as hell lines at the corners of his eyes, his face is all chiseled features and sharp angles, highlighted by a wide mouth and a pair of sensual lips that I'm quite certain he knows how to put to good use.

The only clue that he's in his late forties is the hint of gray at his temples. And that, frankly, is a look I find very, very sexy.

Despite my better judgment, I let myself wonder if the parts of him hidden under that corporate armor are as lean and chiseled. That's certainly the image my imagination is drawing—an image that is not only delicious but has my cheeks heating up all over again. Not to mention other parts of my anatomy.

"A feel," he whispers, his voice little more than a low rumble as he repeats my earlier words. "A *feel* for who you'll be working for." He takes one step toward me, putting him so close that his breath ruffles my hair, now a wavy brown, shoulder-length with copper highlights. "As it happens, if hired, you'll be working directly under me." I hear the slight emphasis on the word *under* and feel the reverberation of that word between my thighs. "So why don't you tell me exactly what kind of *feel* you were hoping for?"

My entire face goes hot, and despite the dim lighting, I know I'm in trouble here. I'm not a woman who can hold her own with high-level sexual banter. But I am a woman with a very vivid imagination. And the moment his eyes meet mine, I'm certain he knows exactly where my mind has gone. But if that twinkle is any indication, he has no problem whatsoever with me picturing him naked. Or getting more than a little wet for him.

I am in serious trouble here.

I glance around, wondering where Clive is. I don't find him. But I do breathe in another whiff of weed and feel my head go a little woozy. As far as drugs, I'm a total lightweight. But tonight, I think that's probably just fine.

Either that or I need to get the hell out of here before I make a complete fool of myself.

Holt takes a step closer, fully crossing the line into my personal space. "You haven't explored the mansion yet, have you?"

I shake my head as I inch away, just to ensure that I can keep my wits. "I'll do that now. Just wander a bit. See what I see."

His fingertips lightly brush my collarbone. "I wouldn't dream of it, Aria. Let me give you a personal tour."

"Oh."

The corner of his mouth twitches, then he says, "Why don't we start here?"

He reaches for the door I'd already tried, but this time when he turns the handle, it unlocks. He glances up at me, then reveals the keycard nestled in his palm. "One of our higher-level rooms."

He holds the door open with the toe of his shoe, then pockets the card before reaching up and tracing his fingertip around the edge of my mask, his eyes never leaving mine.

He's not even touching my skin, yet I still have to work to control my breathing. Too bad I don't have similar control over my quickening heartbeat—especially when he pushes the door open far enough for me to see into the dimly lit room.

In truth, I can't see much, but what I do see is enough to make my nipples go hard. Although that might be because Holt has eased us into the room, and now his back is pressed against the wall, his hands on my breasts as he holds me close. And that's definitely not his belt buckle I feel behind me.

"Pleasure," he whispers, his breath warm against the back of my ear. "These people, they're all here—in this room, at this club—because they understand not only the value of pleasure but how to capture it. How to fight for it. How to be bold and claim it."

I can't see much in the shadows, but I can see enough. The pale white ass and back of a woman straddling a man on sofa. A muscular man spanking the generous breasts of a woman chained to a column. A nude woman on her knees, going down on a man dressed in a suit that probably cost more than Holt's.

I swallow, not sure if I'm uncomfortable or aroused. I think both.

As if to make sure it's the latter, his fingers make slow circles on my right nipple, and though I bite my lip, I can't stifle a groan.

"Pleasure," he repeats, then squeezes my left nipple hard enough that I squeak. "Pleasure and pain. Desire and longing." His tongue teases the edge of my ear, and it's as if a thread of electricity has raced through my body, all the way to my clit, leaving me dangling on a precipice, desperate to fall.

"Tell me you want it, Aria. Beg me to make you come."

I gasp from the bold words, my thighs clenched together as if that can satisfy my need. I want so badly to do exactly what he's ordered, but I know I can't. I don't know what game we're playing, but somehow, I'm certain that if I surrender, I lose.

I draw a breath to gain some control over my body. Then I turn my head, trying to ignore how much I like the feel of his hands on me. "Why did you bring me in here?" I try to add a hard edge to my voice, but it comes out soft. Vulnerable.

"I'm doing you a favor. You're knocking at the door, Aria, asking to come play in my world. I thought you ought to know what you'll be getting into."

For a moment, I'm confused, then I realize he doesn't mean coming to Masque tonight. And he definitely doesn't mean my intent to poke around in the meet-and-greets. Instead, he's talking about my interview with him on Monday.

One hand moves from my breast to my thigh, then starts to slide up, his fingers easing beneath the stretchy material that makes up this very minimalistic tube-style dress. I suck in air and remain perfectly still, determined not to react at all. Not to protest. Not to beg. Not to give him any hint that his touch has lit a fire inside me.

But there's no hiding the truth that he'll so easily find when those wonderful, horrible fingers slip into my very wet, very eager core.

He's close, and it's all I can do to stifle a moan. Hell, it's all I can do not to beg. The hand on my breast tightens, pulling me closer, and he bends to tease my earlobe with his teeth. I feel the whisper-soft brush of his fingertip at the edge of my thong panties, and it's everything I can do not to beg. I'm wet. I'm needy. And though I hate myself for my weakness, I want what he seems so ready to give.

And then he's gone. Still standing behind me, true, but his hands, his tongue, his breath are gone. I make a soft noise of protest, then want to slap my own face for giving him the satisfaction. I whirl around. "Why the hell did you bring me here?"

He puts a finger to his lips, then takes my elbow to ease me back out of the room. I yank free and push past him into the hallway. "What the hell was that?" I demand once the door has clicked shut.

"That was the room where anything is possible. A soft touch. A quick fuck. Maybe you just want to watch. Maybe you're not looking to get involved at all. Less excitement, maybe, but definitely less dangerous."

"Dangerous?" I suppose so. At the moment, I think I'm drowning in a sea of double entendres.

If he notices my confusion, he ignores it. "Or maybe it was simply a preview. Or perhaps a test." His mouth twitches in a way that has already become familiar. "Think of it as a bit of on-the-job orientation."

"This is about my interview?"

"*Personal* Assistant, Ari," he says. "That is the job."

He takes a step closer. There's something about those hard, piercing eyes. Cat's eyes. Familiar. And dangerous. "Be careful, Ari. You're a clever woman with a soul like a bright flame. But you're made of glass."

I think of Jenny. Was she glass? Had she shattered? "Screw that," I snap, practically spitting the words. "I'm titanium."

Instead of responding, he brushes my cheek. "No. You're like the finest blown glass. Beautiful. Fragile. But stronger than it looks. Be careful, Ari," he adds. "You're strong, yes. But not as strong as you think."

I shake my head. "What are you talking about?"

He doesn't answer me. Instead, he gestures to someone behind me. I turn and see a woman with pale, perfect skin and midnight black hair approaching. She's carrying a gift bag, which she hands to Holt, then turns and walks away without saying a word.

"Your date is still ... occupied," he says after glancing at his phone. So please feel free to explore the mansion. Enjoy the perks. The bar at the far end of this level is well-stocked and comfortable if I do say so myself. He hands the gift bag to me. "Stay as long as you wish. Look around. Drink the wine and enjoy the food. Whatever your pleasure, feel free to indulge. Just promise me one thing."

"What's that?"

He indicates the gift bag. "Don't open that until you're home."

"Why?"

Again, he grins. "Because I'm the boss, Ari. And a good assistant knows her place."

SIX

"You okay?"

I twist around to find Clive standing behind the bench where I'm perched. "Oh," I say. "I'm fine."

It's not a lie. I'm pretty sure I am fine. Just overwhelmed. And more than a little turned on. From the way Clive's brow rises, though, I'm guessing he doesn't quite believe me.

"Really," I say. "I had a talk with Holt. Mission accomplished."

He sits on the bench behind me so we are shoulder to shoulder, facing in opposite directions, but also able to talk. "He wasn't pissed off you were here?"

I frown and tilt my head from side to side as I consider that. "Definitely not pissed off."

"Oh, really?" His voice rises with interest and he narrows his eyes as he studies me. "You got laid."

I sit up straighter. "I did not."

"No?" He sounds genuinely perplexed. "I'm never wrong."

"Tonight you are. If I had a maidenhead, it would still be firmly intact. I didn't get banged, boned, or fucked."

He chuckles. "Oh, but you wanted to."

Busted.

What's worse, I didn't even realize how much I wanted to until right now. "Fine. Maybe. Yes." I scowl. "And what's wrong with that? We're in a freaking sex club. Who comes here and walks away without at least wanting to have a go?"

"Oh, girlfriend, you do not have to explain to me." He leans in closer. "He has you on the hook now, though."

"No, he doesn't have me on a—"

"Gift bag," he says, cutting me off. "It's almost cute. Instead of his cock, he gives you a gift bag. It's deviously adorable."

I cross my arms and glare at him. "I'm pretty sure the bag means I got the job. And that there are going to be rules."

"Yeah?" He makes a grab for the bag, but I pull it back.

"One rule is that I open it at home."

"Really?" He fans his face with his hand. "Whatever's in that bag must be smoking hot if you can't open it here."

"The thought crossed my mind," I admit.

"But you're pretty sure you'll get the PA job?"

I nod. "I won't know until I know. But I'll follow his rules."

"In that case, Project Masque was a winner."

I sit up straighter. "You found out about the parties?"

"I found out that none have ever been held here. Holt is a fanatic about not co-mingling his Hardline work and ... whatever you'd call this enterprise."

I nod, frowning as I process this news.

"That's not a happy face. Bad detective work? Or bad result?"

"Neither," I assure him. "You did great." I hold up the bag. "But if he's so cautious, why give me this?"

"Maybe it doesn't have anything to do with the job interview. Hell, maybe it doesn't have a thing to do with Masque. Was he specific?"

I shake my head, now more curious than ever.

A wide grin lights his gorgeous face. "Shall we continue our exploration? Meet and mingle? Make new friends?"

I laugh. "Do you mind if I leave you to friend-hunt alone?" I nod toward the bag. "I really want to get home and see what's in here."

"You are such a rule follower."

I shrug. I'm not, and he knows it. But I'm doing all this for Jenny. If that means I need to follow the rules, then I follow the rules. Besides, I'm about to implode from curiosity.

"Come on," he says, holding out a hand to help me up. "I'll get you in an Uber. And tomorrow," he adds with a definite gleam in his voice, "I'll give you a call and share all my adventures in wicked, dirty detail."

I laugh. "No call," I say. "Drinks. And every detail. It may be vicarious, but a girl's gotta get some, too."

Soon enough, I'm tucked in the back of an Uber, Clive's kiss lingering on my cheek as the driver races toward Burbank at a speed designed to ensure that a) I don't fall asleep, and b) he has plenty of time left to squeeze in at least one more ride tonight.

I'd forgotten to leave the porch light on, so it takes me a moment as I fumble with my key. Then I'm inside, and the instant I step over the threshold, all the tension seeps from my body.

We did it. We'd got into Masque, learned that the club isn't connected to the meet-and-greets, and I'd taken the first step toward landing that job with Holt. And I have to land it. Because if Masque holds no answers, then the truth behind Jenny's death is at Hardline. It has to be, because otherwise I don't know where to look, and I can't let Jenny down.

I glance at the bag I'd left on the table beside the door, then take a step toward it. Then I stop, turning around and head to the kitchen instead. I have no idea what's in that bag, but I sobered up in the cab. And this unwrapping requires wine.

I pour a glass, then take a long swallow as I retrieve the bag. I settle on the couch, then reach in and pull out a bundle wrapped in tissue paper. It feels like clothes, but it's also crunchy. As if the clothes are wrapped in regular paper and not simply the decorative tissue that forms the outer layer.

I don't think a lot about it, though. After all, everything I wrap is in a bag, and the inside gift is never wrapped at all. Just buried under a mountain of tissue. Why? Because I suck at wrapping. And it's not a skill set that I feel particularly obligated to learn.

I stare down at the package that's now in my lap and realize I'm procrastinating. I'm not sure why. It's a gift. Surely a gift won't be bad.

"Fuck it." I gulp the rest of the wine, then rip into the paper. A little too vigorously, because there are regular sheets of typing paper in there. Thirteen, actually. And from the header, the pages form a binding contract regarding the terms of my employment as Mr. Holt's PA. I've already ripped two pages almost in half.

Oops.

I skim the whole document, and though I'm no lawyer it seems straightforward enough. At least until I reach the last paragraph. One clause has been added in by hand, the letters firm and slightly slanted. A masculine hand, I think.

Holt's hand.

The clause is about his property rights. And according to the clause, the property referred to is me. And as for those rights ... well, I'm pretty much handing me to him on a platter.

There's a Post-It on that page of the contract, with another note in that same bold hand: *Open the bundle.*

I do as instructed, my heart beating fast. My body more than a little tingly. I tell myself it's only the lingering thrill of Masque.

Yes, I have mad skills of deception. I can even lie to myself.

My mouth goes dry when I pull away the tissue to reveal what's inside, and I have to take a deep breath before pulling out a skimpy, lace bra that was clearly not designed with support in mind, along with a pair of equally useless matching panties. Thong style, of course.

The two pieces are held together by a piece of paper and a safety pin. That same bold handwriting is on the paper:

All right, Aria. Just how badly do you want this job? You'll wear these on Monday. Whatever you imagine the possibilities are that could flow from these garments—whatever prurient act you might be called upon to perform—remember that act is part of the terms of your PA contract.

Think before you sign. Because once you've signed, I will, quite literally, own your ass.
—MH

Once again, I pick up the garments, this time unpinning them. Silk and lace and undoubtedly expensive. More than that, they're exactly my size.

As I hold them between my fingers, I know that I should step back. Should take a moment to think more clearly. Should pick up the phone, call the guy, and tell him that he's a narcissistic prick with serious boundary issues, and that I should send his gift, his note, and this contract to the local press.

But I don't. I won't. I need answers. And despite the fact that the mere sensation of his hand at my back tonight made me wet, he is still on my Jenny-radar. I may not want to think he could have killed her, but he's strong enough, powerful enough, and arrogant enough to not only think he could get away with murder, but to actually do that very thing.

It's a bracing thought. But I can't ignore it. Not when I'm

holding lacy panties and a contract that signs me over to him, terms put forth by a man who clearly expects to always—*always*—get what he wants.

A trill of trepidation races up my spine, but it's countered by a sensual tightening between my legs.

I shouldn't do this. But I'm going to.

I have to.

And, if I'm being truly honest, I want to.

I grab a pen off the coffee table, then sign the contract with a flourish.

Then I scoot back against the cushions, as if waiting for fireworks. They don't come.

As I sit there, a little shell-shocked, I take in the gravity of what I've done: I've indentured myself to Matthew Holt. And I don't know if that's the best decision I've made in my life, or the thing I will come most to regret.

But so long as it leads me to whatever horror led Jenny to kill herself—if she did kill herself—then maybe this deal with the devil will be worth it.

SEVEN

My field trip to Masque with Clive was on Friday night. Now it's after midnight on Sunday and the earth is spinning fast toward Monday. Which means that for three nights and two days both Jenny and Matthew Holt have been on my mind. One teasing me with decadent promises. The other begging me from behind the veil of death to give her peace through answers.

Or maybe it's only me who wants that peace.

I don't know. Hell, I'm not sure I know anything anymore.

Which is why instead of being tucked into my warm and snuggly bed the night before I return the contract and formally accept Holt's "job" offer, I'm standing on the Glendale-Hyperion Bridge, the glow of distant streetlights casting elongated shadows in the gloomy night. The sturdy bridge seems to sway, and I keep my hands on the rail as I look down at Riverside Drive and the battered ghost of my dead friend.

I had no intention of coming here tonight, and I don't even remember making the decision. One minute I was on the couch, tearing up as I watched the last few minutes of an episode of *How I Met Your Mother,* a friend-centric show that had me missing Jenny all the more. The next thing I knew I was driving along Glendale Boulevard, the bridge's octagonal towers coming into view in front of me. The bridge has thirteen arches—a piece of LA history I picked up somewhere—and I shudder, thinking about that unlucky number.

It was certainly unlucky for Jenny.

I sigh, and despite knowing that I'm standing about where Jenny must have stood in the last moments of her life, I feel safe, like a spectator peering into a distant age. With a sigh, I look down at the river and highway, wondering how many secrets this bridge has kept across the years.

I'm not sure how long I've been standing, lost in thoughts too scattered and fleeting to grasp. It's peaceful here, and I can almost hear Jenny calling to me, ready to reveal all her secrets. I only need to close my eyes and let her in and maybe then I'll—

"What the *hell* are you doing?"

I jump, my heart pounding as I turn to face Bree, stalking toward me on the pedestrian walkway.

"Me?" I snap back. "You can't just sneak up on people like that. She was just about to tell me—you know what? Never mind."

I can tell from her expression that she knows exactly what I was going to say, and I stand up straighter, fully prepared to argue that just because she doesn't get feelings and impressions like I do, that doesn't mean I'm being ridiculous or new-agey or whatever.

But she doesn't say that. Instead, she bites her lower lip and just says, "I'm sorry. I shouldn't have interrupted."

I sag, all the fight going out of me. "It's okay. I don't think she was really going to tell me anything."

She moves closer to stand beside me, both of us looking down at the spot where Jenny's body had been found.

"It's strange, isn't it?"

I shake my head, not knowing what she means.

"She died there, but it's just asphalt. It should have her initials. Or a red X." She wipes away a tear. "Her death made the news, but in a few weeks, no one will even remember."

My chest tightens. "We will."

Beside me, Bree exhales softly. "Yeah. We will."

I shoot her a sideways glance. "So you tracked me?"

She shrugs. "I swung by your place and you weren't there. Then when I saw you here, I got worried."

I reach for her hand and squeeze it. "I'm okay. I'm just—I hate it. Not having answers, you know?"

She nods. "Yeah. I know."

For a moment we just stand there, the hum of traffic underscoring our thoughts before her words break the silence. "Did you learn anything at Masque?"

Oh, yeah. I learned quite a lot.

But I don't say that out loud. I'm not quite ready to tell Bree everything that happened with Holt. "I learned that Clive makes an excellent date," I quip. "Except for that pesky no sex at the end thing."

"Sucks to be you. But what did you learn about those parties? Do you think Matthew is involved in whatever made Jenny kill herself. Or," she adds after I give her the stink-eye, "whatever led someone to murder her?"

"I don't trust him," I say.

"Him—you mean Matthew? Come on. I know he's edgy, but ..."

She trails off as if I'm going to pick up the thread. I don't. She's right about him, and so am I. He's odd and edgy and sexy, but there's something real underneath. I don't want to be attracted to him. He's a gorgeous, powerful man who runs a no-holds-barred sex club. That isn't a man who follows the rules. That's a man with power.

And powerful men believe they can walk through the world

doing anything they want. And they think they can get away with it because usually they can.

I meant what I told her—I don't trust him. But more than that, I don't trust myself around him. And I don't know what to do about the intense longing I feel all the way into my bones every time I think of him.

"Ari—"

"No. You tease me about my hunches but you know I'm usually right. There's something about him. Something dark. Something secret."

"Well, duh. He runs a billion-dollar industry. It would be weird if he didn't have secrets."

I tilt my head from side to side, trying to work out the kinks. "It's more than that," I say as cars whoosh by beneath us. I think of my gift bag and the arrogant, ballsy, and damned enticing gift I found inside it. "He's a man who'll do whatever it takes to get what he wants."

"So will most powerful people. That's how they become powerful. Or stay that way. But that doesn't mean he doesn't have limits. And it sure doesn't mean he'd commit murder."

"You can't be sure of that."

"Then you can't be sure he's dangerous."

"I'm certain," I say. And it's true. I'm one hundred percent certain that Holt has it in him to kill. Not for money. Maybe not even for his reputation. But to protect his secrets? To protect someone else? Yeah, I could see him doing that. And I'm about to throw myself into his lair.

For a moment, I think she's going to argue some more. She doesn't. Instead, she puts her hand over mine. "Then you can't work for him. If he catches you poking around ..."

I steel myself. "It's a risk."

"A risk?" she repeats, her voice rising. Then she shakes her head. "No," she says. "No, he can't be that bad. I mean, come on. I know him. Ash is friends with him."

"He has it in him," I say firmly. "But that doesn't mean he did it. It just means he could. If he had reason enough, he'd probably do it in a heartbeat." I turn to look her in the eye. "Ash could, too. You know he could."

Even in the dim light of the streetlamp, I can see the color drain from her face as her eyes go wide. "Yes," she says, the word barely a whisper. "To protect me, he wouldn't even hesitate."

"Or to protect his sisters and his brother. Or Nikki. Or Damien. Ash has that fire. We both know it. So does Holt."

She bites her lower lip before saying, "You're sure?"

I nod. "And with a man like that, you either trust him or you run like hell. I can't do either."

"Ari—"

"No." The word is soft as a prayer. "I'm going to walk into the lion's den tomorrow, and I'll do whatever I have to do—play whatever role I have to play—but somehow, someway, I will learn the truth. For Jenny."

For a moment, Bree says nothing, then she meets my eyes and nods. "Yes," she says. "For Jenny."

EIGHT

Matthew Holt pressed his palms flat against the marble countertop of his private bath, then leaned forward, looking past his own reflection in the window to the glow that was spreading over the vista. Pale gold, soft pink, even a hint of lavender—the morning light as it illuminated the backlot of Hardline Entertainment's Burbank headquarters and studio.

From this twelfth floor vantage point—the highest on the lot—he could see most of the complex that he'd built over the last two decades. But in his imagination, he still saw the undeveloped land that he'd purchased, betting his every penny on the down payment, then mortgaging himself to the hilt. But he hadn't wavered. He'd moved to LA with a dream to build something huge. Something *his*. And through a combination of ego, bold determination, and the seed money he'd worked so hard to acquire, he'd turned acres of underdeveloped land into a Hollywood force to be reckoned with.

Hollywood? Hell, the world. His empire reached every facet of the entertainment industry from live theater to recording artists to podcasts and movies and television and more.

An entire life built on the profit of his imagination and dreams. And a few unique skills that Fate had forced him to acquire.

He took a step back, casting his gaze around the elegant private bathroom that he'd demanded be included in the architectural plans eleven years ago when Hardline Entertainment moved out of the original cluster of trailers that had once served as office space.

He recalled the day he'd looked at the blueprints that Jackson Steele, his architect, had drawn up. They'd been perfect. His huge office. This bathroom. And a formidable building that reached to the maximum height the Burbank Powers That Be allowed.

He'd loved every minute of the design and building process. And when it had come time to choose paint and tile and furniture and fixtures, he'd wallowed in that as well.

Shallow? Perhaps. But he'd worked his way up from life as a street rat to the most powerful man in Hollywood. And, dammit, he fully intended to wallow in the luxury that represented everything for which he'd worked so hard.

He drew a breath, his gaze drifting over the subtly veined Italian marble floor, sourced from the Apuan Mountains above Carrara. The etched-glass steam shower that took up an entire side of the room, its polished chrome fixtures gleaming in the early morning light now sneaking through the frosted glass window that made up an entire side of the shower.

He'd insisted on controls that allowed him to fine-tune the water temperature, the pressure, the amount of steam. He could take a quick, bracing shower if he needed it, or a longer, therapeutic steam when the day's demands ground him down.

With a sentimental smile, he ran his finger along the marble countertop that stretched the length of the opposite wall, providing plenty of space for dual sinks and the huge mirror that almost filled the wall. Hidden cabinetry kept the area tidy, while the brushed steel fixtures contrasted the cool white and grays of the rest of the space in a way that underscored the room's elegance.

Stunning and efficient, just as he'd wanted. Functional. Inspirational. *His*.

The room sat like a microcosm of his business.

A business that some unknown asshole was now fucking with.

But *he* was the one who did the fucking, not the other way around, and if there was a traitor at Hardline, he would make it his mission to find that person and destroy them.

He clenched his fists, then closed his eyes, letting his head drop as he counted to ten.

Over the last two decades, he'd fulfilled every dream he'd spun during those long years when he'd lived out of a backpack, forced to hustle for his supper.

He was only forty-seven years old, but it felt as if he'd lived a millennium. All those years. All that work.

Had it been worth it?

He pushed away the intrusive thought. Of course it had. He'd started with nothing. Didn't he now have everything he'd ever wanted, with enough money tucked away to buy it all again, thirty times over?

Damn right he did. He had it all. Every tabloid rag in the city said so.

Except that was a lie.

He was close, no doubt. But the truth sneered at him. Whispering that he didn't have forgiveness. Instead, he had regret. Even shame. And he didn't have *her*, the one woman who'd been his touchstone for what felt like a lifetime. A woman he couldn't have but would always crave.

But the tabloids knew nothing about any of that. They saw

his life, his women, his power, and they praised him as a genius. A brilliant strategist. A player who rained pleasure upon a woman's body while toying with her heart.

All true. And at the same time not true at all. How could it be when those reporters and gossips knew nothing about his past. Nothing about the ragged hole that marred his soul. Hell, as far as the Hollywood gossip mill knew, he was like a male Minerva, brought forth fully embodied from the sea in a giant clamshell with Hardline Entertainment borne on his shoulders.

God, he was being maudlin.

And why not?

Somebody was fucking with him.

The rage that had been on a low simmer ever since he'd realized that inescapable truth began to boil. He'd worked too hard to lose everything, but with the girl's death, that was a very real possibility.

No.

No, no, and hell fucking no.

He'd built an entire world for himself. He wasn't about to lose it now.

He drew in a calming breath and shifted his gaze, so that now he focused on the window, not the vista beyond. He met his reflection and silently confessed that he was no stranger to sin.

Sin and danger and pain. He knew the price for success. The body count as he'd climbed on the backs of the conquered. The corporate world was like the damn Roman Empire. Thankfully with suits instead of togas.

True, he'd made it out of the gladiator pit, but he still had to play the game. Had to fight for everything he had and cut down anyone who stood in his way. Over the years, he'd become expert at clearing a path.

Still, no matter how high he flew, those years of secret sin haunted him, and Friday night at Masque had reminded him that more and more often he felt the tug of his ghosts reaching out from their dark hiding places to grab him by the throat.

Every day, he told himself that he'd buried the mistakes of both youth and hubris. Shoved them so far down into his soul that they—and she—would never rise again.

He should have known better.

He wasn't a believer—not really. But his mother had been. Too bad her belief hadn't saved her, and the fact that her god had called her home before he was six years old had taught him the only thing he could truly believe in was himself.

Certainly not his father. Wasn't he still paying for Vincent Larouche's sins along with his own?

He closed his eyes, her image coming unbidden into his mind. The woman he should never have fallen for, much less ever met. He thought he'd gotten rid of her. Had finally, painfully, done away with the last remnant of her, then buried the guilt along with the memories.

He had, dammit. He had.

The only mistake he'd made was not anticipating her ghost.

"*Goddammit.*" Without any conscious intention, he turned to face the mirror and the vain and sentimental man staring back at him. Two long strides and he had the crystal glass in hand. He turned it sideways, letting the toothbrush fall to the floor. Then he took three steps away from the mirror and hauled his arm back even as his mind screamed for him to stop. *Well, fuck that.*

He threw it forward with all the strength he had. It rocketed toward his reflection, then shattered the mirror, destroying his visage and sending shards of glass spilling into the sink, onto the floor, everywhere.

But he remained unscathed.

He stifled a mirthless chuckle.

Once again, he'd dodged a bullet he didn't deserve to dodge.

The pounding at the restroom door came within seconds. "Matthew! Dammit, Matthew, are you okay?"

"I'm fine, Lila," he called. "Everything's fine."

The doorknob rattled. "Open the door."

He pinched the bridge of his nose, fighting the urge to tell her to go the fuck away. He glanced at his watch. Not even six a.m. "What the hell are you doing here so early?"

"Catching up." He heard the metallic scrape of a key going into the lock. He bit back a curse, then opened the door before she could.

Lila Blackstone crossed her arms over her chest and leaned against the now-open door frame. She wore her long, blonde hair up in the style he'd once told her was his favorite. She had cheekbones that could cut glass and green eyes hidden beneath naturally long lashes. She wore a pale pink shift-style dress that he'd seen before. Sleeveless and form fitting, it hugged her hips and waist and breasts in a way that accentuated her Marilyn Monroe-esque curves.

Her makeup was, as usual, perfect. And as he had so many times before, he marveled at her skill in putting herself together so quickly in the morning, taking about a quarter of the time most other women he knew took. In the past, he'd considered that talent of hers a bonus. Today, it was irritating as hell.

With a sigh, he pinched the bridge of his nose in an effort to stave off a headache. "We've talked about this, Li. You're my receptionist. Not my Personal Assistant. I only need you here during your regular working hours. And in case you're confused, the day starts at nine. Embrace it."

She started to speak, but he held up a hand. He saw a hint of irritation flare in her eyes, but he pressed on. "You have two choices. One, stay on my desk, take my calls, usher my appointments into my office, cash your paycheck, and remain my friend. Two, get the hell out of here. I'll soften the blow with a hefty severance package if you choose Door Number Two. We've talked about this before. Hell, the only reason you're even on my desk is because I didn't want you out of work in a shit economy. So make your choice. I won't discuss it again."

She held her hands up in surrender. "Bitchy much? I come in early, and I get chewed out about a job I'm not even applying for?" She softened the words with a smile that was obviously forced.

He winced. The damn headache was still building, and he really didn't need this right now. "Sorry. I didn't sleep much, and I have a full day of interviews to look forward to." He hoped that wasn't the case. Aria Parker was on his calendar as the third appointment of the day. If she came to his office with a signed contract, that would clear his calendar.

With that bit of hope brightening his morning, he offered Lila a smile. "I apologize for snapping."

The way her face brightened was like a time machine, taking him back to those days when they could practically read each other's minds. "Apology accepted. I think we know each other well enough that we can drop the boss/employee routine. Especially before seven a.m."

"True."

"Besides," she added, with a familiar smirk. "I know where all the bodies are buried."

He shook his head, half-amused, half-annoyed as he pointed to the door. "Go. Call maintenance and the janitor and get this mess cleaned up. Then bring me a coffee."

"Of course. And I'll bring the applicant files. There are eight today. I've summarized the pros and cons for each. Since you insist on not letting me undertake the work, I thought the least I could do was help you hire someone competent in the job. You'll find the analysis in the HR folder under today's date. Or would you rather I print them?"

"Aria Parker's the third appointment?"

"That's correct."

"Fine. Bring me the files for the first three applicants. I've already offered the job to Ms. Parker. When she accepts at her interview, you can call and cancel the rest."

"Oh. I see." She tapped her lower lip, something she did when annoyed. He'd seen it often in their years together. "Ms. Parker wasn't at the top of my list. I hate to think that we have a different vision as to what you need in the way of assistance."

He rubbed his temples, the fire going out of him. "Lila."

She moved one step closer. "Matthew."

He felt the tightness in his lower back. God, he was an asshole. "You know how much I rely on you. So thank you. Really. That will be all."

She looked at him, and he remembered how he once thought the gleam in those pale green eyes was a kind of sweet mischief and *joie de vivre*. He knew better now. Knew himself better, too.

Most of all, he knew he was a man who had a long road of atonement ahead of him.

NINE

I've lived in Burbank for a while now, and I've passed the ornate gate that marks the entrance to the Hardline Entertainment complex more times than I can count. But this is the first time I've made the left turn from Victory Boulevard onto Hardline's private drive.

Honestly, it's kind of exciting. And not just because I'm coming to see Matthew Holt.

I stop at the gate, show my ID, then follow the guard's directions to the guest parking area, getting more and more intimidated the deeper into the complex I drive. From my usual vantage point on Victory, I'd never realized how big the place is, much less how many buildings cover the acreage. I pass sound stages, workshops, actors in period costumes, a faux neighborhood, and even a pen of live pigs before I finally make the right turn into the tower's guest parking area.

I keep Harry the Honda running while I check my make-up, then use a hint of powder to get rid of some shine ... and a dab of lip gloss to add a bit.

I pat the steering wheel. "You'll be safe here. Nobody's repossessing you while you're on this lot." And since I'm about to walk through those doors with my signed contract, I've got the money coming in to keep the loan thugs at bay. All for the price of my soul. Or, more accurately, my innocence.

Except that I'm not innocent at all. So, hey, score one for me.

I close my eyes and take a breath, annoyed by my flighty thoughts. I'm nervous, of course, and it's making me a spazz.

But I really can't be a spazz in front of Holt.

For Jenny, I tell myself. *Calm down and don't screw this up.*

Thus chastised, I push open the door, then grab my purse, the signed contract sticking out of the top of it.

After another deep breath, I climb out of the Pilot. I pause for a moment, my hand still resting on the door frame as I gaze at the building that rises in front of me. With twelve floors, the structure gleams in the morning sun, broadcasting success. Power. And for one heart-clenching moment, I wonder if I'm truly up to the task.

Hell, yes, I am.

At first, the words are nothing more than a mental pat on the back. But as soon as I approach the double glass doors, something occurs to me. Matthew Holt may qualify as a Master of the Universe, but like every superhero, he has a weakness. And considering the man conditioned my employment on wearing sexy undies, I'm thinking I know what that weakness is. I may not be rich, I may not be powerful, but I have something he wants.

And, sure, maybe he can get it from another woman, but I'm the one with whom he struck his naughty little deal. I'm the one with the job and the contract.

I'm the one with the lacy bra and tiny panties.

And that means I'm the one with the power.

With renewed confidence, I tug open the door and step over the threshold with my head held high. I have *so* got this.

I get my pass to the twelfth floor from the receptionist—a woman who probably believes the cliche that she'll be discovered by the boss and then thrust into stardom. "Good luck with that," I say before I head to the elevator, leaving her confused behind me.

There's a mirror between the two elevator banks, and as I wait for my car, I do a quick once-over. I look damn good, if I do say so myself. I've got the conservative suit and the sexy-yet-somehow-work-appropriate heels. Everything says polished, professional, reliable. But underneath ....

I look down, my lips pressed together as I hide a smile. I should be pissed that he's playing the perv. That he's diving into all those obnoxious stereotypes and pulling a major Weinstein.

But I'm not.

I feel powerful this morning in a way I hadn't anticipated. I'm going into the lair with a mission—to find out what happened to Jenny. And if Matthew Holt is attracted to me ... well, I've watched enough psychological thrillers to know that puts me in the power position. Not him.

Bottom line? This job is exactly what I need. A way to not only make decent money, but to get in close and poke around. To play detective and try to learn what really happened to Jenny. Who hurt her. And—if she truly did kill herself— then why.

I know the answers may not be here, but I can't think about that now. I have no other ideas, no other leads.

The elevator arrives, the doors sliding open. I step on, shoulders straight and loins girded. If I want to do right by my friend, this is where I have to start.

I press the button for the twelfth floor, and as the doors slide shut, a chill creeps up my spine.

Anticipation, I tell myself. Not nerves. Because today, nerves aren't allowed. Today I'm cool and collected.

Today, I am seriously bad ass. Sexy. Confident. In control.

Matthew Holt doesn't stand a chance against the likes of me, and if he has any secrets, he might as well just spill them now, because I'm going to find out everything.

When the doors open on the twelfth floor, I roll my shoulders back and walk with confidence down the sleek hallway in front of me. His office is at the end, taking up one entire side of the building. Sketches from the design of various Hardline movies hang on the walls as if highlighting a promenade of success leading straight to his office.

I pause outside the door, reminding myself I'm confident and collected. I have the skills for this job. And he's already vetted me.

At the same time, there's no denying the fact that—considering the offer was made at Masque and accompanied by the prerequisite of lingerie—I may not have been hired entirely for my job qualifications.

I sigh, my nerves twitching as my confidence starts to take a dive.

Stop it.

You. Have. Got. This.

I'm not sure that talking with the little voices in my head is actually evidence of confidence, but I press on anyway. Mostly, I'm nervous because I don't know what he wants. Am I really here to be an assistant? Or am I here so he can take an up close and personal tour around the lingerie?

I stop walking for a moment to wipe my damp palms on my skirt as I remind myself that the job details don't matter. I'm here with a mission, and I don't intend to fail. And if that means getting up close and personal with Matthew Freaking Holt, then I need to just roll with the punches and enjoy myself. After all, the guy's hot as sin. And after Friday night, there's no denying that he pushes all my buttons.

Then again, naughty time with a hot guy is one thing. Naughty time with a hot, egotistical guy who probably has a god complex and who may have killed your friend is something else altogether.

Clearly, I'm not entirely sane.

I continue on until I've reached the end of the hall and stand facing the floor to ceiling door with M. Holt, CEO stenciled on it in crisp gold letters. And, no, I'm not intimidated at all.

I bite back a self-deprecating chuckle. I excel at lying, which is probably not something to brag about, though it's true.

What's also true is that I excel at lying to myself. And right now, I'm not sure if I was entirely honest with myself when I decided that taking this job was a good idea.

Yes, I want answers for Jenny. Because she deserves them, and because I want them. For me. For her. For her family and friends. But maybe swan-diving into the lion's den wasn't the most brilliant plan ever.

I'm about to turn around, find the ladies room, then call Bree and lay into her for not putting an end to this particular manifestation of my insanity, but of course that's when the door opens. A burly guy in a poorly tailored suit with hair the color of sweet potatoes steps out, pausing for a second to look me up and down. He smiles, almost shyly, then says "good luck," before continuing down the hallway.

Whoa. Another applicant? I've already signed the damn contract. So what the actual fuck?

"Ms. Parker?"

I jump a little, then realize that while Opie disappeared down the hall, the door had stayed open. Now the space is occupied by a curvy, elegant blonde in a sexy-but-conservative shift-style dress that reveals shapely legs that seem to go on forever.

Not intimidated. Not one little bit.

She extends her hand. "I'm Lila Blackstone. We spoke on the phone."

"Right." I take her hand to shake, noting that her skin is as smooth as her voice. "The scheduling call." I glance behind me, then back at her. "How was my competition?"

She only smiles and laughs politely. I seethe as she ushers me into the reception area, which is all smooth lines and perfect polish. The efficient yet stylish reception desk. The leather sofa and matching chairs for guests. The coffee table neatly displaying today's *Hollywood Reporter* and various fan magazines.

The room holds one surprise, too. Unlike the hallway, which had boasted Hardline-related art, this room is all about classic abstract art. I recognize a Rothko and a Kandinsky right away. Whoever Holt's decorator and art consultant are, they made good choices.

"Stunning pieces, aren't they?"

"They really are." I offer a smile, hoping to lighten her up. "I approve of Mr. Holt's decorator."

I think I hear a hint of disdain as she says, "Mr. Holt is more than capable of choosing his own furniture and artwork. In fact, those two are both signed and numbered serigraphs from his personal collection."

"Oh." I feel duly chastised. Considering Holt's ego, I would have expected framed memorabilia—photos of him accepting a Best Picture Oscar. Stills from his movies. Articles blaring out the box office gross. Photos of him standing arm-in-arm with the industry's hottest stars.

But there's none of that in this room.

Strangely, the disconnect between my expectations and his reality makes the butterflies start up in my belly. And then all the confidence I'd gathered during the trek from my car to this office grabs onto those butterfly wings and flies far, far away, leaving me alone with the nerves I'd tricked myself into ignoring.

Fuck.

I'm about to tell Lila I need a moment in the ladies' room when I realize she's reached the grand double-doors on the far side of the room. She turns the nob, pushes the floor-to-ceiling door open, and steps inside.

Then she looks over her shoulder at me, her expression making very clear that I should be at her side. Her lips purse as she holds the door open and says, "Ms. Parker is here."

Flustered—and annoyed that she didn't give me even a moment to get my bearings, I hurry across the room, then step into Holt's private sanctuary just as he's rising from behind his huge desk, his finger tapping the earpiece of a headset.

He's dressed in a suit that probably cost more than the sticker price of my car, and he looks as perfect and polished as any movie star heartthrob. The truth is, just looking at him takes my breath away, and when my mind un-jumbles and I remember what I have on underneath my own suit, my mouth goes dry ... and my southern hemisphere has the exact opposite reaction.

"Ariadne Parker," he says, with a nod and a gesture to the seating area on the far side of the room. "Please have a seat. Would you care for coffee?"

"I'm fine. And I mostly go by Ari." My mom's a huge fan of spiders, which is how I ended up saddled with Ariadne. It's different, even kind of cool. But I think spiders are creepy as fuck. So after years of explaining my name, I registered for college as Ari. And that's the name that's stuck.

"Ari, then." He looks to Lila. "Thank you. That will be all."

She smiles, her gaze sliding over me once more before she slips out of the office and closes the door behind her. There's absolutely nothing odd about her expression, but I feel a chill nonetheless.

"I apologize," Matthew says, indicating an earpiece. "But I need to address this immediately."

"Sure," I say, taking a seat as he turns to face the window while taking the call. Though I try to eavesdrop, his voice is low enough that I can hear nothing except a brief hint of irritation that matches the sharp line of his posture.

I want to hear more, but since I can't, I use the delay to gather myself in this overwhelming and—frankly—intimidating space that's so much more impressive and imposing than my imagination had conjured.

When Bree was the Starks' nanny, she occasionally took the kids to Stark Tower to see their dad. So she's not only been to his office in downtown LA, she's also described it to me in all of its elegant, polished, and undoubtedly expensive glory.

I haven't seen it myself, but I'm more than certain Holt's office puts Damien's to shame. This is a space that demands attention.

Yet at the same time, it seems a perfect fit for a man with Matthew's innate command and poise. It feels like a throne room, the place from where the king wields his power.

And that, I think, is exactly what it is. What *he* is.

Two of the walls are entirely glass, revealing his kingdom as well as the spread of the San Fernando Valley beyond, all the way to the mountains rising near Santa Clarita. The entire room feels drenched in light, casting shadows that seem to dance across the leather furniture and Holt's expansive desk that must be at least as large as a queen-size bed, and clearly designed to intimidate anyone not sitting in the black leather throne.

Like, for example, me.

Still, despite the glitz and glam, the room doesn't feel ostentatious, but it does feel like power. More than that, it feels like Holt.

"He doesn't need to know we talked." Matthew's voice is still low, his back still to me, but he's moved closer to his desk, and the acoustics must be better because I can just make out his steely-edged words. "I'll shoot him a text. I want the revised event budget in my inbox with his annotations in two hours, along with notes explaining every flagged discrepancy."

He bends over and scribbles something on a notepad. "I'll dig into that. Okay, see ya," he adds, the words seeming strangely informal considering the tone of this conversation.

He taps the earpiece to end the call, and I watch his back as he rolls his shoulders, then takes off the headset and tosses it onto his desk, a shadow in his eyes. "A friend?" I ask, then immediately regret the question.

He slides his hands into his pockets and turns, his gaze landing on me with a weight that sends a shiver down my spine. "Pardon?"

"Oh, I didn't mean to eavesdrop. I just heard you say 'see ya.'" I shrug. "I always pictured CEO offices as bastions of proper English."

If there was a shadow before, it's gone now. In fact, for a moment, I can see nothing in his expression, and I wonder if he's still lost in whatever crisis he was dealing with on that call. Then he steps out from behind his desk, and the lingering tension seems to melt away, leaving a man who is completely confident and one hundred percent in control.

"Ah, the *see ya* maneuver." He walks toward me, and I stand to meet him. "That's my trademark bamboozle. I use it in the midst of every multi-million-dollar negotiation. It always throws the other side off their game."

He flashes a crooked smile as he looks me over with a slow,

practiced assessment, his gaze lingering in a way that leaves no doubt he knows exactly what I'm wearing—and precisely what it's doing to me.

I fight the urge to cross my arms, to close myself off from the effect he's clearly having. But I don't. I can't. I'm here for a reason, even if that reason feels like it's shifting, slipping out of my control with each second under his watchful gaze.

I'm in over my head.

The thought spins through my mind even as a smile lights his face.

"No," he says.

I blink, confused. I'm *not* in over my head?

"I have no trademark bamboozle," he explains his jest, apparently seeing my confusion.

"Oh." I grimace, feeling like an idiot.

"Perhaps I should get one." His voice is gentle, and I realize he's taking pity on me. And though I know my assessment might change in an instant, right then, I actually trust Matthew Holt.

For a moment, we both stand in silence. Then he says, "Ms. Parker," in a voice that's smooth as silk, but there's a thread of something darker, too. Something that destroys that nascent trust even while sending a surge of heat through me.

"Um? Yes?"

"I believe that's for me?" He nods to my purse and the document that's poking out of it.

"Yes," I manage, my voice steadier than I feel.

"Signed?" His expression doesn't change, but the fire in his voice is undeniable, and like Pavlov's dog, I react, my nipples going tight as I fight the urge to squeeze my thighs together.

"Yes."

He extends his hand, and I pull the contract free then pass it to him. He flips through it, checking every one of the pages for my initials and my full signature at the end.

Without a word, he turns his back to me, then crosses to his desk. I hear a drawer open and close, the contract disappearing inside.

I expect him to return, but instead he sits, godlike, behind that massive desk, his eyes locked on mine.

Then, with clear deliberation, he slides his gaze down, pausing at my breasts. My skirt. "You've met all my conditions?"

I nod, and he lifts his hand, bending his fingers in a *come here* gesture. I hesitate, but comply, my movements feeling unnatural as I walk forward under his unblinking gaze.

I stop when I can put my hand on the desktop. I'm close enough I can smell an intoxicating hint of his familiar cologne. Tension stretches between us, taut and undeniable. My entire body is warm, and I wonder if he can hear my heartbeat.

Suddenly, I'm acutely aware of the whisper of lace beneath my clothes, and I fear that every secret thought and every wild desire I have is now on display for him.

For one terrifying moment, I'm certain he's going to tell me to take a step back. To unbutton my blouse. To lift my skirt just enough to confirm that I really am playing this game.

And so help me, I want to.

But he doesn't. Instead, he taps a button on his desk. I hear the echo of a low buzz, and a moment later, Lila steps into the office.

"Please cancel the rest of the interviews. Ms. Parker will be joining us as of today."

"Of course," she says, then disappears with a look of quiet efficiency.

I stand taller, thinking of Opie and feeling strangely smug that I got the job instead of him. As if the fact that it was my choice to sign the contract somehow really did make me the best candidate.

A delusional thought, but I cling to it. It feels safer than the knowledge that I'm here because I'm playing a naughty game with Holt. Not to mention that I'm here because I'm also playing my own secret game of *Clue*, and I had to win this job in order to get in close, get info, and somehow vindicate Jenny.

Except I'm not there yet. I haven't any idea where to start looking for clues, and in the meantime, I have to make good on Holt's demands. So I wait, my body tingling with expectation as I stand in front of his desk. Any moment, he's going to demand that I unbutton my blouse or inch up my skirt. Hell, maybe he wants me to crawl over his desk, sex kitten style.

I don't know.

All I do know is something's coming. He'll want proof of my compliance. More than that, he'll want to take what he bargained for.

But he says nothing. Not one single word.

For what feels like an eon, he simply holds my gaze, a faint smile tugging at the corner of his mouth, as if we're playing a strange game of chicken. And with every beat of my heart, I feel my nipples hard against the lace of the bra and my core tighten with a familiar need. I make no sound, though. I don't squirm, I don't lick my lips.

There is no way I'm giving the bastard that satisfaction. I'm here for Jenny. And if sex games are the price, well, then game fucking on.

Finally, he leans back, the chair creaking just slightly as he says, his voice low, "Shall we get down to business?"

"All right." It's a simple response, but even I can hear my eagerness. An eagerness that fades with a surge of furious disappointment when he gestures for me to sit in the guest chair I'm standing beside, saying, "I have a number of documents I need you to review and sort."

I meet his eyes, certain he can see both my need and my

anger. But I take a seat, my eyes never leaving his. "Sounds good," I say, and in that moment, I hate him with the wildest of furies.

But, dammit, I hate myself more.

TEN

The morning unfolds like a minefield. I feel like I'm a psychic who knows an attack is coming, but has no idea when. I'm walking on eggshells—wearing the proof of his expectation under my clothes—but in all the hours between my arrival and lunch, he's barely even looked at me. Much less suggested he's going to sweep his desk clean, lay me over it, and fuck me senseless.

I tell myself that's a good thing.

It's not a good thing.

The anticipation is killing me. Not because I dread the inevitable, but because I crave it. And, yeah, I hate myself a little because what I should be doing is trying to gather information on Jenny and the parties.

I tell myself it's only my first day and I need to be careful—how much poking around can I really manage on Day One? But that's cold comfort. Jenny's counting on me, and I'm sitting here fantasizing about Holt, a man who may well be tied in with her demise.

With a sigh, I focus on the stack of documents in front of me. At least I have an actual office, which is the first time in my run of many, many jobs that I can say that. It's a strange little place, though. A hidden room located behind Lila's desk. Access is through either a door camouflaged in the wood paneling of the reception area or a door that connects the north side of my office directly to Holt's.

Right now, the door to reception is closed. The door to Holt's office is open, per his instructions. Good, because it allows me to eavesdrop, hoping for some mention of Jenny or parties or any potentially nefarious activity. Bad because Holt is a pacer. Which means that as he takes his various calls, he walks back and forth along the length of his office, that silky voice and magnificent body catching my attention with each and every pass by my doorframe.

"Why?" I'd asked when he told me about the open-door rule. "I'm sure I'll be able to concentrate better with the door closed, and these phones must have an intercom, right?"

"Because you're my PA, Aria." He'd held my gaze, emphasizing each word. "Personal. Assistant. That means I need you to be available at all times."

"Oh." Had I imagined the heat in his voice? I still wasn't sure. But the heat in my veins had suddenly pooled between my thighs as I remembered that line from *Pretty Woman*. Apparently, I really am Holt's beck-and-call girl, just like Clive had said.

Frankly, I like the sound of it more than I should, especially since I'm here so I can snoop around for any evidence that he or Hardline had a role in Jenny's death. But there's no denying the attraction, and until I'm certain Holt is in on it … well, they do say to be careful with pillow talk. Folks tend to reveal too much.

And what, I wonder, will Holt say once he calls in the lingerie marker I'm wearing and we're sharing that pillow? Or couch. Or desk.

The latter, I'm thinking, might be more his style.

So why the hell hasn't he made a move? If he's not planning to touch me, to close that gap between us—then why all the head games?

Because he gets off on it. He's playing cat and mouse, and I'm the mouse.

He's manipulating me. And knowing that truth only turns me on more.

As if to prove that point, my thoughts have been in a constant spin all morning as I've tried to organize a stack of files containing his notes, staff memos, scripts, budgets, union requests, guild queries, and on and on and on.

Who would have thought a company that works in visual media would generate so much paperwork?

There seems to be no rhyme or reason to the stack, but since its organization requires my full attention, I'm having a hard time eavesdropping on his calls.

I've spent the morning trying to tune into words like *Jenny* or *party* or *suicide* or *meet-and-greet* or anything that might be related to my friend. So far, I've got bupkis.

"A mess isn't it?" Lila says, making me jump when she appears in the reception-side doorway. She shakes her head and makes a *tsk*ing sound. "As I explained this morning, notes should be written directly into a computer file using the desktop template. But Matthew has a habit of scribbling on whatever paper happens to be on his desk. It's the sign of a creative mind."

"So that's what it is," I say dryly.

She just stares at me.

So much for female bonding.

As far as I can tell, Lila's poised, well-spoken, intelligent, and determined—the perfect buffer between Holt and What Lies Beyond The Office Door. In other words, she's giving off massive Watch Dog vibes, which means if I'm going to have any hope gaining enough alone time to do some serious poking around about Jenny, I'm going to have to suck up to her big time.

It's high school all over again. And I really hated high school.

She nods to the pile on my desk. "You'll be scanning those once you organize them. And remember, you're not just skimming, you need to read. If anything seems urgent or creatively intriguing, bring it to Matthew's attention."

I nod, surprised at my visceral—and unpleasant—reaction to her using his first name. "No problem," I say, though how I'm supposed to know what *creatively intriguing* means is anyone's guess.

She continues to stand, her head tilted as if she's waiting for me to say more.

"Uh, is there anything else you need?"

"It's three-past noon." There's a haughtiness to her voice, and I'm thinking that calling her the *watch dog* wasn't quite right. She's female, after all. The nickname requires a tad more specificity.

"Sorry," I say as I push back from my desk and stand. "And thank you for offering to show me around." *Insisted* is more like it, but that's probably par for the course with a Watch Bitch.

I fight a tiny smile, amused at my own inner monologue. Then I see Holt pass by the open door, deep in conversation about an option for some newbie's screenplay.

I mentally cringe. "Should I ...." I begin, not sure if I can just leave or if I need to catch his attention, and when I turn back to Lila, I think she looks a little smug. As if my confusion has validated her as the Top Dog in the office.

Like I was confused about that.

"It's fine," she says. "From twelve to one, you're on your own time. If you go to lunch early or late or take additional time off, tell him or send him a text—but first make sure he doesn't need you. You have his cell number?"

I nod. I'm now swimming in numbers, having been loaded down early in the day with cell numbers, office numbers, key-code numbers, and any number of other numbers.

"Then off we go."

I almost say that I'm happy to go to the employee dining room myself—after all, Lila intimidates the shit out of me—but she's also giving me the full tour and taking me to Human Resources so I can sign all the documents I completed electronically. And so I can pick up my keycard and ID. Since that's definitely a priority, I force myself to smile and follow her lead. After all, she probably knows him better than anyone. Who knows what I might learn by spending time with her?

As it turns out, I learn very little. About Matthew, anyway.

In truth, Lila's an excellent—if somewhat condescending—guide, and she knows the history of the company backward-and-forward. So well, in fact, that even though I feel my lacy under-things with every step, I soon manage to tune out that wicked question mark and simply let her words flow over me as she lays out the story of how Matthew worked and saved until he was able to produce his first film, a minor hit that got him some Hollywood attention.

"Because of that," she continues, her voice lyrical with pride, "he was able to find enough investors to fully fund his next three films, two of which went on to win numerous Academy Awards."

"And he's never taken the company public," I say. "Right?"

I think I see a bit of respect in the sidelong glance she shoots my direction, and I give myself a pat on the back for doing my homework.

"That's true. He's been approached multiple times, but he has no interest in a public company. This business is his only true love. In fact, he bought out his original investors before acquiring the land for this location."

"Impressive," I say.

"Very. And I've been with him for most of that journey." She looks at me, her expression somehow both amused and hard. "I know where all the bodies are buried."

"Are there a lot of bodies?" I hope my voice sounds casual. Just a little joke between new friends.

"Of course." Her mouth curves in the tiniest of smiles, and she starts walking again, her stride long and her heels clicking on the polished wood floor as I hurry to keep up for the rest of the tour.

Soon enough, all my paperwork is signed and I have my magic ID card that doubles as a key. It gets me through the Victory Boulevard gate and access to pretty much everywhere in the building, including my own little alcove. And—because I'm his PA and just signed eight billion NDAs and consents to be flogged if I use my key unwisely—I even have access to Matthew's office.

Okay, the flogging thing is an exaggeration. I think. I didn't actually read the documents. I mean, who reads the fine print?

I frown as I hold my keycard tight, thinking about my mission. And despite the possibility of flogging, I wonder if the card unlocks his file drawers as well. Because that could be very, very handy indeed.

When we return with to-go curry from the Dining Room, the door between my office and Holt's is closed. Odd since my edict was to keep it open. But when I sit at my desk to dig into my meal, I check his schedule, and immediately see why. Apparently, he's behind that door with two of my favorite actors and an up-and-coming director whose current movie is going gangbusters.

It takes all my willpower not to pretend I'm unaware and

just yank open the connecting door and waltz right in, but I manage. Partly, because I don't want to look like an idiot to Hollywood royalty. Mostly because if I'm going to have leeway to snoop around, Holt has to trust me, wholly and completely.

I hug myself, wondering if that's even possible. Bree's the only person in the world I trust that deeply, and that's true even though I love my parents to the moon and back. Love them, yes. But I haven't been able to step over the trust line since I was a little girl and they left me alone with monsters.

The thought is like cold water on my good mood, and I want to kick myself. I'm not a truster.

But most people aren't like me.

I'll win Holt's trust. I'm certain of it.

But whether I'll ever trust him? On that, I wouldn't lay odds.

ELEVEN

Holt pauses in front of the open door, the headset in his hand making clear that he's no longer on the phone. "How's your first day going?"

"Oh. Fine. Getting settled and digging in." I'm pushed back from my desk, my shoes kicked off and my feet on a box of unfiled documents. Since that seems a little too casual for a conversation with the boss, I start to move my legs.

"Don't," he says, his gaze leaving a trail of fire as it drifts from my toes to the hem of my skirt, then up over my thighs, then my breasts, then higher still until he meets my eyes. "I like you this way. Comfortable. Doing my bidding."

A smile tugs at the corner of his mouth. My own mouth is dry. Unlike certain other parts of me.

"All of my bidding," he adds.

I lick my lips as I try to think of something clever and flirtatious to say. I'm supposed to be the femme fatale in this particular drama. The woman who's invaded his private domain in order to find the truth and render justice, and right now, he's snared firmly in my web.

Unfortunately, I don't actually have a web, and my mind's

entirely forgotten how to function. All I see is him. All I feel is a slow burn spreading through my body, its growing intensity promising a wild burst of flame any second.

"Let me see," he demands. "Show me that you've met all the conditions for being in my office."

I tilt my head in what I hope is a flirtatious manner. "If you want to take a peek, nobody's stopping you."

"No?" He moves a step closer, his fingertips barely grazing the top of my foot, then easing higher as he inches closer. Soon, he's standing by my hip, his fingertips butterfly-soft on the skin above my knee and just below the hem of my skirt.

My breath catches in my throat, and my eyes meet his, only to look away for fear I might get burned by the heat I see there.

Then he's inching my skirt up, higher and higher, his fingers stroking soft, sensitive skin, and I'm trying so hard not to squirm, so hard not to crave his touch. I imagine the stroke of his finger along the edge of the panties, his soft touch as he slips under and inside me. The low growl when he—

"Aria?"

The fantasy shatters.

I jump to my feet, my heart pounding in my chest as I turn to see Lila standing at my reception-side door, her arms crossed as she looks at me with a furrowed brow.

"Sorry," I say, hoping she can't read my mind. "Just resting my eyes before another round of computer entries."

"Hmm." She taps her watch, her brow furrowed as if she can see all my prurient thoughts. "I leave at three on Mondays and Fridays. I've switched the reception phone to your desk." She nods to the door that leads to Holt's office, still closed. "I expect he'll be at least another half-hour in this meeting. I know your work history is ... checkered. Can you handle his calls for the rest of the day?"

I assure her I can, trying to keep the glee out of my voice.

She gives me a dubious look, then continues to linger in the doorway. So long, in fact, that if another minute passes, I might just end up confessing everything.

Thankfully, her eyes do another quick run over me, then she nods and strides out of my tiny space. My computer can access the floor's security video, and as soon as I see her disappear into the elevator, I do a little fist pump.

Let the snooping begin.

I hurry out of my alcove and into the reception area, then park myself behind Lila's desk. I can't access her computer, of course, but Holt's policy is to keep hard copies of anything important. Which means that what I'm really interested in are the file drawers built into the cabinetry behind her workstation. Too bad I don't know exactly what I'm looking for. A file labeled *Garland, Jenny*? Probably not. And while I might hope for *Illegal Activities*, that seems unlikely, too.

Which means I'm going to have to rifle through as much as I can, and hope for the best.

Since I don't want interruptions during this project—and since I don't have the benefit of the hall camera from out here—I hurry over to the door and lock it, even though Holt has an open-door policy, and it's supposed to be unlocked from ten to five.

Well, let them knock.

With luck, there won't be any visitors.

With more luck, neither Holt nor his guests will burst out of his office.

I swivel the chair and tug on a file drawer. Nothing happens.

I try again. Nothing. There's no indication that the lock is electronic, but I swipe my key card along the top and front just in case.

Nada.

There are ten file drawers behind Lila's desk, and every single one of them is locked. So are the desk drawers. And since there's no keyhole that I see, I think the lock must be electronic. Or biometric. Or some other fancy security set-up that's part of the Billionaire Office Security Package, and therefore above my pay grade.

I could probably jimmy them—but since I haven't a clue how to do that, they'd end up mangled by me banging the end of a screwdriver with a hammer. Not the subtle sneaky approach I'm going for. Plus, Holt would probably hear the banging. Plus, I don't have a screwdriver or a hammer on me.

A pity, especially since something incriminating might be tucked into these drawers.

But the truth is, I don't really believe that. Holt's too careful. He wouldn't trust someone else to hide his red flags, not even Lila, who's his right-hand gal. At least she thinks so.

No, if it's important—if it's dangerous or inculpatory—he's going to keep it close.

Which means I don't need Lila's files. I need Holt's. And that is something that's clearly not happening. At least not now. And probably not tomorrow. That kind of access requires either criminal-level sneakiness or a hefty dose of trust. Normally, I'd go for sneaky, but in this case, I think trust will be easier. After all, Matthew set the terms of my employment, and the simple fact is that sex often morphs into trust. That's Psych 101.

And that's what I'm counting on.

With a little moan, I squeeze my legs together, my body still tingling after my daydream, and since Lila's gone, I allow my overactive imagination to conjure the glorious sensation of his fingers inside the silky, lacy thong.

Soon, I think. Sex first, then snooping.

It's what makes women such excellent spies.

With my freshly hatched sex-then-files plan, I feel more

centered, but not enough to just sit around. And I do have one avenue I can investigate right now.

With that thought, I press the intercom button. "I'm sorry to interrupt, Mr. Holt," I say in my Officious Assistant voice, "but Ms. Blackstone's left for the day and I need to run down to Human Resources. More new hire paperwork."

"That's fine," he says. "Just leave the placard on Lila's desk."

He's referring to the "Please Have a Seat" sign that she'd shown me earlier. I plop it on the desktop, then hurry into the hall, giddy with the prospect of action.

The same clerk's minding the Human Resources desk when I arrive. I tell her what I need, then take a seat as she disappears into what must be the vault from the last scene of *Raiders of the Lost Ark* because it takes her forever to return.

"I'm sorry," she says, pushing a red curl off her forehead. "I can't locate it." She's a bit out of breath, and I believe her when she adds that she looked everywhere she could think of.

"What's missing?" Lila's soul sister approaches the clerk, then turns to me as if I'm some sort of troublemaker.

I resist the urge to put my hands up and take a step back. Instead, I tell her that I'm Mr. Holt's new PA and that I'm trying to locate Jenny Garland's personnel file for my boss. "She was a background actor on at least one film," I add, hoping the extra info helps.

"I've looked everywhere," the clerk says.

The stern woman looks down her nose at me. "You must have misunderstood Mr. Holt."

I freeze, certain she's going to call Holt, and since he's no dummy, he'll realize that I'm nosing around about who killed Jenny, and I'll lose this job, attract the attention of the bad guys —assuming Holt's not leading them—and end up tossed over a bridge myself.

None of that happens.

But what she does say is almost as terrifying. "Mr. Holt requested that file himself about two weeks ago. If he's misplaced it, I can check the server for the scanned backup, but—"

"No, no. You're absolutely right. I realize now that misunderstood. I assumed I had to come down here, when really he was very clear." I've taken two steps back. Now I add a turn toward the door. "I'm so sorry to have bothered you. I really didn't mean to take up your time."

And with that, I yank open the door and disappear into the hall, my heels clattering as I walk-run to the elevator before one of them decides to follow and interrogate me.

It's not until I'm on the elevator that the bottom line sinks in. *Holt has Jenny's file.* And he pulled it not long after she died.

Why?

Does this mean he really did have something to do with her death? Or is he just a man with such a need for control that he doesn't want anyone else—like the police—looking at it without going through it first himself?

Except surely the police already looked at it, assuming they were interested at all. As far as the LAPD is concerned, Jenny Garland committed suicide. End of story.

So why does he have it? I don't know, but it's a pretty good guess that the file includes something incriminating ... and that her death was somehow tied to Hardline Entertainment.

I'm shaking my head as the elevator slides to a halt on twelve, hating that scenario. And the truth is, the file could be completely bland, and Holt requested it simply because of her death.

I just don't know. And the only way to figure it out is to find the file in Holt's office and do what I came here to do. *Snoop.*

The doors open, and I gasp as Francesca Muratti, the acclaimed actress, steps on as I step off. I'm a huge fan, but I'm so muddled up in thoughts of Jenny that I don't even introduce myself as Holt's PA.

I'm still feeling muddled and uneasy and very, very confused when I arrive back at the office. Only Matthew is there, and the double doors between reception and his private office are wide open. He's standing by the window, his back to the door, his headset on. One hand is in his pocket, and although I know that he may turn and see me at any time, I can't help but step closer, trying to hear as he speaks in a low, firm voice.

I catch only a few words—something about a report and PR implications, followed by, "Dammit, that's not what I want to hear, and you know it. And as for the functions, the moment they become a liability, we shut it down. If we get audited because someone's not accounting for expenses the way we discussed, there will be hell to pay. And these were never intended to be a profit-making program, so we need to revisit that at the next board meeting."

I hold my breath as he stays silent, listening.

"Fine," he says after a significant pause. "Tell Joel to get his ass up here tomorrow. And, yes, I know he's new here, but that's not an excuse for unilaterally deciding that budgetary restrictions don't apply to him. He can call Lila in the morning and she'll squeeze him in. No excuses."

He ends the call abruptly, then turns around, his attention going right to me.

I freeze, only relaxing when a flicker of amusement crosses his face. "Damn windows are like mirrors," he says. "And now you're wondering if that was one of my intentional design choices or just a happy coincidence."

"You don't seem to be a man who lives by coincidence, Mr. Holt."

"If there are no guests in the office, then 'Matthew' is fine," he says, motioning for me to enter.

"Sure, um, Matthew," I say, surprised by how much I like the feel of his name on my tongue.

His desk is littered with dozens of file folders labeled with films and shows in various stages of development or production. But what really catches my attention are the booklets of word games—everything from Wordle to crosswords to Jumble. Bree and Jenny and I were anagram fiends back in high school, and this tiny little connection to Matthew leaves a surprisingly warm feeling in my belly.

I try to act casual as I stack and shuffle, as if tidying is the reason he'd beckoned for me. It wasn't, of course. But I'm not sure if I'm about to be chastised for eavesdropping or if he's finally going to acknowledge what I'm wearing under my suit.

The thought of the first rattles me, but the second rattles me even more. I've been waiting all day, and if his goal was to have me spend the day half-lost in sensual anticipation, he has very much achieved that objective.

"Trouble with the press?" I ask, my voice carefully neutral. "I didn't mean to eavesdrop, but I heard you mention PR."

He waves it off. "There's always trouble, Ms. Parker. It's the way of the world." He gives me a smile that feels half genuine, half predatory. "The business world, at any rate."

He stands for a moment, watching me work. There's something oddly intimate about having his attention like that, and it's making me more than a little fidgety. I'm about to pretend that my phone's buzzed in my pocket when I notice the yellow pad on the corner of his desk blotter. His handwriting covers it, mostly scribbled words and numbers. But in the bottom right, I see the letters JG. They've been overwritten with multiple pens, and circled, too. As if JG were something weighing on his mind.

My stomach goes tight, and I force myself to continue stacking papers, putting several other pads on top of that one.

If he's noticed my reaction he doesn't show it. On the contrary, he waves a hand to indicate the couch. "Come sit and tell me about your first day."

I comply, telling myself that JG could mean anything. He was talking on the phone with someone named Joel, after all. For all I know, Joel's last name is Gotlieb.

It's a valid point, and I cram it through my thick, suspicious head as I take a seat.

"Drink?" he asks, so casually, I have to assume the note meant nothing. Otherwise, wouldn't he have told me to ignore the desk in the first place?

"I'd love a drink," I say, which right then is *so* very true. I look around for a bar, and since I don't see one, I expect him to pull a bottle of bourbon from a drawer in his desk.

Instead, he moves across the room and opens the top hemisphere of an antique globe to reveal a small bar.

I clap my hand over my mouth to muffle my little squeak of surprise and delight.

He turns to me, brows raised in question.

"The bar," I explain. "I've wanted one of those since I was a kid and my parents showed me—"

"*Dr. No,*" we say in unison, then laugh.

He holds up a bottle of Glenfiddich 50-Year-Old, a seriously impressive bottle, but I just shrug. "What? No vodka martini, shaken not stirred?"

"I can do that if you'd rather," he says, calling my bluff.

"No, no. I give up. I want the Glenfiddich."

"I don't know. We shared a Bond moment. Maybe—"

"Give me the damn whisky," I say, making him laugh.

"Neat?"

"That vintage? Hell, yes."

He pours, then brings me the liquid gold. Our fingers brush and I feel a jolt that's from more than anticipation of this rare drink.

I take it carefully so as not to spill. And I definitely don't confess that I've never had such an expensive drink.

He pours his own, then joins me on the couch. He lifts his glass and we clink a toast. "Thank you," I say, hoping he hears the sincerity.

"A whisky this special is meant to be shared."

"In that case, thank you for sharing it with me."

Our eyes meet. "You're very welcome."

We both take a sip, and I savor the taste, noticing that he's doing the same. "Amazing." I practically purr the word, which doesn't do the drink justice at all.

"I like to collect amazing things. Things that inspire me or challenge me. Sometimes I collect something just because I want to understand it better."

"Oh?" I take another sip, trying to hide my certainty that he's talking about me. "Like what?"

"Well, whisky, actually. And Kentucky bourbon. I even dipped a toe into gin, but that wasn't a good fit."

"You wanted to understand them?"

He chuckles, clearly hearing my wry tone. "I did. I was twenty-three and even though my dad was a drunk, I didn't have a clue about spirits. I grew up dirt poor, so we never had something like this. Not unless my dad snatched it, anyway."

I realize I'm leaning forward, and he has my complete attention. "Did he do that? Steal?"

Matthew meets my eyes, then nods slowly. "From time to time. Or, more accurately, every damn day. Point being, I wanted to learn about whisky. Bond might be a vodka man, but I'd seen enough by then to know that deals were made in rooms where men drank. And the richer the men, the pricier the drink. I was dirt poor, and I couldn't fix that."

I tilt my head. "Um, look around you."

"I couldn't fix it overnight," he says with a nod to my correction. "I figured if I didn't have money, I could have knowledge. If I knew about The Dalmore 62, then wouldn't folks assume I was someone who could afford it?"

"So you went to Scotland?"

"And Kentucky and a number of other places. Spent a year learning and walked away a connoisseur."

"And did it work? You could name the good stuff, so did folks assume you could afford it, too?"

His grin is more than a little smug. "Like you said—look around you."

I laugh, genuinely impressed. Then I lean back, letting myself settle into the cushion and get more comfortable than I probably should with this man. But right or wrong, I trust him a little bit more now.

That, I think, was probably what he was hoping for. But I can't fault him for it. I believe the story, and if it's a lie, well, at least it was entertaining. No surprise there, I suppose. Entertainment is part of his company's name.

"And now you have a whole world filled with the good stuff," I say, nodding to his globe.

"I guess I do."

"I was barely ten when I saw the movie," I tell him. "The couch, my dad, and a big bowl of popcorn. I wanted it for toys. I thought hiding Mr. Quack and the rest in the center of the world was the coolest idea ever."

"Mr. Quack?"

I feel my cheeks heat. "A stuffed duck I had when I was a kid." I don't mention that I still have him.

"I was thirteen the first time I saw it," he says. "It was at a revival house in Manhattan. I snuck in. Decided right then I wanted to be James Bond."

"Is that your way of telling me that you're a spy pretending to be a movie mogul?"

He gives me a long, dry stare. "I could tell you, but then I'd have to kill you."

I try to fight my grin but fail. "Your secrets are safe with me."

He tilts his head as if studying me. As if wondering if I really mean that. Honestly, I think maybe I do.

One corner of his mouth curves up. "That would be quite a burden," he says. "I have so many." He shifts on the sofa. Now he's positioned so that he could put his hand on my leg. But he's not so close that he's in my personal space.

I kind of want him to slide into my personal space.

I clear my throat. "Why not tell me one? I'll prove to you I can keep your secret, and you can relieve yourself of a burden. Sounds like a win-win to me."

His smile lights his face, and he leans back, his right arm stretched along the top of the couch behind me. It's not touching me, but I'm overly aware of it, as if the air between my back and his arm is warmer than the rest of the room. "Already she's trying to move up in my organization."

I shake my head, not understanding.

"Your excellent negotiating skills," he says. "You won't stay a PA for long."

I tilt my head and meet his gaze dead on, taking control of the moment. "Maybe I like the job. *Personal* assistant, I mean."

I'm playing with fire, and I know it. But the plan was to get close. And so far, what's under my outfit hasn't worked as the first-string play, despite Matthew having chosen that play himself.

That's when I realize that while I'm still wearing my suit

jacket, he's not wearing his jacket or his tie. The first two buttons of his shirt are undone, and I can see just a smattering of hair on his chest. He must have shed the corporate uniform when his meeting ended.

In a whoosh, the ease and control I'd felt moments earlier slips away with the stealth of James Bond himself. I'm no longer cool and calm, and butterflies are doing the Rumba in my stomach.

I start to take a sip of my drink—I need it—but he lifts his hand to stop me. "What shall we drink to?"

I hesitate, then look him straight in the eye as I say, "To friendship and loyalty."

He nods. If he reads anything into my words, he doesn't show it. "And to new beginnings," he adds, then clinks my glass. His gaze lingers on mine, and while it might be my imagination, I think I catch a hint of challenge in his eyes.

"And new adventures," I add before taking a sip. The words feel bold, but his smile deepens, as if I've passed some sort of test.

He tilts his head, studying me over the rim of his glass. "This industry can be ... challenging," he says, his voice low. "Especially for those who don't know what they're getting into."

"And we're talking about me?"

"On the contrary. I think you know exactly what you're getting into. I think you like a challenge. An adventure." As he speaks, his gaze dips briefly—almost imperceptibly—to the hem of my skirt, currently sitting midway up my thigh.

I feel his words as if they're a physical touch, skimming over the lace he knows I'm wearing. He hasn't mentioned the lingerie, but every glance, every pause in his speech reminds me of it, keeping me acutely aware that beneath my professional facade, I've followed his every command.

I cast about for a clever retort, but one doesn't come, and I'm left with the rather mortifying realization that even though I know this man may very well be complicit in Jenny's death, all I want in this moment is his touch. His hands on my skin. His mouth on my lips. It's been too long since I've felt the kind of tug I feel with Holt, like I'm a live wire ready to spark.

I work to steady my breath, hoping he can't hear my heartbeat. I take a long sip of my whisky, needing to feel that burn.

I'm lost in a sea of frustration, wanting to beg, but knowing that would take me out of the game.

And that's when I realize the truth—this is a game. The job, the lingerie, even the desire in his eyes. It's real. I don't think I'm fooling myself about that. But the rest of this—the commanding manner, the sexy underthings, the hand on my thigh. The arm behind my back.

Even the buzz from the whisky. It's a game of control. And every move is him telling me that he's won.

I should be furious. I'm not.

Instead, I'm more desperate than ever for his touch. Not that I'm going to tell him that.

In fact—damn him—I do the only thing I can do to shift the score back to my side of the court. I slide away from him, then study his face, looking for a sign that I've broken from the script.

But he's as unreadable as ever.

"I should get going," I say, expecting him to reach for me. To pull me back. To tell me I can't leave until I show him that I obeyed. That I'm wearing the underwear he sent with the contract.

He doesn't say a word. He doesn't try to pull me back.

"Nine tomorrow?" I ask once I'm standing.

He leans back against the smooth leather, both arms spread, one hand slowly swirling his drink. "Nine sharp. And Aria," he adds with a cocky half-smile, "welcome to the team."

TWELVE

Matthew kept a loose hand on the wheel, letting the low purr of the Aston Martin's engine act as a balm on his frayed nerves as he navigated the straights and curves of Mulholland Drive, his headlights the only illumination on this moonless night.

To his right, night spread over the Valley like a glitter-covered shroud, the soft twinkle of lights seeming to mock him, whispering that he was an idiot, a cornered man who'd chosen to dance with danger, and now he was paying the price.

With a low growl, he shifted gears, taking the next curve at a speed that could only be described as foolish. But tonight he was dancing with the devil. And when Satan has you in his clutches, the only way to survive is to boogie on to the bitter end.

The rawness in his gut taunted him. A gnawing uncertainty that had been growing over the past few weeks. Jenny Garland's death was a crack in the foundation of his empire, and if he wasn't careful, the house of cards he'd risked so much to build would come tumbling down.

He hit the accelerator hard, hugging the curve as thoughts of Aria taunted him. The way she looked at him, as if she could see behind every mask he wore. She was trouble, he had no doubt about that. And he had to rein her in before she became yet another crack in the foundation.

He almost smiled, because he knew exactly how to distract her. And the good news was that he would enjoy it. Hell, they both would. Not to mention all the other upsides: Keep her close. Keep her occupied. Keep her busy. Keep her safe.

Not a bad assignment for himself. Not bad at all.

And that twinge of guilt? Well, he knew better than anyone how to quash guilt. How to box it up and hide it behind your heart. A heavy load, maybe, but he'd had years to learn how to carry the burden.

A jolt of anger roared through him and he shifted gears, speeding up as he took a sharp turn. His thoughts raced as fast as the little red Vantage, careening through the tangled mess of secrets and lies buried deep within the company he'd built.

He had to move carefully. Stealthily.

For years, the city had tagged him as one of Hollywood's bad boys.

Well, they had no idea.

This bad boy had a plan. Wheels already set in motion. And when it was all over, he'd be the one on top. That much he swore on the memory of the stone he'd named the Duck, the biggest gem he ever stole. The yellow diamond that had put him on the path to the man he was today.

A respected man. An honored man.

And, yes, a dangerous man.

And now someone was fucking with him? Trying to hold him back?

Someone was going to lose.

Matthew Alexander Holt did not get fucked. Quite the opposite. And if everybody in this town didn't already know that, they soon would.

But first he had to do something about Aria before she

unraveled the entire thing—and got caught in barbed wire in the process.

Damn her.

Damn her and the way she looked at him, the fire in her eyes making his heart go soft and his cock go hard. Damn her for picking the worst time to start poking around in his business.

Most of all, damn her for making him feel things he had no business feeling.

She was poison wrapped in temptation, and if he wasn't careful, she'd destroy him.

With a guttural growl, Matthew shifted gears again, steering off the treacherous road as he executed a dangerous U-turn. He didn't want her involved in this—not in any way. The risks were too high, and she had no idea just how deadly was the snake that she was poking.

He told himself to just go home. What was that saying? *Sufficient unto the day is the evil thereof.*

That about summed it up. He should head home, crawl into bed, and sleep it off. Not alcohol, but the day itself. Tomorrow would come soon enough, with more than enough problems to tackle.

But somehow his car refused to head higher into the hills to his home. Instead, he found himself back down in Burbank, maneuvering through a quiet, residential neighborhood. He made a right, then a left, then tapped the brakes when he found it—an unassuming one-story tucked in between other cookie-cutter houses. Nothing like the magnificent home of glass and wood and steel he'd designed, as much a work of contemporary art as his collection.

It didn't matter. This little suburban home was like an anchor. A reminder of something simpler. Purer.

Something he'd never had, but had always wanted. How

had he jumped right over that, from poverty to opulence? Had he been lucky? A prodigy? Or just a damn fool?

He didn't know. For that matter, he didn't care. There was only one certainty in the world as far as he was concerned, and that was the fact that you couldn't go back. No matter how much it might suck, the only option was forward.

So here he was, parked across the street. He'd cut the engine, but his pulse still thrummed, the adrenaline from his drive refusing to fade. But as he thought of her, the tension began to ease.

She soothed him. Her sharp tongue. Her contagious laugh. It was dangerous, letting her get under his skin like this. Dangerous and stupid.

He drummed his fingers on the wheel, his gaze drifting to her doorstep, thinking of her behind those walls. His balls tightened, his cock going hard as he imagined her in the lingerie he'd selected, his fingers stroking her skin, pulling off the silk and lace, laying her bare before him.

He groaned, something dark and primal twisting inside him. He hated himself for it, but he couldn't stop the way his imagination ran wild, picturing her wide open for him, her confidence mingling with just a hint of vulnerability.

He couldn't afford to let her distract him, no matter how much she got under his skin.

But she already had, hadn't she? She was in his thoughts, his plans, his blood. As much as he wanted to keep her out of this mess, he knew it was too late. She was already in the game. And whether he wanted to protect her or control her, only one thing was certain—he couldn't let her go, not even if he wanted to. Whether to save her or silence her, he wasn't sure. All he knew was that she was his now, whether she realized it or not.

He turned the key, the engine roaring back to life. He spared one last glance at her house before pulling away, his jaw set and his mind racing. He just needed a little more time. A little more space to tie up the loose ends and take control of the situation.

And as for Aria? He'd keep her close. Watch her. Protect her if he could. Stop her if he had to.

Because this game wasn't over. Not by a long shot.

THIRTEEN

The monsters are back.

I feel them pressing me down into the rough carpet of the living room, their voices filled with scornful laughter as I stare up at the ceiling, too scared to breathe, too small to fight back. Their words slither over each other, talking around me, through me, but I can't make out what they're saying.

I'm trapped.

Terrified.

A scream locks in my throat and tears fill my eyes. I want to move. I want to leave.

But all I can do is hide inside myself, counting the seconds until they leave me alone.

Will they ever leave me alone?

I tremble, wanting to lash out. To pound and scratch and bite, but I'm too small, and they're monsters. How could I ever beat the monsters?

And then he's there. The Stair Man.

My eyes widen, and I'm about to cry out, but he lifts a finger to his lips. He's halfway up the staircase, hidden inside the shadows as he looks down at me, strong and silent, waiting for the right moment to pull me away from this. From them.

And then, before I even know what's happened, the monsters are gone, and I'm standing tall and straight, no longer a child but a woman clothed in nothing but lace and silk, soft against my skin.

My nipples are hard, and when I look up, The Stair Man is right in front of me.

Not the shadowed figure of my childhood, but Matthew Holt. Those intense, green eyes trace over me, sending a lingering heat spiraling through me. He steps forward, and his gaze is as potent as a touch.

"Please," I whisper, and his only answer is a slow, sexy smile as he traces a finger from my lace-covered breasts all the way down to the band of the tiny thong.

My heart pounds, anticipating what comes next. His finger slipping beneath the band, finding my core. Then sliding inside me as he pulls me close for a kiss so wild and passionate that it will send me over the edge, spiraling into a whirlwind of pleasure.

"Please," I repeat, but the word catches in my throat as I see movement behind him. A shadow. A woman.

Lila.

She's standing just beyond him, watching us with a cold, dark malice.

"You're a fool not to realize he's playing you. He's a magician, you know. An expert at sleight of hand. You see what he wants you to see."

"No," I begin, but my words are cut off as the room shifts under me, everything twisting and blurring. The silk and lace are gone. I'm naked. Vulnerable. Trapped.

A scream rips out of me, and I thrust myself upright as my

eyes fly open. I gasp, confused, my skin hot, my body tangled in my sheets.

Then I see Mr. Quack's adorable yellow face on the night-stand, and my body goes limp with relief.

A dream. It had only been a dream.

But even so, my core is wet and my nipples are tight—and the featherlight touch of his fingers lingers like a ghost against my skin.

———

I'm curled up under a blanket on the couch, the television on mute, the images only for company. I take another sip of the wine I'd poured, telling myself the hour doesn't matter. I need wine now to steady my nerves.

Holt.

With a sigh, I drag my fingers through my newly-conservative hairstyle as the reality of my plan settles around me.

A bad plan. A dangerous plan.

Jenny's initials were right there on his desk blotter. And that conversation I overheard? A PR nightmare? Hardline events that were a liability? That had to be the meet-and-greets, didn't it?

I can't be sure, but the knot in my gut says yes, and I try to steady my nerves. Even in dreams, he's got me wrapped around his finger, and he doesn't even know it.

Or maybe he does.

Maybe that's the most dangerous part.

I force myself to take long, slow breaths. This is a bad idea. A very bad idea. Whatever's going on at those parties, Hardline's in the middle of it. Somehow, Hardline's responsible for Jenny's death. I may not have concrete proof, but I know what I know, and in my gut, I'm positive. And even though Bree would say it's just woo bullshit, my gut is hardly ever wrong.

But if Hardline is at the center, then so is Matthew Holt.

A equals A, after all.

Fuck.

I toss back the rest of my wine, then head into my kitchen for another bottle. I refill my glass, then pace my living room as I empty it in four long swallows. And pour once again.

I don't want those thoughts in my head. I don't want to believe he's bad. I've laughed with him. Craved him. Shared drinks with him.

Hell, I've admired him. The way he built that company. The command he exercises over everyone he employs. The way he worked his way to the top. The confidence he always exudes.

Or is it just a fake confidence based on lies? Are the stories about his rise fiction? Instead of climbing his way up using intellect and talent as footholds, did he really claw his way to the top, with lies and deceit and violence?

I close my eyes, fighting the urge to hug myself.

He can't be the bad guy. A man like that—he should be the hero.

The words echo through me as I finish off the bottle, then plop down on the sofa, my blood too full of wine, my head too full of that man.

No.

I don't want him in my head.

I don't want to believe any of the thoughts swirling through my brain.

Mostly, I don't want to want him.

But I can't erase him. I've left sober behind, and my thoughts no longer obey my commands. Even if I was stone cold steady, I'm not sure I could banish him, no matter how much I might tell myself I want to.

Fuck it.

I stand and start pacing, albeit unsteadily. I need him out of my head. I need to step back so I can have some perspective on this man. On who he is. On what I fear he's done.

The next thing I know, my phone's in my hand, and the line is ringing.

It rings twice before he picks up. "Hey, stranger," he says, his words full of heat.

The sound of his voice snaps me back, and I hang up, my heart pounding even harder. *Stupid, stupid, stupid.*

The screen lights up as he calls me back immediately. I consider ignoring it, but I push the damn button anyway.

"Sorry," I say, trying to sound casual. "That was a butt dial."

"Sure it was." I can practically hear him smirking on the other end. "I can come over. Bring some wine. Or maybe something stronger ..."

Something about his tone both entices and disappoints. Like he's too eager, too quick to slip into that role.

"Tempting," I say. "But no."

"You sure? I'm—"

But I don't know what he is because I've ended the call.

Then I pull up my contacts, find the entry for Decker and hit *block*. I don't want a fast fuck with my go-to FWB.

I want Holt. And I hate myself for that weakness.

God, I'm a mess.

Without thinking, I dial another number—Bree's. One ring. Another. Then another.

When it kicks to voicemail I glance at the time. Almost midnight.

Well, damn.

I toss my phone onto the coffee table and pull the snuggly blanket up around my shoulders. I should be tired, but I'm not. I guess my cat nap took care of that. So instead of moving to the bedroom and sliding into bed, I use the remote to click on the television, then randomly poke around the various streaming menus until I stumble on *Jagged Edge*. I haven't seen it in years, so I hit play, pick up my wine, and settle back to watch this movie where a man kills the woman he's sleeping with.

And how fucked up is that?

FOURTEEN

The rattle of a key in the lock jolts me awake, and I leap off the couch, slamming my shin against the coffee table in the process. My heart pounds as my gaze darts around the dim room. For one insane second, I'm certain that Jack Forrester is here, and it's not Glenn Close he's come to kill, but me.

Then I realize that I'm not lost inside *Jagged Edge*. It's Bree.

"Are you insane?" I howl, clutching my leg as pain radiates through my entire body. My voice is sharp with irritation and laced with lingering fear. "You scared me to death."

"Sorry! I'm sorry! But you freaked me out, too. You called. You hung up. What was I supposed to do?"

"Assume I hit the wrong speed dial?" I press my fingers to my temples, then stumble toward the kitchen, desperate for some Ibuprofen.

"I know—I just ..."

"What?" I sag with relief when I find three pills still in the bottle. I swallow them dry, then wash them down with a gulp of wine as Bree gives me the stink-eye.

"You're a mess, my friend."

"And that," I say, "is why I hung up. You don't need to be

dealing with my mess right now. You're leaving the country in just a few hours. That gives you a complete and total pass on all my drama."

"I can sleep on the plane." She flops onto the sofa, then leans forward, her hands on her knees as she looks at me hard. "I'm worried about you."

"I'm fine," I say, the words coming as automatically as *please* or *thank you*.

"The hell you are. Jenny is dead. And maybe it was suicide, and that's a tragedy. But maybe she didn't kill herself. And you're in the thick of it, my friend. If there was foul play—" She cuts herself off with a shake of her head. "Dammit, Ari. I can't lose you. Not ever."

I bite my lower lip as tears prick my eyes. "I love you, too. You know that right?"

"Well, duh."

We both laugh, and I plop my ass onto the sofa next to her, then scrub my hands over my face. "Ash is going to kill me."

She waves a hand in dismissal. "He respects the Girl Code. Besides, he's pulling an all-nighter to prep for a call at six in the freaking morning. Then we head out. We'll both sleep on the plane."

"What time do you have to be at the airport?"

She shrugs. "It's flexible. We're taking one of Damien's jets. Grayson's piloting."

"Poor little rich bitch," I say, fighting a smile.

She laughs. "I know, right? My in-laws rock. I mean, I love Ash, but skipping the TSA line? That's a reason to get married right there."

"You're not wrong," I say, and we share a grin that lasts a good twenty seconds before hers fades.

"I can stay if you need me. Truly."

"The hell you can. Besides, I'm fine."

From the way her eyes narrow, I can tell she doesn't believe me. Doesn't matter, because no way am I holding my BFF back from the Grand Prix. "I've got this," I say. "Big girl. All grown up."

She lifts a shoulder. "Sometimes I wonder."

I cock my head, then flip her the bird.

"Really? That's your best comeback?"

"What can I say? It's late. And I've had a hell of a long day." I drop back onto the couch beside her, then hook an arm around her shoulder.

"I wish I could help more," she says.

I shrug. "It would be weird if both of us applied to work at Hardline. And the man's producing your movie. Not to be crass, but you don't want to piss him off before it hits theaters. Me?" I shrug. "I'm nothing to him."

"Oh, please," she says. "The man bought you lingerie. He flirted at Masque. And I saw the way he looked at you that time by Damien's pool."

"No way," I say, hoping I don't sound as pleased as I am to hear that little tidbit of info.

"Way," she says. "Definitely way." She shifts on the sofa to look at me more directly. "And I saw the way you looked at him, too."

The words hang there, waiting for me to deny them. But I can't. They're true. And if I try to lie ... well, this is Bree. Lying isn't an option.

"He can't be involved," I whisper. "Someone in Hardline, maybe, but not Holt himself."

I see her shift, ready to argue, but all she does is nod, then squeeze my hand. "No," she says, "he can't."

I draw a breath, telling myself I'm confident in his innocence. Because how the hell could I so desperately want the kind of man who could kill a sweetheart like Jenny?

A shiver runs up my spine.

Bree's brow furrows. "You okay?"

"What? Yes. Of course. I'm just sitting here stewing in jealousy," I add, in a not-too-subtle attempt to change the subject. "You're going to Monte Carlo with the man you love. You're living the dream, my friend."

"I guess I am." She squeezes my hand. "I want that for you, too."

"Someday." I say the word casually, as if it's no big deal. But the truth is that there's an image in my mind. A man standing with his hand extended, waiting for me to start a life with him. *Matthew Holt.*

No.

Matthew isn't the kind of guy who'll settle down. He owns a sex club. He's married to his business.

He's ruthless.

And he's the kind of man who would kill to protect whatever or whoever he loves.

The thought comes unbidden and I shiver, because as much as Matthew might push all my good buttons, I know it's true.

A wave of cold horror crashes over me as I realize what that means. If he has it in him to kill, then as much as the idea disgusts and terrifies me, maybe he did kill Jenny. And if so, who or what was he trying to protect?

Minutes later, the thought still lingers as I stand on the porch, leaning against one of the posts as I wave Bree off and tell myself that I'm not jealous. Not jealous at all.

And I'm not. I'm beyond happy for her. No one deserves romance and bliss more than that girl, who's been through so damn much, and is still standing. I don't begrudge her a single moment of happiness. Truly.

And yet ...

I sigh, hating my own thoughts. Hating this envy that runs

through my core. It's buried deep enough that I can hide it, but it's part of me, and though I try to deny it, the truth is that I want what she has—love and laughter and a life with a man who adores her.

I tell myself it's just a matter of time. That one day, Prince Charming will ride in and rescue me. But there are only so many princes in the world and fairy tales are fiction.

My best friend may have won the lottery—but that just means the odds really aren't in my favor.

"Fuck it," I whisper as I turn to head back into the house and, finally, get some sleep. As I do, the headlights from a passing car illuminate the porch. That's when I see it. A small purple bag tucked in behind a large pot that—maybe someday—will actually have a plant inside it. The purple blends with the shadows cast by the dim porch light, and I suppose that's why neither Bree nor I noticed it earlier.

Matthew Holt.

I scoop up the bag, certain it's from him, then hurry inside. I hesitate only a moment before I dump out the contents—then feel a distinctive tug between my legs and a tightening in my breasts as I look down at the small, tissue-wrapped bundle. There's no card, just a handwritten note taped to the package—*for tomorrow.*

I should be annoyed, but I'm not. On the contrary, every one of my cells is firing. And the Siren's call of my bed? Yeah, I'm not sleepy at all anymore.

I tell myself I should be angry. He's playing games with me, and damned inappropriate ones.

Plus, it's not like he's Prince Charming. No matter how much I might be attracted to him, I know I should back away. He's controlling. Manipulative. Quite possibly dangerous.

So what if he makes my heart race or inspires a variety of bedtime fantasies? So what if the thing I want more than anything is to know for certain that he isn't tied in with Jenny's death?

I close my eyes and fist my hands. *So what if he makes me a horny, needy mess?*

I take a breath and square my shoulders, soldiering myself for action. I'll call him up. Tell him he's an idiot if he thinks I'm going to just put this on and head to work in the morning, because—

I stop, my body having gone stiff from the force of the plan that now dominates my thoughts. *I'm not wearing these tomorrow.*

Hell, no.

I'm wearing them tonight.

He wants to play games? Fine. I'm taking the game to him.

FIFTEEN

Holt's address is a well-kept secret, but it turns out that as his shiny new PA, I'll have the privilege of schlepping things to him when he works at home. Which is why his address and the number for his landline are both right there on the Key Information sheet that Lila emailed to me earlier in the day.

Even better, for those occasions when I might have to deliver something when he's not home, I have the code to his front door.

As far as I'm concerned, that pretty much makes my mission pre-ordained.

Now, I'm standing on the dark street, well out of the circle of light thrown by the single streetlamp. It's a dead-end, and Holt's house is at the very end, the front door accessed by a staircase that dips down into the canyon. I take the steps slowly, appreciating the dim illumination built into the railing. I pause at the first landing, realizing the home is built like a treehouse. It sits atop a massive concrete pole buried deep into the hills. The pole—which I assume encloses an elevator, rises up to the stunning, round home at which I'm currently gaping.

It takes me a moment to find the entrance, and by the time

my finger is hovering over the doorbell, I think of Jenny and almost lose my nerve. After all, I still haven't got a clue what really happened to her.

That's the point. I haven't got a clue what happened to her.

I'm here to get answers from Holt. Or at least to get closer so I can ask the right questions. And, yes, maybe I'm stepping into the hornet's nest. And, yes, maybe I'm a fool. But whether he's involved in something nefarious or not, I can't make myself believe that Matthew Holt will hurt me.

Which means I'm either very perceptive or far too trusting.

Dammit.

I jam my finger on the glowing yellow button before I can talk myself out of it. Then I push it again and again and again in defense against my lingering urge to bolt.

I'm about to use the key-code when the porch light snaps on. Seconds later, the speaker crackles. "*Aria.*"

The heat in his voice is palpable, and once again, my nerve begins to fade.

"Since we're very much past working hours, I hope this is a social call."

I glance up and around until I find the security camera. Then I stare directly at it. "We need to talk."

I expect a reply—probably something snarky about my timing—and when I don't get one, I fear he's gone back to sleep, probably after pushing some button that makes sure he neither sees nor hears anything more from me.

Screw that.

I pull out my phone so I can call up the key code, but before I can get to it, the locks click, the door swings open, and there's Matthew Holt, disheveled in a way that makes him look both dangerous and wildly sexy.

I hear myself release a breathy little *oh* as I take in the black tee clinging to his broad, muscular chest. The faded jeans sitting low on his hips. The tousled hair and unshaved jaw.

He doesn't look like a CEO right now. He looks like trouble. More than that, he looks like delicious, lickable sin, and when I try to speak, I find that my mouth's desert dry. I swallow, trying to remember why the hell I'm here.

"I'm going to guess you're not selling Girl Scout cookies."

"I'm not selling anything," I say with what I hope is a saucy smile. "I'm giving it away."

His brows rise, and I wink before stepping inside a space that can only be described as breathtaking. Floor-to-ceiling windows wrap around the entire living room, and the lights from the Valley glitter like stars against the inky blackness. The house feels weightless, perched so high above the world that it seems suspended in air. It's like the tower of a castle from which Holt looks out over his domain.

"—for free?"

I shake my head, realizing I missed most of what he'd said. "I'm sorry, what?"

"I asked about the valuable commodity you're giving away for free." He takes a step back and makes a show of looking me up and down. "Shall I tell you what I'm hoping for?"

"Legal advice," I say firmly. "I'm not really a lawyer, but with your help, I could play one on TV."

I see the way his eyes crinkle as he presses his lips together, clearly fighting a laugh. After a moment, he tilts his head in a nod. "It's a foolish CEO who ignores free legal advice. But the law always seems to go down better with a drink. Can I offer you anything? It's not yet last call."

"Maybe not by the clock, but I think that bell has rung for me." Mostly because I want to keep my wits. But I don't tell him that part.

"Orange juice, then? Or coffee?"

"Now you're speaking my language. Coffee would be great."

"Follow me."

I have an excellent view of his excellent ass as we move into the kitchen. The man rocks a suit like nobody's business, but a man with a nice ass in jeans is one of God's gifts to women.

The kitchen is well-lit and shiny, without any of the stereo-typical bachelor clutter. I wonder if he's neat—in which case he's a better person than I—or if he has help.

I'm betting on the latter.

As I watch, he pushes some buttons on a fancy machine that either makes coffee or mines Bitcoin. Until the moment he puts the cup of caffeinated goodness in my hand, I figure it could have gone either way.

As for my host, he pours himself a scotch, then hits me with an expression so deadpan I almost have to laugh. "I have a feeling I'll need it," he says.

Considering it's the middle of the night and I barged in without an explanation, he's playing it pretty damn suave. James Bond, indeed.

"So, legal advice," he prompts, leading me back to the open area. He gestures for me to take a seat in one of the overstuffed chairs while he stands, his back against glass, so that he appears to float over the San Fernando Valley's grid of lights.

"It's about the gifts," I say, intentionally crossing my legs. I'm wearing a sundress that buttons up the front, from hem to collar. I haven't, however, fastened all the buttons, and the skirt falls open to mid-thigh.

I've slipped out of the red pumps I'd worn into the house, and I see his eyes drift from my silk-covered toes all the way up to my crossed thighs and the hint of black garter peeking out from the floral print dress.

"Black today," I say. "White yesterday."

He lifts a brow. "Makes you wonder what color tomorrow

will be. Or is that the trouble? You don't like the color? Hardly seems grounds for legal action."

I sip my coffee, more to hide my amusement than for the hit of caffeine. "I guess men like you don't have time for a broad view of the world. I bet you only watch the entertainment news and financial channels."

"You're suggesting I'm not well-rounded?"

I uncross my legs and lean forward, my elbows on my knees. It's a position that I know offers a nice little peek at the girls, high and plump in the lacy bra he sent, and pushed so close together he could probably fuck my cleavage and get off.

Then again, maybe that was the idea.

"I'm suggesting you may not be familiar with some concerns that are front and center at most companies."

"Oh?" He shifts, as if getting more comfortable against the window.

"Sexual harassment. It's been in the news. You may have heard of it."

I'm already having a hard time fighting my smile, so when he shakes his head slowly and murmurs, "Not ringing a bell," I have to bite the inside of my cheek not to laugh. And, okay, I know it's not funny. If the bastard were actually harassing me—in a way other than making me wait far too long—I'd report him so fast it would make his head spin.

But this? What we're playing at? It's far more dangerous than a federal crime.

"Harassment," he repeats, then pushes away from the glass. He moves across the room, a man with as much control over his body as he has over his empire. When he's right in front of me, he stops, and it's only when the room seems to dim that I realize I've forgotten to breathe.

He extends his hand, and I take it, letting him help me to my feet. He's only a head taller than me, but he overshadows me, making me feel small and vulnerable in a way that I like. I want to be overpowered. *Claimed.* And as he slowly unbuttons my dress, I squeeze my legs together, already wet. Already desperate for him.

When all the buttons are open, he pushes the dress off my shoulders, letting it fall to the floor. He steps closer, then strokes his fingers down my arm before he leans in and whispers, "Sweetheart, the only way I'm harassing you is by not fucking you."

He's so damn right about that.

He eases back and looks me up and down, the inspection making me more aware of my body than I've ever been. "Beautiful," he whispers, and my breath hitches as he traces a fingertip over the swell of my breast, then along the edge of the bra before continuing down my side—over my ribs, along the curve of my waist, and then along the band of these barely-there panties.

His eyes meet mine as he hooks a finger in the band, then tugs me forward before removing the finger and extending that hand to me. I take it, then let him lead me to a bedroom. It isn't his. It has too much of a designer feel to it. The master bedroom, I'm certain, has an elegant masculinity. And not even the hint of a designer touch.

All thoughts of art and paint colors are shoved out of my head when he pushes me onto the bed. My body is on fire, and in that moment, I know that I will do anything he asks of me, a point I prove when he tells me to, "Lie back. Spread your legs. Close your eyes."

I let myself slip into the dark world of sensation, relishing the feel of his fingertip easing up my leg. The curve of my calf, the inside of my thigh. The soft crease between my thigh and my sex. Then along the edge of the thong, lower and lower until he's right where I want him. Until I'm silently begging him to push the minuscule bit of material aside and slide inside me.

Fingers, tongue, cock. I want them all. I want to feel every sensation he can give me.

I want him to light me on fire.

"Please," I whisper, then break the rules by opening my eyes. I meet his, and they are so full of need and desire and lust, that I almost come right then.

He's still fully dressed, sitting on the edge of the bed, his body twisted so that he can lean over me, one hand on the mattress for support as the other gently grazes the soft area between my thigh and my sex.

I whimper. I'm so ready. And from the way he's seated, I can see the bulge of his cock, hard behind the denim.

He's ready, too.

"Please," I repeat, the word filled with a lifetime of need.

He gives me a slow smile, then slides down the bed and kisses me just below my belly button. Then another, just a bit lower. And another until he reaches the band of the thong.

"Do you have any idea how much I want you?"

"Tell me."

He shakes his head. "More than you can imagine. And for longer than you've known."

"What do you mean?"

He doesn't answer. Instead, he shifts his hand and cups my pussy over the thong. I arch up, awash in a storm of sensation.

Then his hand is gone and he's standing as my body tingles with anticipation. I watch, expecting him to strip. Instead, he takes the sheet and pulls it gently over me. "Get some sleep, Aria."

I sit bolt upright, need morphing into anger. And disappointment. "Wait. What?"

The corner of his mouth twitches. "Anticipation, sweetheart. All the best things are worth waiting for."

"I—" But he's gone, the door closed behind him. I start to

throw the sheet aside, but something stops me. I think about his touch. About how much I want him. About this delicious confirmation that he wants me, too.

And, yes, about the fact that it's the middle of the night.

Next time, I think. Next time you better take me to the moon, or else ...

But I don't manage to finish the threat, because exhaustion sweeps over me, and my last thought before falling headlong into sleep is that I haven't helped Jenny at all.

SIXTEEN

I roll over, my eyes fluttering open as golden streaks filter through the windows, warm against my skin. Still half in a dream, I blink up at the unfamiliar ceiling. The bed beneath me is too soft, the sheets too luxurious, the quiet too absolute.

My stomach clenches. *Where am I?*

Then I remember. *Matthew.*

My body tingles with the memory of his touch—and clenches in frustration at the memory of him walking away.

I really need to get out of here.

I sit up, looking around for my phone and finding it on the bedside table. I check the time, then bolt upright when I see that it's already ten past eight. I have to get home. Get dressed. Get to work.

Then a dose of sanity kicks me in the head. Considering whose house I'm in, I probably don't have to worry about the boss looking askance if I drift in after nine. But after the night we had (almost had?) I'm not sure I want him looking at me at all.

I shove the covers down as I move to sit on the side of the bed. I'm in only a bra and a thong, and I look frantically around, relieved to find my wrinkled dress folded over the back of a chair.

I spy a smudge of mascara on the white pillowcase, then promptly flip the pillow. If only all my problems were so easy to hide. I stand up, knowing I have to make it from here to the front door.

I hit pay dirt when I pop into the attached bath. I almost jump into the luxurious shower, but I make do with the plastic-wrapped travel toothbrush and toothpaste I find in a decorative basket. There's a hairbrush, too, and since I don't know where my purse is, I use it to tame the rat's nest that is now my hair.

I head back into the bedroom, then put on the dress, buttoning it from the very top to the very bottom. I glance around for my shoes, but don't see them. Apparently, they're out partying with my purse.

With a quick glance toward the door, I debate my options. Walk of shame? Slipping out quietly has its appeal. No awkward small talk, no "so, what now?" moments. No, "I wanted to beg for you to keep touching me like that ... and more" confessions. But my stomach growls, a sharp, insistent reminder that I haven't eaten since last night. Or was it yesterday afternoon?

Coffee.

I need coffee.

And I need it bad enough that I'm not sneaking out. Instead, I'm pulling up my big girl panties and heading out to find that elixir of life.

And Matthew.

As I head barefoot to the door, I smooth the wrinkled dress, or try to, anyway. Then I give up and tug open the door. Immediately, I'm thrust into Foodie Heaven as the scent of frying bacon wafts around me. My stomach growls, and I follow the aroma like a cartoon character being lured by an invisible hand.

But as soon as I can see the kitchen, I stop dead in my tracks. The splendiferous aroma of bacon can't hold a candle to what's in front of me—Matthew at the stove, his bare back to me, a tapestry of muscles and sinew that seem more like a sculpture than a living, breathing man.

And it gets better. The gray sweats he wears hang just low enough on his hips to make my fingers itch and my mouth go dry.

I must not have been as stealthy as I'd thought, because he looks over his shoulder at me, his face shadowed by morning stubble and his hair slightly mussed. I know he's in his late forties, but right now he looks young and eager. And—though I'm not sure how it's possible—

even more attractive.

He looks like a man just starting out and knowing full well that he's going to take the world by storm.

"Good morning, beautiful." He points to a place setting at the counter. "Take a seat. I'll bring you a coffee."

The kitchen is even more stunning in the daylight. Open and bright, with sleek countertops and massive windows that let in the morning light. The kind of space that invites you to linger.

I glance toward the H.G. Wellsian machine that had brewed coffee for us last night, but it seems to be dormant.

"I know how much coffee you drink before noon. I thought a pot would be better." He nods to a coffee maker with so many buttons and knobs it puts my Mr. Coffee to shame. But when he brings me a cup, I can't deny that it makes a damn good brew.

"How do you know how much coffee I drink?" I ask after my first life-giving sip.

He flashes an enigmatic grin. "I pay attention," he says as he slides two eggs—over easy—onto a plate, then adds bacon and a piece of toast before sliding the plate in front of me.

"To my coffee intake?"

"That, and other things."

I study him, not sure what he means. Then I glance down at my plate. "Coincidence, or did you know that eggs over easy are my fave?"

"I knew," he says, so casually it makes me pause.

My fork freezes halfway to my mouth. "How on earth could you know that?"

He leans against the refrigerator holding a piece of bacon. "Do you remember a brunch by the Starks' pool a few years ago? A birthday celebration for one of their kids. There were Mickey Mouse waffles."

I smile at the memory. "Sure. Nicholas wore that silly cat costume the entire party. That kid is just too adorable."

"He is," Matthew says. "But it was an adorable woman who drew my attention."

It's still early, and I've not made a dent in the coffee, so I cut myself some slack for taking a moment to realize that he's talking about me. The moment I do, though, a kickline of butterflies start dancing in my belly. And despite how the moment makes me feel—flattered, special, *seen*—all I manage to say is, "Oh."

From his small smile and the gleam in his eyes, I think my response was just fine.

"I don't remember seeing you there," I admit, the confession surprising me. Especially since I've had a little lust thing going for Matthew since I met him in that bar line ... which was also at the Stark House.

How could I not have noticed him at a kid's birthday party?

As if in response to my unanswered question, he shrugs, saying, "I only dropped by to give Damien something for an upcoming project. I had to leave right after to catch a plane. But

I saw you." His gaze softens. "You were ordering eggs at the cook station. Over easy."

"Oh." My mouth has gone suddenly dry.

"I remember exactly what you were wearing, too. A green dress with little white flowers. Strappy sandals. Your hair was shorter and darker, and the tips were pink and purple. You looked like a fairy princess sparkling in the sun.

My stomach flips, and not because of the food. "You noticed all that?"

"You caught my attention that morning," he says simply, and there's something in his tone that makes the air between us hum. "Actually, you've had it for a long time."

My pulse quickens, and I suddenly feel exposed in a way I'm not used to. "Why?" I ask, my voice barely above a whisper.

He hesitates, clearly searching for words. "Because you're you," he finally says, his expression open, as if he has nothing to hide from me. "Sharp, bold, unafraid to speak your mind." His attention is so fully on me that I feel as if I'm under a spotlight. "But that's not the only reason you've been on my radar."

"It's not?" The words sound lame, but I'm having trouble thinking.

He steps closer, until he's only an arms-length away. "It's because of what's between us. The sizzle. The pop," he adds, with just a tiny bit of humor. "I felt it the first time we met." He reaches for me, his fingertips stroking my face as he tucks a strand of hair behind my ear. "I think you did, too."

"Oh." I don't know what else to say. My chest feels tight, my skin too warm. "I—"

I cut myself off. I have no idea where that sentence was going, and I need space—now. Grabbing my coffee and a strip of bacon, I push back from the stool and wander into the living area, which seems like a different room in the light of day. The huge windows offer a panoramic view of the Valley. Beneath the panes, bookshelves filled with novels, scripts, and rows of DVDs line the walls.

I sip my coffee, letting the rich flavor ground me as I scan the various titles. My gaze catches on an entire shelf of DVDs with familiar titles. I pull one out and see Vivien Lorainne's striking face. I turn, holding the case up for Matthew to see. "There are so many. Do you have all of her films?"

"Every last one. I've been a fan for years."

"Me, too. I love her movies. I was practically weaned on them." Vivien Lorainne was one of the biggest stars during Hollywood's Golden Age, an exceptional accomplishment considering her time in front of the camera was cut short when she was brutally murdered. An act which, some say, bore a curse.

"She was a brilliant actor," Matthew says. "Range like that doesn't come around often. We should watch one soon," he adds. "A movie. Popcorn. My sofa's comfy."

I glance around at the plush seating and panoramic view. "Just one tiny problem. You don't have a TV."

"Don't I? Huh." He turns in a circle as if checking out his living room. "Well, that's odd. And considering my job, that's a little embarrassing."

I bite back a fit of giggles. "Let me guess. There's one in the bedroom."

"Not at the moment," he says. "But whatever the lady wants," he adds, sounding more than a little lascivious.

I laugh. "Sorry. Bedroom's off limits." I smile sweetly. "I don't think I can survive another night on the edge."

"Oh?" He steps closer, his voice low and his presence magnetic. "Are you suggesting that you want fall ?"

My mouth goes dry, and my heart flutters as his scent—a mix of soap, bacon, and something distinctly him—fills the air between us. "You heard me," I whisper.

His grin is as bright as the sun. "I think we can make that happen. Some wine. A movie. And so many possibilities."

"And still, you have no TV," I remind him, my tone teasing.

"Ye of little faith. Eight? You bring you. I'll take care of everything else."

I should say no. I'm supposed to be getting closer to him because I'm investigating Jenny's death. Not because he makes me laugh. And certainly not because the memory of his fingers on me is enough to make me want to drop onto the sofa right now and say yes to everything.

"Did I lose you?"

"Just trying to remember if I had plans tonight." I flash a playful smile. "You slid right into the only empty slot in my very active social calendar."

"Did I?"

"Yup. It's a good thing you didn't suggest tomorrow. That's when I have to clean the breadcrumbs out of my toaster and shave my legs."

"And how could I compete with that?"

We share a smile, and I realize that I don't want to leave. "My family actually knew her." I blurt it out without preamble, but he knows exactly who I mean.

"Really? How?"

"My great-grandfather made the tiara she wore in *Starlight Serenade*. Well, it's really a diadem. But when I was little, I called it a tiara. I was so in love with it. The diamonds were real, not paste. It was a gift from the studio to Vivien. A thank you for bringing in those box-office dollars. Well, all the stones except for that huge yellow diamond at the point of the diadem. That was from her private collection. Some prince gave it to her before she turned down his marriage proposal. Apparently, it was priceless."

He's actually taken a step back, and I do a mental fingernail buff, because how many folks can blow the mind of a guy like Matthew Holt?

"That's incredible," he says, and I hear genuine admiration in his voice. "I remember reading that it was lost after her husband murdered her."

"It wasn't." I put a finger to my lips, indicating a secret. "She'd given it to my family a few years before she died, humongous diamond and all."

He shakes his head slowly. I'm not surprised. For anyone who's a fan of Vivien Lorainne and knows any Hollywood lore, this is one of those Cool Industry Stories. To me, it's a tale of trauma and loss. But everything's about perspective, isn't it?

"Why did she give it to your family?" Matthew asks. "The curse?"

"You believe in that?"

"In curses? I do," he says. "But I think most people are under a curse of their own making."

He's right about that. As for his question...

"Honestly, I have no idea why she'd want to give away something that valuable. My mom said Vivien had a dream and knew she had to. Another theory is that there'd been whispers of a heist, and she wanted to make sure it was safe. There's even a rumor that she'd had an affair with my Great Grandpa and just wanted him to have it. All I know is that everyone in the family says that having that diadem seemed to bring him back to life. I guess he'd been depressed or something. Out of work, broke. The diadem changed things for him. It changed things for my entire family."

"How?"

I lift a shoulder in a casual shrug. "I wasn't even born when she gave it to our family. All I know are the stories. But the way my family talks ... well, it was more than a diadem. It was hope."

I shrug again, as if to emphasize that this really isn't important. "But that was a long time ago."

Something shifts in his expression. It's subtle, but I catch it —a flicker of tension, I think. Or maybe that's his *forced to look interested* expression. I wince. "Sorry. I'm probably boring you with family history."

"Hardly. I'm just ... awed." There's a weight in his words I can't place. "I didn't know any of that."

"Why would you? Anyway, it was stolen. The Cat took it. Fucking bastard." I grimace. "Sorry. Touchy subject."

I look around for my phone, but don't have it. And I don't see a clock. "We should get going, right? I mean, Lila might not give *you* the stink-eye ..."

"Trust me. She gives everyone the stink-eye. But she's a damn good gatekeeper. And a lifelong friend."

"Even so ..." I start to turn toward the guest room, but he reaches for me, his fingers finding my bare arm. Even that simple touch is enough to send my senses reeling.

"Matthew," I whisper, "we have to go."

"We will. But don't leave me in suspense about this Cat thing. I'm picturing Garfield in a diadem. You have to save me from that image."

"A jewel thief," I explain, frowning as I remember the stories my parents told. "There was this cat burglar active in New York when I was a kid. My parents always thought he was the one who took it."

"It was stolen." It's a statement, not a question.

I nod. "Doesn't matter. The diadem's gone, and so is he. Fucking cat-bastard destroyed my family."

"Destroyed?"

I sag a little. "For a while at least, yeah. We almost lost everything—our house, our stability. My parents fought constantly. Apparently, my dad had arranged to borrow money to keep us from losing our house. The diadem was going to be collateral, but before the deal went down, it was stolen. And we were fucked."

I glance at Matthew, expecting polite sympathy. Instead, his jaw is tight, his blue eyes locked on mine with an intensity that humbles me.

"I know," I whisper. "Vile. And if I ever find out who he is," I add, my voice low and hard, "I will fucking destroy him."

Matthew's gaze doesn't waver. "I don't blame you," he says. "That's exactly what I'd do."

SEVENTEEN

I'm running late for obvious reasons when I screech to a stop in front of my house, slamming Harry the Honda into park with a satisfying jolt. My brain is already spinning possible excuses to toss at Lila as to why I'm so late—and since *oh, I stayed at Matthew's last night but didn't have a change of clothes for today*—probably won't go over well, I'm hoping to brainstorm something a tad more creative. But I'm distracted from spinning my deceptive tales when I spot my elderly neighbor—Tilda? Zelda?—standing on my porch, taping something to my front door.

Great.

I sigh, half hoping she'll scuttle away before I get out of the car. But no, she hears me as soon as I open the car door, her head snapping up like she's been caught committing a crime.

"Oh! Ellie, I thought you were at work!" she exclaims, pulling down the piece of paper and handing it to me.

Ellie—I have a letter for you. Tilda.

"Thanks." I resist the urge to correct my name even as I wonder if someone on the block named *Ellie* is missing her mail.

I smile again, mostly because I don't know what to say, and she takes that opportunity to pass me a brown paper bag that rattles when I shake it. Which makes me pretty certain there's more in there than a letter.

She must see the confusion on my face, because she smiles, pats my arm, then says, "I know how much you single girls like candy. I had some left over from Halloween and thought I should spread the love."

"Great." I somehow manage a smile as I imagine biting into an eight-month-old, sugar-coated gummy concoction. "It was sweet of you to think of me," I add, because it's true. Even if delivering misdirected mail with a side of stale candy is more than a little odd.

She just stands there, and I'm not sure if I'm supposed to tip her or make conversation. I decide to go for a polite-but-bland smile. "I'm *so* late for work." I pause, hoping she takes the hint. "Just one of those days," I add, when she continues to linger.

"Hmm," she says, squinting at me with the sharp, discerning gaze of someone who's about to launch into a story I don't have time for.

But all she says is, "Long night?" and I feel heat bloom across my cheeks.

"Something like that," I mutter, willing her to just saunter back to her house. But no, now she's shifting her weight and adjusting her oversized purse like we're settling in for a chat.

"The letter in there was mis-delivered weeks ago," she says. "I'm sorry to have held onto it so long. I've been away—an Australian cruise. So magnificent! And my dear, you would not believe the kangaroos. They're so—"

"That sounds fabulous" I interrupt, my voice a little too high-pitched. "But I'm terribly late for a meeting."

Not true, of course, but the mental image of Lila's stony-eyed glare is enough to put the fear of God into me. I start shifting from foot to foot, hoping this universal sign of urgency will get her to wrap things up.

"Oh, of course. You working girls. Always busy. My Betsy goes a mile a minute, and I can't ever seem to—"

"I'm *really* sorry. But you know I work at Hardline, and I have a conference call with Steven Spielberg in less than an hour, so I really need to run."

She presses a hand to her heart. "Indiana Jones is absolutely delicious, isn't he?"

"Hell, yes," I say, and right then, I'm being totally sincere.

"Well, I won't keep you." She finally starts tottering down the steps, moving at the speed of molasses.

I sigh again, then hurry to her side, taking an arm to steady her as she makes her way down, chattering all the while about koalas.

By the time I manage to get inside the house and close the door behind me, I'm practically vibrating with impatience. I toss the bag carelessly onto the entry table and sprint to my room, not even bothering to scope out the candy situation. I have zero need to apply fun-size Snickers directly to my ass in the days before I'm—hopefully—going to be up close and very personal with Matthew.

Besides, I bet Tilda only buys the cheap stuff for the little witches and warlocks.

Twenty minutes later, right when I'm finally showered, dressed, and ready to bolt out the door, my phone screen lights up with a text from Lila.

If you are running late, policy is to check in. If you are out sick, policy is the same.

I groan, then type a quick reply. *Sorry. On my way.*

I toss the phone onto the desk, then run my hands through my hair, frustration churning through me. I need time to think, but Lila won't tolerate me blowing off work—especially not on my second day. And the last thing I need is her breathing down my neck.

I'm going to have to sacrifice something to the Business Gods, because despite being ridiculously late, Lila gave me no grief at all. I'm not sure if that's because Matthew told her that I'd been working at home (a nice cover for which I was grateful) or because she's had an epiphany and both likes and values me as a co-worker now.

I'm going to with option two. Because I'm just that kind of optimistic gal.

Even better, she's out of the office now, leaving me to my own devices. I have no idea where she's gone, but I sent up a silent thank you to whoever drew her away, even though that leaves me alone to handle the office despite not fully knowing all the ropes. But Matthew's in his office tackling dozens of return phone calls, so if I'm desperate I can catch him between the time one light on the phone goes out and another lights up. Or, I can try.

Besides, the work Lila left on my desk doesn't require an in-depth knowledge of the company or the entertainment business. Filing only requires the alphabet, and I've had that down pat for years.

By the time I'm three hours into the project, however, my chipper mood fades. Life, I'm beginning to think, might be a lot easier if the Phoenicians had left well enough alone.

I've reached a point where the Alphabet Song is going non-stop through my head and I'm seriously considering a lobotomy when there's a tap at my door. Then Matthew pokes his head in, his smile as refreshing as a cool glass of water. "I thought you looked incredible last night, but you may have one-upped yourself today."

I think he's joking, but there's real heat in his expression, and I do a quick mental assessment. I'm wearing reading glasses, my hair is pulled back with a messy fringe tickling my face, and my fitted tank only barely passes as work attire. Hardly a look to drive men wild.

"What?" I say defensively as he lingers, still silently scoping me out.

"Nothing." His grin widens. "I'm just trying to figure out if it's the sexy librarian vibe or the chaos of your desk that's doing it for me."

I fight a smile as I lean back in my chair. "It's the chaos. Your sadistic side gets off on watching people suffer."

He doesn't miss a beat. "Only if they look good doing it." He steps closer. "And you, Ms. Parker, make filing look like an art form."

I lift a brow, feigning nonchalance. "You get off watching me file?"

"Maybe." His tone drops, low and teasing. "But it's not just the filing. Or the tank top. Or the way your hair keeps falling in your eyes no matter how many times you push it back."

I wait for him to continue, but he stays silent. "What then?"

"It's the way you jump into things headfirst." His voice is soft, his grin fading into something more serious. "Like you're ready to conquer the world. It's kind of irresistible."

My heart skips a beat, his words hitting me harder than I want to admit. For a moment, I let myself wonder if he really sees me that way—if maybe, just maybe, there's more to this thing between us than banter and chemistry.

Then his grin returns, and he steps back, shattering the moment with a wink. "But yeah, it's mostly the filing."

I laugh, the tension breaking, though my pulse is still racing. "Good to know where I stand."

"Right at the top of the organizational hierarchy." He backs toward the door. "I'll leave you to it. But don't forget—I never play fair."

My stomach growls, and I glance at the clock. Already past one. I reach to press the intercom, then sway in my chair, silently debating. Finally, I go for it. "Mr. Holt?"

I can hear the smile in his voice as he says, "Yes, Ms. Parker?"

"Lila texted that she'll be back in fifteen. I think I'm going to step out for lunch. Have you eaten?"

"Actually, I'm having lunch in Santa Monica."

"Oh. That sounds like fun." I wait a beat, expecting him to invite me, then kick myself for being unreasonably disappointed when he doesn't. I remind myself that we're not dating—*Are we dating?*—and even if we are, we wouldn't be flouting it during working hours.

Plus, when I check his calendar, I can see that it's a business lunch.

I'd still rather grab a bite with him, but my ego is assuaged. Besides, the Hardline Dining Room serves amazing sushi.

"Then I'll see you after your lunch," I say.

"I won't be coming back to the office."

"Oh."

I'm shocked by the depth of disappointment that crashes through me. I've never been one to fall hard or fast, but that's what's happening with Matthew. My relief is palpable when he adds, "But we're still on for eight?"

I smile so wide my mouth aches. I couldn't play coy with this man right now if I tried. And despite having walked into this office with a mission, the truth is I don't want to go down that road. For better or worse, I trust him.

"Eight o'clock," I repeat. "Absolutely."

"Good," he says, his tone low. "I can't wait."

"Neither can I." The words, so true, send a bolt of fear

cutting through me. I'm falling for this guy like I've never fallen before. Faster and deeper. So much, that I feel a little out of control.

Honestly, I like the feeling.

But at the same time, I know that if this goes sideways—if I'm wrong about him—it won't just be my heart on the line.

It'll be everything.

I think of Jenny, and a chill cuts through me.

It could even be my life.

EIGHTEEN

It's seven fifty-nine, and I'm sitting in my car on his street. I've been here for fifteen minutes already, forcing myself to clear out emails on my phone rather than skip to his front door and blatantly reveal just how much I've been looking forward to tonight.

Not because I love Vivien Lorainne's movies.

Not even because this is a chance to get close to him and maybe learn something about Jenny's death. And, yes, that should be my motivation. Hell, it *is* my motivation. I'm not going to give up on Jenny—not ever.

But as much as I want those answers, that's not why I'm so eager that I spent forty minutes deciding what to wear. It's not why I arrived far too early. And it's not why there are butterflies doing a wild dance in my belly.

I want him.

No great revelation there. After all, I've been attracted to this man for a very long time, and after the other night, I'm certain he wants me, too.

But Matthew Holt is a man I shouldn't want. A man whose secrets I'm trying to discover.

A man who may be complicit in the death of my friend.

But so help me, I *do* want him. More than that, I want him to be innocent.

If he's guilty, going back into his home to suss out answers could be the last bad decision I ever make.

If he's innocent, going back into that house to suss out answers could be a betrayal he'll never forgive.

And there it is. The real reason I've been sitting in this car. I'm damned if I do, and I'm damned if I don't. And no matter how this whole thing shakes out, I can already see the end.

Matthew Holt will never be mine.

I blink back tears as I tell myself that's okay.

I tell myself that I'm doing this for Jenny.

And I tell myself that even if I only get one night with him, that will be enough.

Fortunately, I'm a good liar. And the person I've always lied best to is myself.

I glance at the clock. Five after eight. Now or never time.

I suck in a breath, check my hair and makeup in the visor mirror, then climb out of the car and head for his door, trying desperately to look like a woman who's there only for a movie ... and whatever delicious interlude might come after.

I press the buzzer, and the door opens so quickly that my heart does a little leap from the knowledge that he must have been waiting for me.

"I saw you park the car," he says, apparently seeing my surprise.

"Oh." A wash of heat spreads over me in what I'm sure is a full-body blush. "I, um ... oh, hell. I was wasting time. Checking emails and then checking my makeup." I smile up at him. "I didn't want to look too eager."

"I get it," he says, ushering me inside. "I only noticed because I've been checking the exterior cams for the last ten minutes. So if it's a competition to see who's more eager, I think I may have won the trophy."

His smile is warm and teasing, and my stomach does a little flip. "Maybe we've both won," I say, my voice barely above a whisper.

"Yeah," he says, closing the door behind me. "I wonder what we'll get as a prize?"

I turn back, smiling at the devilish gleam in his eyes. "Something fabulous, I hope."

For a moment, we just stand there, both of us taking the other in. It should be awkward—like teens on a first date who aren't sure where to go in the house to avoid mom and dad. Except it's not awkward at all. Just the opposite. It feels like a welcome. Like in some weird way, this is my space, too.

I shake my head, certain my thoughts are getting way ahead of his reality.

I remind myself to be careful. I know the man I want him to be. I know the man he seems to be.

But I don't yet know the man he really is. Or what that man may have done.

"You look stunning," he says, sending a warm rush of pleasure careening through my blood.

I flash a quick smile. "What? This old thing?"

The dress is one I'd picked up on sale about a year ago. On a hanger, it looks plain. Even dull. A bit like a long, clingy, sleeveless shirt with a deep scoop neck and criss-crossing straps across the back. It's midnight black and made out of some stretchy blend, that hugs me in all the right places.

The neck is low enough to show a hint of bra, but the material is tight enough that a bra's not really necessary. I'd considered showing a daring hint of red lace but decided that letting the girls roam free was more fun. From the way Holt's eyes keep dipping to my cleavage, I think I made the right choice.

As for the rest of the dress, it hugs my hips and thighs, but not so tight that it reveals the band of the silky thong he'd given me with the contract. I figured it was only fair for him to have a peek.

But where it really shines is on my ass, because the material perfectly hugs and accentuates those curves. More important, the same Louboutins I wore to Masque are on my feet, adding a bit of height and a bit more curve to my rear end.

All in all, I think I look hot. And from what I can see, Matthew agrees with that assessment.

"Come on," he says, extending his hand. I take it, then let him lead me to the kitchen where a bottle of Pappy Van Winkle bourbon sits on the counter next to a carafe of coffee.

I raise a brow as I turn to look at him, sure my awe is reflected all over my face. That shit is both rare and pricey.

He shrugs, a smile tugging at the corner of his mouth. "I wasn't sure which you'd prefer. I also have Coke, Diet Coke, possibly Dr. Pepper, a full bar if bourbon's not your poison tonight, and a variety of wines."

"A full service host."

"We aim to please."

I eye the bottle of Pappy. "Is that the fifteen year? Isn't that almost impossible to get?"

He moves to the counter and pulls out the cork, then pours just a taste. "Anything can be had for a price," he says. He holds the glass out for me. "Even rare and delicious things."

A shiver runs up my spine at his words, and I almost turn away. Almost tell him that this is a mistake and I shouldn't even have signed on as his PA. But I don't know if I'd be running because I fear him or because I want him.

Probably both.

Both are a reason to stay as much as they are to go. I want answers, after all. And, yes, I want him, too.

I sniff the bourbon, then take a small taste, letting it sit, feeling the burn. I don't know much about bourbon—or any alcohol, really. But I know what I like. And this is exceptional.

He chuckles. "Give me the glass and I'll pour you a full shot."

I do, then watch as he pours double shots of Pappy for both of us. "Guess the coffee will come in handy later," I say, pointedly looking at the bottle he's picked up along with his glass.

"Won't hurt," he says, and we share a smile as we head into the living area.

As soon as we're in the middle of the room, I come to a stop, then turn in a full circle. It looks exactly the same as before. I take a sip of my drink, put the glass down on a table that runs along the back of the sofa, then turn to him. "False pretenses, Mr. Holt?"

"Excuse me?" He takes a seat on the sofa, gesturing for me to do the same.

I comply, then recover my drink from the table before I point at the huge windows and the view of the Valley beyond. "Unless Vivien Lorainne filmed Public Service Announcements about living in the Valley, I'm going out on a limb and saying nothing has changed."

He makes a show of looking around. "Damn. you're right. Same old living room. How the hell could I have forgotten to buy a television?"

He slides closer to me, then meets my eyes. I stifle a sigh, enjoying the way my heart starts racing. Then enjoying even more the way my skin heats as he traces a fingertip down my bare arm, so slowly I think I'm going to go a little mad. When he reaches my hand—now holding my drink—he slides his finger in, dampening the tip.

"Matthew ..." My voice is low. Needy. "What are you doing?"

"Hush," he says, then traces his finger over my lips in a caress that ignites a flurry of sparks inside me. Sparks that sizzle and pop and want and need.

He leans closer. "Who needs a television when we have other forms of entertainment?"

"But we—" My words hang there, part of me wanting to lecture him about luring me here under false pretenses. Another part of me wanting to surrender completely, loving the fact that he got me here under false pretenses.

"Shhh," he murmurs. "Close your eyes." I do, then feel the pressure of his finger beneath my chin. I expect him to turn my head toward him, then melt me with a kiss. All around us, soft music begins to play. Something romantic and familiar. Something I—

Starlight Serenade.

I open my eyes and find myself looking at the opening scene of the movie on a huge screen that's descended from the ceiling. The musical score seems to surround us, and all the lights in this exotic treehouse have gone dim.

"You rat," I say, laughing. "You tricked me."

"Mad?"

I shake my head, absolutely delighted. "Furious."

He grins, then puts his arm around my shoulder, and I lean against him, sighing happily as I settle in to watch the innocent Darla Parks turn the tables on that bitch Veronica, thus catching the attention of Peter Cain, the roguish mob boss and nightclub owner who confesses his crimes and goes straight—well, mostly —in order to win Darla's love.

By the time it's over, I'm praising whoever invented waterproof mascara and trying very hard to hide the tears that are trickling down my cheeks. Matthew passes me a tissue, and I grimace. "I thought I was being subtle."

"You were," he assures me. "That's why I didn't pass you the entire box."

"It's not fair," I say. "Now you know I'm the type of girl who cries at everything."

His brows rise, amusement lighting his face. "Everything?"

"You think I'm exaggerating. But I'm not."

The corner of his mouth twitches. "Uh-huh."

"You know that car commercial with the broken down Chevy on graduation day that dad and the daughter fix up together?"

He lifts a dubious brow. "Really?"

"Oh, yeah. I bawl like a baby. And that toilet paper commercial with the little kid running half-naked through the formal dinner party. And that dog food one, with the huge bulldog who lets the little terrier eat first." I press a hand to my heart and try to blink back the tears the last one has conjured.

"Now you're just messing with me."

"I wish I were," I say, wiping away a tear that got away. "I'm a total softy. So don't hurt me, okay?"

The words are out of my mouth before I can call them back, and I regret them immediately. Too much, too fast, and what the hell was I thinking? "I'm sorry. I don't have a lot of filters, and I—"

But he presses a finger to my lips before I can get the words out. "I won't. I promise."

"That was a stupid thing for me to say." I shake my head, feeling like an idiot. "I mean, that's not the kind of thing you say on a first date." I bite my lower lip, then cock my head as I look at him. "This is a first date, right?"

"It's a date," he says. "It's not our first."

"Really?" I lean back, amused. "I'm pretty sure I'd remember if we'd gone out before. And considering I came over uninvited last time to give you grief, I don't think it counts. No matter what direction the, um, encounter ended up going.

"Fair enough. But there've been dates. At least a half dozen times."

I gape at him. "Did each goodnight kiss steal my memories? Because I'm a hundred percent sure I'd remember going out with you."

"Well, the dates might have only been in my head." He grins. "But they were so vivid I would have thought you'd remember them, too."

I laugh, delighted by this man. "So they were good?"

"Damn good. Beyond good."

I let out a long sigh. "Well, that's a relief. It's those imaginary dates that you really want to rock. If you can't come across as awesome in someone else's fantasies, you've got some pretty big problems."

He chuckles, then moves a bit closer and rests his hand on my thigh.

I'm suddenly extremely aware of my body. And in the best possible way. "So, we've had all these dates," I say, my voice low. "Tell me about them. Especially the first one. How did that happen?"

For a moment, I think he's going to blow off my question, but just when I fear I'm going to have to come up with a new topic, he says, "I've watched you for a while, Aria."

"Oh." I lick my lips. The truth is, I've watched him, too. But since he's so often in magazines and on entertainment-related news, that's not too hard. Or too odd.

"Um, was that watching in a creepy, stalker way?"

He laughs. "No. Wait," he adds, his brow furrowing. "Are the cameras I planted in your house creepy?"

I use the pillow in my lap to smack him, making him laugh, and definitely lightening the moment.

"I just mean that I've seen you out in the world. And I might have asked Nikki what you're like."

"Really? No wonder she gave me the—never mind."

He laughs. "The masks for Masque? Yeah, I should send her some flowers for that."

"What can I say? I wanted in."

"Why?"

I open my mouth to tell him—then I remember that he's still on my suspect list. He's falling further and further down the list with each moment our banter goes on, and I tell myself sternly that I have to be strong. I can't trust him just because I'm hot for him.

But maybe I'll be able to learn more since he's hot for me, too...

"Masque," he urges. "Why did you want in?"

"I just ... you know." I lift a shoulder. "You hear stories. I didn't even realize it was your place. I just thought it sounded ... interesting."

"It can be," he says. "And sometimes it's *interesting* just staying home."

"Yes," I say, meeting his eyes as my heart does a little squeeze. It's a heated moment, full of possibility, and I have no idea why I break it, but I do, dropping my eyes, then looking back up at him with a slightly embarrassed smile. "When you asked Nikki what I was like, why didn't you ask her to set us up?"

He takes my hand, the action so smooth and natural I'm almost certain he doesn't even realize he's done it. "You haven't exactly been alone," he says.

"Oh, believe me, I have." I think of Dexter and my other guy friends, some of whom are more friendly than others. "There've been some guys on my arm now and again, but nothing was going anywhere with them."

"Well, I didn't know that. Besides," he adds. "I'm twenty years older than you. I didn't think you'd be interested."

"Oh." I lick my lips. "You should have asked." I hold his gaze, then boldly climb onto his lap to straddle him. "Because it's actually only nineteen and a half years. And I am interested. I'm very interested."

He shakes his head slowly. "Don't," he says, even as his hands move to cup my ass in a way that feels warm and familiar and enticingly naughty. "Don't play games with me."

"I don't play games," I tell him. My skirt has ridden up my thighs and is now bunched up at my hips. "A couple of decades don't scare me. I like a man with enough experience to know who he is. Who knows how not to play games."

"Except we are playing games."

"No," I say, though the word is a lie. Or a partial lie, at least. My need isn't a game. The heat between my thighs isn't a game. The craving for his mouth on mine isn't a game.

And yet, this whole night is a game. Because wanting and craving and needing be damned. No matter how I feel about this man, I came here to get close enough to push open the door to his secrets. To find out the truth about Jenny.

And then—if I have to—to bring Holt and anyone else involved down.

But now ... oh, god, right now I don't know anything about the meet-and-greets. I know nothing about what truly happened to Jenny. I have theories and suspicions but no facts I can act on.

The only thing I have that's one-hundred percent real is the way I feel about this man. The way he's looking at me. The intensity with which he wants me.

Maybe it's stupid. Maybe I'll regret it.

But tonight, I'm going to take it. And I'm pretty sure that Jenny would understand.

NINETEEN

I can't remember ever feeling so turned on by a man. And it's not just because I'm grinding against him, his cock so hard I think it will probably burst out of his jeans.

It's the feel of his hand on my hip. The press of his other hand as it cups the back of my head. His low, guttural groan of pleasure, the sound of which makes me so damn wet.

It's all of those things, each part making up a wild and sensual whole.

Mostly, though, it's his eyes. Those vibrant eyes that are locked on mine, as if challenging me to ride him harder. Faster.

"Aria, oh, god, Aria ..."

My name from those lips works on me like an aphrodisiac—not that I need any help in that regard. Matthew Holt is the literal embodiment of everything I want in a man. Everything I've wanted for years, though I've tweaked my mental checklist here and there over the last two decades. Elementary school Aria hadn't considered the benefits of sensuality. College Aria did.

Strong. Powerful. Sexy. Successful. Protective. This man is

everything I've craved. *And ruthless. And determined. And arrogant.*

And dangerous.

Possibly very, very dangerous.

I know my mind's little voice speaks the truth, but right now, I don't care. How can I when I'm half-naked, grinding myself against him and edging close to the best damn orgasm I've had in my life?

"Matthew," I whisper, partly because I can't hold the fullness of this feeling inside me any longer. Partly to shut up that tiny, bitchy part of my brain.

"Oh, baby, yes," he murmurs, his head bent back as I move my hips, stroking myself against him, the tiny silk triangle of my thong rubbing the denim of his jeans, making me hot and needy and very, very wet.

It's wild and raw and glorious—and I want so much more. And unless his Academy Award collection includes one for acting, I know that he does, too.

"Matthew," I whisper. I keep one hand twined in his hair. With the other, I reach down between us to find the button on his jeans.

He stops my hand. "No."

I whimper. "Please. I want—"

But he cuts off my words by tugging my head down to his and claiming my mouth in a kiss that's wild and hot and so damn sensual I truly believe I could come just from this. Except I won't have to, because while his mouth is busy pushing me toward heaven, his fingers are about to finish the job.

"That's it, baby," he whispers, two fingers snaking under my thong, then teasing my clit before thrusting inside me. "You are so damn wet."

"Please," I beg again, because it's the only word I can find at the moment. The only way to let him know how close I am to shattering in his arms. How much I want him inside me.

As if in answer, he runs his hands up my legs, his fingers grasping the dress still bunched-up around my hips. I'm straddling him, my hands on his shoulders for balance and my bent legs on the leather upholstery. Now, I rise up, lifting my arms above my head so he can pull the dress all the way off.

"Good girl," he murmurs, tossing the garment carelessly aside. It's one of my favorites, but I hardly notice. I'm too obsessed with the way his hands are teasing my breasts.

I watch as he licks the pad of one thumb, then gasp when he brushes it over a nipple. It's as if he's found a magic button that triggers a flurry of sparks that rush from my breasts all the way down to my core.

"Oh, baby," he murmurs as I cry out in response to yet another brush of his fingertip, this time on my other nipple. "I love how responsive you are."

I swallow, barely managing words when I say, "Well, I love what you're doing."

"I can tell." I hear the masculine satisfaction in his voice, then see it when he meets my eyes. He holds my gaze as he slides his hand along my cleavage, then over my belly, making me tremble with longing, only to whimper when he halts his sensual exploration right at the band of the thong.

"Don't stop," I beg, and though I expect him to torture me a little bit more, he complies, his hand moving lower and lower under that tiny bit of silk until his finger finds my clit and sends a chorus line of pleasure dancing through me.

With a low moan, I close my eyes and arch back, my knees pressed against his hips and my hands clutching the edge of the leather couch cushions for balance as his fingers stroke and tease, sparking every cell in my body—and promising a bigger explosion to come.

I'm ready—so ready, and I don't even realize I'm grinding hard against the denim-clad bulge of his cock until he says, "That's it, baby. That's so fucking hot."

I need more—hell, I need him—and as he holds my hips—as I continue to grind against him—my fingers go to work on the buttons of his shirt. But I can't focus. I'm too turned on. Too wild. Too lost.

"Fuck it," he says, then grabs his shirt just below the collar and rips the damn thing open.

I meet his eyes, and we both laugh. Then he takes my chin and tilts my head up, capturing me in the kind of deep, hot kiss that's at least as intimate as fucking. "I liked that shirt," he whispers after he breaks the kiss. "Let's make this worth it."

He grins, and I laugh again, trying and failing to remember when I've wanted a guy as much.

But there's only Matthew. Hell, I can't even remember any other man. They're all a blur. Just appetizers while I'd waited for the main course.

His body is perfect. Hard, defined muscles, but not so much that he's overly ripped. Instead, his bare chest looks as sensual and perfect as he does when he's in a suit. As if his body is flipping the bird to anyone who tries to judge him, because try as I might, I can't find a flaw.

On the contrary, he's warm and perfect, and I sigh with feminine pleasure as I trace my fingertips over the lines that define his chest and abs.

I don't finish, though. I want more than fingers on flesh, and so I cup his neck, then rise up a bit as his fingers tighten in my hair, pulling me closer for a long, deep kiss, our tongues warring as I rock my hips, teasing his cock. Wanting. Needing.

Before, I'd been enjoying the anticipation. Now, I'm impatient. I want him inside me, and I bend forward, my lips brushing his ear as I whisper his name. And all the while, my fingers are still fumbling for the button on his jeans, then the zipper.

I hesitate, expecting him to order me to slow down. To savor.

But he says nothing, and I make quick work of it, then exhale a little *oh* when his cock springs free, revealing the very obvious fact that he was wearing nothing under his jeans. He's huge and hard, and just seeing how turned on he is makes me melt a little bit more.

And makes me wetter than I ever imagined I could be.

"Aria ..."

My name is both a wish and a command, and I don't have to ask what he wants. What we both want. I rise up on my knees, then bend forward, enjoying the erotic sensation as the hard, hot length of him strokes my most sensitive parts. I slide my palms along his torso, then up to his chest and over his own hard nipples.

"Please tell me you have a condom," I whisper, and see his answering smile before he leans over me and pulls one from a bedside drawer. He rolls it on, managing even though his eyes never leave mine. Then he flashes that cocky grin as his fingers tighten in my hair, and he pulls my mouth to his in a deep, claiming kiss.

As his tongue teases my mouth, his hands find my hips and he lifts me up until the tip of his cock is right there and I hear myself begging him to fuck me, to just please fuck me *now*.

And then he's there, and I arch back as he enters me in one exquisite thrust, the kind where pain melds with pleasure and then melts into a sensation of bliss. I cry out, and he silences me with a long, deep kiss, his tongue mimicking the thrust of his cock inside me.

"Aria," he murmurs, and the sound of my name on his lips turns me on even more. I put my hands on his shoulders while his stay on my hips as I ride him, slow at first, then faster and deeper until it's no longer me doing the work but him controlling my movements, his cock going deeper inside me than any guy before him. So deep it feels as if he's touched my soul.

"Matthew," I murmur, but I'm not even sure that I spoke aloud. I'm lost in a sensual haze, my body on the verge of exploding, the atoms spinning out of control.

I feel that distinctive pressure building inside me, and his soft orders for me to come with him. To go over. To explode. And I'm close—so very close. My clit rubs against his skin and the dark hairs that trace a line from his torso to his cock. And his cock is working its own magic, the thrusts teasing all the sensitive spots hidden inside me.

But it's the brush of his fingertip over my ass that finally sends me over. That unexpected, naughty, erotic touch that pushes me over the edge and has my core clenching tight around him as I arch back and gasp with wild pleasure even as he cries out, too, his orgasm melding with mine as we lose control together.

I'm breathing hard, my mind spinning as if I lost time simply from the force of that explosion. I'm limp. Sated. But when I lean back and meet his eyes, I see that his are still full of fire and need. And though his cock's not quite hard again, it's definitely working toward that goal.

"You're insatiable," I say.

"How about you?" There's a tease in his voice. "Think you can keep up with me?"

I feel that delicious tug in my pussy and grin. "I think I can give you a run for your money."

He makes a show of looking me up and down. "I do love a woman who can keep up."

"And I love a man with stamina."

He winks at me, then tugs his jeans—now down around his

ankles—all the way off. He's essentially naked, the ripped open shirt his only garment.

He stands, then holds out his hand to me, his body so sculpted and perfect that I have to take a moment simply to soak it in.

"Come on," he urges, and I slide my hand into his without thinking.

"Where?"

"Bedroom," he says. "I want to fuck you properly."

"Oh." Since that sounds like a perfectly lovely idea, I follow him around the curve of the house to the double doors that lead to a massive bedroom overlooking the canyon, the trees of which are glowing in the light of a huge full moon.

"Beautiful," I say.

"Very," he says, and it takes me a moment to realize he's talking about me.

My skin heats in a blush, ridiculous considering what we just did, but there's something about the look in his eye that makes me shy. A need. A longing. And it's me that's the source of that look.

It's humbling.

And it's a little wonderful, too.

He crooks a finger, and I go to him. I'm naked. Vulnerable. And he slowly looks me up and down. "You're perfect," he says.

I shake my head. "I'm really not."

His fingertips stroke my cheek. "I'm your boss. Don't argue with me."

I laugh. "I'm pretty sure that since you're my boss we're not supposed to be doing this."

He lifts a brow. "Feeling harassed?"

"Very much the opposite," I tell him, and we share another grin.

"How about now?" he asks as he scoops me up and tosses me on the bed.

I gasp, then laugh. "Yeah, now maybe a little."

He climbs onto the bed, then straddles me, pinning me down as I lay on my back. "As a dutiful boss, I guess I need to make up for that by treating you very, very well."

His voice has lost the playful tone, replaced by something dark and needy.

"Tell me you want me."

"I want you," I say, the words heavy with truth.

"Tell me to fuck you."

"Fuck me." A shiver runs through me. "Matthew, please. Please fuck me."

I see the heat in his eyes. The tightening of his cheek. The flash of primal lust across his features. And, oh, how my body responds.

He leans in, his lips finding mine as his cock teases my entrance. I hold my breath, anticipating the pleasure of him filling me. But it doesn't come. Not until I beg him. Then he slides inside me, his hands just above my shoulders, his mouth pressed to mine, and his cock thrusting deep.

I move just a little, watching his face, seeing the need grow. "Deeper," he murmurs, the word little more than a groan, and it mirrors the way I feel, my body on fire, desperate and needy.

I want him. I want every inch of him, and then I want more. I want all. Every bit of this man who fills me up. Who fascinates me, excites me. This isn't just sex, it's a joining.

I tremble, feeling excited. Alive.

And this is the moment I realize that I may have fucked up.

Because however much I might crave this man, I might literally be in bed with the enemy.

TWENTY

Matthew tried to hold back. Tried to stay still and revel in the pure, raw joy of being deep inside her. The feel of her. The scent of her. He was rock hard—harder than he could ever remember being, and right then, his entire world was Aria.

He needed claim her. To go full-on caveman and make her his. To bury himself even deeper inside her. To lay her out, bend her knees up and watch ecstasy play out on her face as he fucked her hard.

But not yet.

Right now, he just wanted to revel in the fact that she wanted him, too.

He loomed over her, his hands on either side of her as he let his eyes drift over her perfection, as he moved slowly inside her. As he listened to her soft, erotic moans of pleasure. Of her whispers as she begged for more.

He tilted his head, his eyes grazing over her nipples, tight and dark. A contrast to the way the rest of her skin glowed, as if she was lit from within.

"Please," she murmured, her eyes fluttering open. "Matthew, please."

But he only shook his head, his cock still inside her, but unmoving in a delicious torment he knew was driving them both wild.

"You're beautiful," he whispered. "Beautiful and sexy and I think I might die if you walked away right now."

Her eyes fluttered open, and the delight he saw there humbled him. "Matthew." His name was only a whisper, but it said everything he wanted to hear. A promise. A plea.

And who was he to say no?

He lowered himself, letting her take more of his weight as he moved in slow, steady strokes designed to drive her—and him—right to the brink.

"Pleas—" she began, but he cut her off with a kiss, gentle at first, but when she cupped his head and pulled him closer, he lost all will to hold back and tease. Now he wanted to ravage. To consume. To make her his.

The kiss was hard and hot, their tongues moving in time with the thrust of his cock and her hips moving in time with him. It was the most sensual of dances, and it was magical.

He'd wanted this—wanted her—for so long, and now here she was. No longer a fantasy wrapped in a memory. She was real, she was naked.

And she was his.

For now, at least.

The unwelcome thought crashed through him, and he almost pulled away.

She was his for now, yes. But when she learned the truth ... when she understood who he really was. What he'd done.

A shock of cold dread pierced his heart, and he drew back slightly.

"Don't stop," she murmured, her eyes fluttering open, her expression one of pure, sensual need.

"Never," he said, willing it to be true. Telling himself he had nothing to fear. There was no reason for her to know the truth.

She was his now ... and his she would remain.

She lay on her stomach, propped up on her elbows as he sat up, his back against the upholstered headboard. She was naked, her feet crossed in the air, her hair mussed and wild around her face, her lips red and swollen. She looked well-fucked and beautiful, and very much at home.

Her hands were flat on the mattress in front of her, fingers spread, and he was tracing his own finger along the outline of her right hand.

"You're not thinking loud enough," he said, making her laugh.

"Impossible." She grinned up at him. "Everyone says I'm the loudest thinker they know."

"Already keeping secrets from me?" He said the words as a joke, but immediately wanted to kick himself. Even if she was keeping secrets, he was hardly one to talk.

"Not a secret. On the contrary. I was just thinking about what I told you before." Her voice was teasing, and the way she bit her lower lip when she finished speaking was almost enough to have him rolling her over and taking her hard once again.

As tempting as that was—and as hard as the thought made him—he said only, "Told me what?"

She pushed herself up onto her knees, then moved to straddle him. He'd pulled the sheet up to his waist, but even so, the pressure of her body against his cock was enough to breathe new life into him. "Careful. Or we may never get out of this bed."

"Maybe that's my plan."

He chuckled. "Maybe I like the way you think." He brushed his fingers over her breasts—not to get anything started, but just because she was so damn beautiful. And, yes, because he wanted to claim her. "But right now," he continued, "I want to hear the secret."

"It's not really a secret. More of a fantasy."

"Oh, is it?" He settled back, making a show of getting more comfortable. "Do tell."

She traced her fingertip along his chest, and he was certain her motives were the same as his—she was marking him as her territory. And he had no problem with that at all.

"You know how I said I liked older men?"

"I have a vague recollection. And for the record, I'm not yet in need of a walker."

A smile tugged at her mouth. "The truth is, I've had this fantasy for pretty much my entire life. Ever since I started getting interested in sex, anyway."

Her cheeks bloomed pink, which delighted him. Because his Aria was not a woman who blushed easily.

"And?"

"Honestly, it's not much of a story. Just that every time I have a sex dream, the guy is always older. Even if I'm awake and fantasizing, he might start out around thirty, but by the time he's undressing me, he has at least a decade on me. Usually two."

"That's it?"

She scowled at him. "I told you. It's not much of a story."

"But that's not the whole story, is it?"

She rolled her eyes. "Okay, fine. The rest of it's a little silly. A different dream, though they overlap sometimes. And in the dream, I'm always out in the world and something happens. Godzilla attacks. Or gangs are chasing me. Monsters, you know. All different kinds of monsters. And then this older guy swoops in and saves me. Sometimes he does fancy kickboxing stuff.

Sometimes he magically transports me away. But he always wins. He always protects me." She shrugged. "He sweeps me off my feet."

She bit her lower lip, then looked up at him, the blush back in her cheeks. "Sometimes it's you, Matthew. You've been in my dreams since the first time we met. I guess that makes you my dream man."

He wanted to pull her close. To claim her once and for all.

But he didn't.

He couldn't.

"Oh, hell," she said, leaning back. "I've totally scared you away."

"No." His heart felt about to burst. "Hell, no."

He could see the relief flow through her.

"Another reason to like older men," she said. "You don't play games."

"Sweetheart, I play all kinds of games. Don't ever make the mistake of looking at me and thinking that I have it all figured out."

She studied his face, those clever eyes narrowing. "Why?"

He frowned. "Why what?"

"Why are you screwing with me?" She made finger quotes as she said, "You play games? You don't have it figured out?" She indicated her body with a wave. I'm sitting here naked, desperate to have you inside me again, and you're saying words designed to push me away."

"No," he lied, even as he realized that was exactly what he was doing.

"Do you want me to go?" He heard the catch in her voice, and the sound both humbled him and tormented him.

He stayed silent.

"Dammit, Matthew." She slid toward the edge of the bed. He reached out and snatched her arm just above the elbow.

She froze, her eyes meeting his. "Let go of me."

He did, releasing his hold as he said, very simply, "Stay."

For a moment, she only looked at him, and he could read nothing on her face. "Why should I?"

"You shouldn't," he said. "If you were smart, you'd go." He reached for her hand, relieved when she didn't yank it back. "I want you, Aria. Make no mistake. I think you may be the most amazing woman I've ever met, much less touched. You're already under my skin. Here," he said, pressing his hand to his heart. "And here," he continued, touching his head.

"I want you, and I'm used to getting what I want. But, sweetheart, I'm not a good man. I've done things I regret. Lots of things. Bad things. If you were smart, you'd walk away right now."

Her expression was flat, unreadable as she said, "Maybe I'm not that smart. I mean, hell, I can't even keep a job for more than a few months."

"I'm serious. You know what the press says. That I'm ruthless. That I'll do whatever it takes. That my business is all I care about."

She met his eyes, and it felt like she was looking straight down into the dark depths of his soul.

"Is that true? Is it all that you care about?"

He looked away. He wanted to say yes. Wanted to push her away once and for all. Wanted to finally do the right thing and get her out of the circle of his life.

Instead, he looked back at her, awed by her beauty and humbled by her desire. "No," he said. "That's not all."

For a moment, their eyes held. Then she nodded slowly. "Thank you for the warning, but I think I'll stay. Just promise you won't lie to me. I—I don't trust easily. I'm not sure I trust at all. Except maybe Bree."

He hesitated, then nodded. "I promise," he said, hoping the

word wouldn't be a lie by tomorrow. Knowing it already was just because of the secrets he was keeping.

The sunshine of her smile erased all his doubts. "In that case," she said as she moved to straddle him, "I'm staying." She grinned. "So tell me, old man. Have you got enough in you for one more round?"

He felt his cock go hard as a wave of pure joy crashed through him. "Yeah," he said. "I think I can totter my way through just fine."

TWENTY-ONE

My head rests on his lap, the sheet soft against my cheek as he gently strokes my hair.

"What happened to you being a noisy thinker?" he whispers. "I can't hear a damn thing."

I laugh. "So sorry."

"How can I tell if you enjoyed our movie night if I can't get into that head of yours?"

I twist around, then resettle on my side with my head on a pillow. He does the same so that we're facing each other, the giant bed spread out like an ocean around us.

I reach out and stroke his hair, smiling at the touch of gray at his temples. It really is so damn sexy. "Will you believe me if I say that I was thinking about how incredible you are? And how amazing you made me feel."

I slide my hand along his side, taking the sheet with me until he's just as naked and exposed as I am. "I like you better this way," I say, resting my palm on his bare hip. "And I definitely like the view."

His brow rises. "You're breaking the rules, Ms. Parker. We agreed there'd be no more touching."

"Because we need sleep," I say, parroting our agreement. "And because touching leads to activities that are a tad more energetic than shut-eye."

"Exactly," he says.

I expel an intentionally dramatic sigh. "That's what I get for dating old men. I guess it's time to just settle in and head off to sleepy-town."

He shakes his head, then clicks his tongue. "Honestly, babe. I don't know that this is going to work. I need a woman who can keep up." He makes a show of looking me up and down. "Someone a bit younger. With more stamina."

"Oh, you're in trouble now." I laugh, then roll on top of him. "You want stamina? I'll show you stamina." But he counters by flipping me onto my back, then straddling me.

He kisses me, long and hard and deep, and when he pulls back, my body is once again tingling with need.

"That's to keep you craving the next time," he says, pulling me close and spooning against me, his cock half-hard against the curve of my ass. "But if we still want to fuck tonight, we can do that in our dreams."

"I like the sound of that," I murmur as I snuggle my backside against him. But even as I do, I'm glad he can't see my face. I'm thinking about what he said. *If we still want to fuck.* And I can't help but wonder if that's all this is to him. A good time. A fast fuck.

For better or for worse, this night has pushed me fully over the threshold into Matthew Land. That crush I've had since the day I saw him on the Starks' patio—it wasn't just about the sensual fantasies that grew and bloomed for years. No. It was about *him.*

It was a crush that grew deeper and wider with everything I learned about him, whether from an article, a casual mention by a friend, a radio interview, or even overhearing a wannabe actor/waiter talking about Holt's many, many accomplishments.

That first moment of lust I'd felt upon seeing the man had taken root and grown into something deeper and truer. And now here I am, head over heels for the whole of who he is. A talented, vibrant man who seems to check every box in the What I Want list that has been growing in my brain since junior high. His talent. His mind. His ambition.

Plus, he's gorgeous, and that's definitely icing on the Matthew Cake.

Now that I seem to have him, though, I can't help but wonder if I can keep him. What could a guy like that see in a woman like me? A woman who's almost thirty and still hasn't settled into a career. A woman who would actually take a job where sex is so obviously part of the equation.

Of course he only wants to fuck me.

And that, I tell myself, is all I should want, too. I'm here on a mission, after all. And I should know better than to let good sex and a crush mess with my head.

I should ... but apparently, I don't.

With a sigh, I roll over, putting my back to him, then using a corner of the sheet to dry my tears. I draw a breath and tell myself it doesn't matter if he's only here for a few good fucks. This is all about Jenny. And the less there is between Holt and me, the easier it will be to take him down.

But when he rolls over in his sleep and puts his arms around me, I have to wonder if that's really true. I can tell myself a hundred lies, but the truth is that I want this man. I have for a very long time.

So am I really here to help my dead friend, or did I take on this challenge to get close to Holt?

And if it's the latter, what kind of shitty friend does that make me?

The aroma of bacon rouses me from a dream involving a naked Matthew, a convertible Porsche, and a three-ring circus going full steam in the parking lot behind Vons.

I almost register a complaint when I reach the kitchen—I really, really wanted to know where that dream was going to land—but all thoughts of fast cars and circuses evaporate when I see the man standing by the stove, showered and dressed and looking ironically sexy in nothing but sweatpants that sit low on his hips and a floral print apron tied behind his neck and back.

I let out a low whistle, then raise my phone. "How much do you think *The Hollywood Reporter* would pay for this picture?"

He points kitchen tongs at me. "One, I don't serve bacon to women who threaten my masculinity."

My lips twitch. "I'll be fine. I'm sure I have a granola bar somewhere in my car."

"Two, the apron was my mother's. I found it in a box after she died."

I nod, as if considering that. "I didn't know your mom, but I'll take a wild guess that she'd have been on my side."

From his scowl, I know I played that right.

"And three," he says, moving the bacon to a paper-towel covered plate, "anyone who messes with my cooking vibe will find herself getting no more bacon at all."

"I told you. Granola—"

"And just to be clear, 'bacon' is a metaphor for sex."

"I see," I say, working very hard not to laugh. I slide my phone onto the counter. "The public doesn't need to know everything," I say. "But, damn, you look hot. The apron is a serious turn-on."

And, frankly, it kind of is. He looks a little ridiculous, very adorable, and wildly sexy.

I'm not sure if that's an empirical assessment or if my take means I'm falling hard.

I have a feeling it's the latter.

"Over easy again? Or do you want to be wild and split a mushroom and cheddar omelet?"

I press a hand to my heart. "Sharing food. Better be careful. You're going to get caught in my web."

He meets my eyes. "Ah, Ariadne. I can't think of a better trap to fall into."

I smirk as I think of my Jenny mission. I should tell him the truth—surely this man couldn't have hurt Jenny. More, he could help me find out what really happened.

But instead of telling him the truth, I smile, as if it's all just silly banter. Because I'm standing too close now to really see the truth. And just like I told Bree—Matthew Holt is a man who could kill. He could, I think, kill to protect me.

And he could kill to protect himself, too.

It's in him. That ruthlessness. But what would it take for him to hurt a woman like Jenny? Could he even do it at all?

That, I still don't know.

"It wasn't supposed to be a trick question."

I jump, pulled from my reverie. "Oh. Sorry. I'm not quite awake."

He points to the coffee maker. "Grab some elixir. So, yes to the omelet?"

I nod, then make a beeline for the coffee. I'm in the midst of pouring when his phone rings. Not his cell, but some hidden landline that is now chiming throughout the house.

He taps a button on his watch, then says, "Holt."

"You have a meeting at eleven." Lila's voice filters into the room through speakers hidden somewhere above us. I presume you'll be here in time to review the file."

"And a good morning to you, too. It's only nine-fifteen. I don't think it's time to send a helicopter for me just yet."

"It's my job to make sure your calendar runs smoothly, Matthew. Try not to make my job more difficult."

"I'll do my level best," he says. "If there's nothing else, my breakfast is getting cold."

"Actually, I thought you'd want to know that Ms. Parker hasn't come in yet. As I'd feared, I don't think she fully understands the depth of responsibility her job contains."

"Nonsense. She's so responsible she came here. It's a working breakfast."

"I see."

For twenty-seven seconds, the line is completely silent. As it turns out, twenty-seven seconds is a lot more time than you'd think.

"In that case," Lila says, continuing as if there'd been no pause at all, "ask her to stop by the *Widow Bluff* set on her way in. Accounting needs the cost overrun reports by the end of day."

"Done," he says. "Which also describes my omelet. I'll see you soon, Lila. You can fill me in on the rest then."

"You need—"

But I don't hear what else Matthew needs, because he's tapped his watch again and the ceiling goes silent.

I glance up toward the hidden speakers and mics. "I can't decide if that's cool or creepy."

"Cool," he says, then flashes a tight smile. "Sorry about that. I'm sure you've already noticed that she's a bit overprotective."

"Understatement much?"

He gestures to the small table by the window, and I take a seat. He joins moments later with the omelet, some fried potatoes I didn't realize he'd been heating up, and toast. He slides the plates onto the table, then leaves, returning in a few seconds with two carafes—OJ and coffee.

"I would have helped."

"Maybe I like waiting on you. Besides, that's everything. Unless you need ketchup or something?"

"Nope. I'm all good." I start to pick up my fork, then hesitate. "Are you?"

"Am I what? Good?"

He sounds genuinely confused, and I shrug, feeling a little confused myself.

"Aria?"

"I—" I shake my head, feeling like an idiot. "I just—oh, hell. Is there ... I mean, you and Lila. Is there something there?"

"No," he says.

"But—"

"No."

I nod, then focus on my meal. Which isn't difficult since it's freaking delicious. All of it. Omelet. Bacon. Toast. OJ. Coffee.

Coffee refill.

And then there's no more food ... which means no more distractions.

I lean back in my chair, my finger tapping a rhythm on the tabletop. He sighs, then reaches across the table to take my hand. "There's nothing romantic or sexual between Lila and me." His voice is soft. Earnest. "But there've been times when she's made it more than clear that she wants there to be. And maybe even some times when she thought we were heading that direction. But, no. There's nothing now. There hasn't been anything for a very long time."

"Oh. So there was."

"We were in our early twenties. We were working together. It was casual, just one time. We were celebrating something."

His eyes meet mine, and I see only regret. "It didn't last. The friendship did."

"I shouldn't have asked. It's not my business."

"Oh?" His eyes meet mine. "I kind of hoped it was."

"Yeah?" My question is so soft, it's a wonder he can hear me.

But he can, and he nods, then grins. "Where exactly have you been the last couple of days? Because if that's not something you picked up on, I'm going to have to rethink your role as my PA. I mean, I need an assistant who gets me." He reaches for my hand. "I thought you got me."

I match his grin, feeling both full up and very light all at the same time. "I think I do. But I'm certain you've got me. And that you get me, too. Does that count?"

His brow furrows as he sways from side to side as if pondering some internal debate. "Judges say yes."

"Well, good. I'm glad I'm still in the game."

"In it?" He squeezes my fingers. "Baby, you won it."

For a moment, we just look at each other. It's one of those moments that seems removed from both time and reality. "Is this —are we—I mean, we're moving awfully fast."

I regret the words the moment I say them. I don't want him to pull back. And not because I need to be close if I'm going to find out what happened to Jenny. This moment is only about Matthew. And me.

"In case you hadn't noticed, I make up my own rules. And I think we're moving at the speed of us."

I tear up a bit, delighted by his words. "Yeah. I guess we are." I hesitate. "Except ..."

His eyes narrow, and he strokes the pad of his thumb lightly along my hand. "No. No exceptions."

"It's just that I don't think Lila likes me. And I have a feeling that *the speed of us* isn't something she's going to understand."

"She's my receptionist, not my mother or my shrink or my relationship counselor."

I notice that he doesn't deny my assessment as to Lila's utter lack of love for me.

"But she's also my right hand," he adds. "I won't fire her. There's too much history there." The corner of his mouth quirks up. "She knows where all the bodies are buried."

His tone is teasing, but I go cold nonetheless. I take a sip of coffee, then look at him over the mug. "And how many bodies are there?"

"I don't know," he says. "But I battled Hardline into existence. And for every person who looks at a plot of land and sees a historic battleground, there's someone else who looks at it and sees a graveyard."

He reaches across the table and squeezes my hand. "My rise in this business was fast but legit. I may have killed my competition, but only metaphorically. Don't worry," he says, "Once Lila gets to know you better, she'll like you just fine."

He says it, but I don't believe it. It doesn't matter, though, because I trust Matthew. More than I ever thought I would.

Hopefully not more than I should.

I take another sip of coffee, trying to wrap my head around how I feel about this man. It hasn't even been twenty-four hours since I arrived for movie night, and yet it feels like we've lived a lifetime. Like he is—and always has been—right by my side.

"Penny for your thoughts," he murmurs, his voice low and rich, a vibration I feel all the way to my toes.

I glance up, meeting his gaze. "I was just thinking about how you make me feel."

"Yeah? How's that?"

"Like I'm safe." I hesitate, feeling a vulnerability that almost scares me. But he's here, watching me with those fathomless eyes, and somehow I know I can be honest. "Like I'm right where I'm supposed to be."

"You are," he says simply, his words wrapping around me like a promise.

For a moment, neither of us speaks, and I let myself bask in the quiet intimacy of the moment. Then, of course, I have to dive back into deep waters. "Lila," I say. "You really think she doesn't want you back?"

He shakes his head. "There's no *back*. I told you, we weren't together that way except for the one time. And that was a drunken, celebratory mistake."

"It's just that ... well, it's obvious she doesn't like the idea of me and you."

"She's protective. We go way back, and without her I never would have gotten my first films made. We made a good team, but ..."

"But?" I prompt, sensing the weight behind the word.

"But we had some rough months, then went our separate ways. She hit hard times, and I let her back in. I owed her."

"Owed her?"

"She—well, let's just say she was instrumental in getting me on this path. I owe her a lot. And we're friends. Good friends."

"I never saw you as the kind of businessman who would hire someone just out of obligation."

He leans back. "I'm not. She also happens to be great at what she does. More than that, I trust her completely."

The silence hangs between us, heavy with things unspoken. "I'm sorry," I say. "We're barely together—I don't even know if it would be fair to say we're dating—and I'm getting all bent out of shape about something that's clearly in the past."

His face is unreadable, but I see the way his body relaxes. "One, we are dating. Exclusively," he adds, in a voice that makes me want to drag him right back to bed.

"It'll be a challenge, but I guess I can live with that."

"Two," he says, fighting the smile that tugs at his mouth, "Lila's seeing someone."

"Oh. Who?" The question is automatic. It's not as if I've been around long enough to know Lila's paramour.

"Elias Trent" he says. "He's—"

"—head of Talent Relations."

His brows raise. "I'm impressed."

I flash a modest smile. "I want to do a good job. I studied the corporate chart. Other than that, I know nothing about the guy."

So maybe Matthew is right. Maybe Lila's just protective and prickly, and I'm reading too much into things.

But even as I tell myself that, a little part of me can't help but wonder if he's blind to what's right in front of him. And if there really is something dark and scary happening at those parties.

And if so, does Lila know?

TWENTY-TWO

Wednesday passes in a glorious blur. I have errands all over the studio lot, so I'm able to mostly avoid Lila. Something I consider a good thing, since I'm pretty sure she'd read *I Had Sex With Matthew* with just one good look at my face.

Still, despite my honed and sharpened acting skills (not), I can't help but float through the day. And while Matthew and I play it purely professional, I catch Lila's sharp gaze more than once. And by the end of the day, I can't shake the feeling that she knows.

"Don't worry about it," Matthew tells me when we're tucked away in his office sorting documents. (*Not* a euphemism.) "Lila's a big girl, and I already told you there's nothing between us."

"You also told me that she'd like there to be. Which I think makes me her archnemesis."

"And you'll look damn cute in the bodysuit and cape."

"Don't make light of it."

We're working on the sofa in his office, the documents spread out on the coffee table. Now, he reaches for my hand and squeezes it. "I'm not," he says. "I respect how she felt about me in the past. But she's seeing someone now, remember? Whatever she might have felt for me is history."

"Maybe," I say. "Maybe not. But if this thing between us is going to go anywhere—"

"Thing?" He arches a brow.

"—then you need to tell her," I finish, my voice firm.

He's still holding my hand. Now he lifts it and kisses my knuckles. "This is more than a thing," he says, with so much heat in his voice I feel a little undone. "And you're right. She's my oldest friend, and she deserves to know. I've got a morning meeting, but I'll talk to her after that. Sound good?"

"Sounds perfect," I say, in a voice that's more chipper than I feel. I do think Lila deserves to know. That doesn't mean I'm entirely certain it's going to be all hugs and puppies and congratulations once Matthew lays it out.

But I'll worry about that tomorrow. In the meantime, there's something thrilling about sneaking kisses in his office when no one's looking.

And something even more thrilling about going home with him and sharing his bed that night.

He wakes me Thursday with a kiss, and when my eyes flutter open, my heart does a little flip-flop. Not only am I looking at an exceptional face with a radiant smile, but I'm in the bed of a man I've fallen for fast and hard.

Although maybe it's not that fast when I think about all the years I've watched and wanted, never believing I could ever have him.

The real miracle is that he's fallen just as hard for me.

"I've got Lila duty," he says, taking a seat on the edge of the bed and brushing my hair off my face.

My stomach flutters. Today is the day he's telling her. "Call me after you talk," I say.

He nods. "I will. But don't worry. We're all adults. It will be fine."

I nod.

"Want me to drop you at your house on the way? Or do you want to lounge in bed a little longer?"

"Lounge," I say. "Who knows when I'll have another opportunity to ransack your house and learn all your secrets?"

For a second, I think I see a shadow cross his face. But by the time I say, "I'm kidding—hello?" I'm pretty sure that was my imagination.

"Just so long as you don't sell them to *Variety*," he says, making me tap a finger on my temple and say, "Now there's an idea."

"Careful," he says. "I'd love an excuse to spank you."

I lift a brow. "Oh, really?"

"Then again, perhaps that's not a punishment." Mischief dances on his face, and he leans closer, his breath tickling my ear as he says, "I'll just withhold sex."

"I'll be good," I say, crossing my heart. "Nary a snoop."

He chuckles, then gives me a goodbye kiss that is sweet and sexy and full of promise. "I'll see you at the office," he whispers. "And I'll see more of you tonight."

"Damn right," I say, then snuggle back against the pillow as he heads out to—hopefully—not make an enemy of Lila.

Since I actually have a hefty pile of work at the office, I don't luxuriate in the sheets for long. Instead, I luxuriate in the steam shower—*how have I never experienced one of these before?*—then order an Uber since my car's been on the Hardline lot since yesterday morning.

Since I don't have a clean outfit at the treehouse, I have the Uber driver drop me at home. I'm running later than I'd planned, and as I rush inside, I toss my purse on the entry table, accidentally knocking off the brown paper bag I'd left there after Tilda's visit. A handful of bite-sized candy bars burst out, along with a white envelope, half-protruding from the paper bag.

A letter. I'd completely forgotten that the candy bag also held a letter for me that had been mistakenly delivered next door.

The envelope is only partly revealed, and as I bend down to scoop up the spilled candy, all I can see is the return label. There's no name, just a familiar address.

Whitsett Avenue. Valley Village, California.

My whole body goes cold.

Jenny.

The letter is from Jenny.

My knees give out, and before I know it, I'm on the floor, staring at the envelope like it might explode. The postmark shows that it was mailed the day before she died, and my hands shake as I pick it up, then rip it open without any ceremony. A single sheet of paper flutters out, landing on the floor beside me. I grab it, my pulse thundering in my ears as I look at the words scrawled in green Sharpie in Jenny's messy handwriting.

I AM THESE TORN LINES.
JG
PS: I'm driving on, driving out. Forgive me, this tangled knot.

The words blur as my stomach lurches. I drop the paper and stagger to my feet, stumbling toward the bathroom. I barely make it to the toilet before I'm vomiting, my body shaking from the force of it.

When I'm done, I sit back against the cold tile, clutching my stomach as I try to catch my breath. My mind is racing, spinning with possibilities I can't piece together.

I don't know if I sit there for minutes or days, but finally I push myself to my feet, wipe my mouth, and stagger out of the bathroom.

Jenny.

That note.

What the hell does it mean?

The question swirls through my mind as I stumble out of the bathroom. I don't remember heading to the back of the house, but the next thing I know I'm in my office—the room that used to be Bree's bedroom. It's a mess. Bookshelves crammed to the brim and papers spilling onto the desk. But I'm here for a reason, and I drop to my knees in front of one of the shelves and start pulling out books until I find my senior yearbook. I flip to the back, where dozens of autographs crowd the pages.

It's all there—the promises, the jokes, the signatures from kids I swore I'd be friends with forever but haven't seen in years. I flip faster, skimming the pages until I find it. The big green heart.

Inside the heart, the words jump out at me, written in that same familiar handwriting: *Madam, I am Adam—and Adam, we're the word masters.*

I trace the words with my finger, my heart pounding. It's signed by the three of us—Jenny, Bree, and me. We'd written this in each other's yearbooks, proud of our ridiculous wordplay.

It had been Jenny's thing at first. She'd loved word games. So, of course, she'd sucked me and Bree into the madness. We weren't as into them as she was, but it made for a fun thing to share—and hiding messages in silly sentences turned out to be the thing I would most remember from high school.

I blink, realizing that my vision has gone blurry with tears. *She sent me a message.*

If I'd gotten it in time, would I have been able to save her?

I reach for my phone, thinking that I have to call Bree. But I hesitate. She's off on the trip of a lifetime, and I don't want to ruin that for her. Not unless I truly, desperately need the help.

I'm holding a clue in my hand, and it must lead somewhere. Either to the darkness in her head that led to suicide ... or to murder. So I'll follow it until I hit a dead end. And then—maybe —I'll drag Bree in.

Until then? Well, I guess she can enjoy her nights having wild sex in Monaco.

I reach for a pen and a notepad, intending to start unscrambling, but as I do, my phone buzzes, the screen lighting up with a text from Lila. I grimace. All I can see on the preview is *Has the policy re running late slip—*

I start to tap to open the text, but I hesitate, not sure if Matthew's talked to her yet. But surely he would have texted me if he had.

Fuck it.

I tap, then I type back a quick reply. *Sorry. I was with Matthew. He said he would tell you I would be in late.*

I hit *send*, knowing it's a bit passive-aggressive, but not really caring. Except it's going to put her in a pissy mood.

I sigh, then almost text Matthew and tell him not to talk to her today. But I shove the thought aside. If I have to deal with Lila, I will. But right now, I'm going to focus on Jenny.

I tuck the note back into the envelope. I don't know if it's a clue or a suicide note.

Either way, I have to unscramble the message.

I only hope that I can.

By the time I get to work, my nerves are frayed. My mind keeps replaying Jenny's note, the lines of green Sharpie etched into my memory as if I'd written them myself.

I am these torn lines.

PS: *I'm driving on, driving out. Forgive me, this tangled knot.*

What was she trying to say? Was it a goodbye? A warning? Something else entirely?

I'd spun those letters around and around in my head for the entire ride to Hardline. Now, I'm in the elevator, staring at the photo of the letter I'd taken before locking the original in my desk. I try to will the letters to jump into their proper order, but nothing happens. The words are nonsense, and they're determined to stay that way.

My stomach twists. This letter is the only hope I have of learning what happened to Jenny. She'd written out the anagram. She'd mailed the letter to me. It was some sort of cry for help. And while I have no idea why she didn't call and just talk to me, it doesn't matter now.

This letter is what I have left—and I *will* learn the truth.

But apparently not today.

With a frown, I lock my phone as the elevator doors slide open. I step out, tilt my head down, then head toward the office where another challenge awaits me: Lila.

If she's looking, I know Lila can see me on the security camera, but I take my time, anyway. I need the extra moments to try to clear my head and make sure my face isn't reflecting any errant thoughts. Easier said than done since I'm about as good at hiding my emotions as I am at acrobatics. As in, not at all.

I watch the pattern of the carpet as I walk, hoping that I'll somehow grok my next best step by the time I reach the door. What I *want* is to show Matthew the note, and it guts me to acknowledge that I can't. Jenny's death is the reason I'm at Hardline. The reason I applied for the job. The reason I wanted to get close to Matthew. Well, that and my long-standing crush.

I fight the urge to fake a stomach bug and just turn around and go home. But I can't. I got into this for Jenny, and I'm going to see it through. I can't back off now, even if I am slowly unraveling with every step toward that door. Even if I know that there are only two people in the whole world who could help me hold it together right now. One's in Monaco. And the other might very well be the man who took Jenny from me in the first place.

No. No, I can't believe that.

But that's my heart talking. My brain is quietly whispering that I can't let myself be stupid.

Would it be stupid?

I know the man. I've seen his heart.

And what about what you told Bree? That he and Ash are alike. That they could kill to protect what they love.

But how on earth could Jenny have been a threat? A wannabe actress? It makes no sense.

And it won't. Not until you know the truth.

I hesitate at the office door, knowing the little demon in my head is right. I won't know until I know. And I have absolutely no idea how to take the next step toward truth.

Lila says only, "Good morning," when I walk in, but I'm sure there's a dark message underneath. Something like, *"Welcome back, bitch, and stay away from the man I want."*

I give a slight nod of acknowledgment, keep my head down, and hurry into my office. I shut the door that leads to reception. Then I glance toward the door between me and Matthew's private office, noting that it's already closed.

Good. I need a few minutes to think. I even go so far as to pull up Bree on my phone. I'm about to tap the icon to call her, but then I remember two things. One, I can't drag her into this when she's overseas. And two, I have no idea what time it is over there, but I'm guessing that it's not a good time to call.

And that's when the heavens open up, angels sing, and shafts of gold light shoot down from above.

Because I know what to do.

I'll tell Matthew.

Not that I came to Hardline because of Jenny. Not even that I know that Jenny went to Hardline's meet-and-greets.

No, I'll just tell him that my friend Jenny was trying to break into acting, that I need to figure out why she committed suicide, and since he's Matthew Freaking Holt, then maybe he has a way to find out if something happened before she died. Like maybe she'd bombed an audition for Hardline or some other producer in town.

That way Matthew never has to know I suspected him for a second. Plus, he'll be able to help me figure this out. Because, of course, he's completely innocent.

And if I'm wrong about that ... well, in that case, hopefully I'll be able to tell. And as much as it might break my heart, I'll take him down.

But I'm not wrong. I've been naked with this man. Joked with him. Made love with him. Cooked and laughed with him.

I'm not wrong.

I can't be wrong.

And because I can't, I open my phone to the photo of the letter, then stand up and go to our connecting door. I'm about to tap on it when I realize that it's already slightly ajar, which means if I knock, it will just fly open. Fine if he's alone, bad protocol if he's got someone in there.

I bend forward, my ear to the crack. At first, I hear just a slight murmur, as if he might be on the phone. I start to push the door a bit more, just for a peek, when I freeze, every ounce of blood in my body going cold from the single word I've heard.

Gardner.

TWENTY-THREE

I hold my breath, then lean closer, straining to hear. Had I really heard him say *Gardner*?

And even if he did, was he talking about Jenny? Maybe he was talking about an actual gardener. After all, the studio grounds are gorgeous. There must be dozens of gardeners on payroll.

Or maybe I'm trying too hard.

Or maybe I need to quit guessing, keep listening, and try to gather some facts.

I bend over, putting my ear closer to the crack. I still can't make out the actual conversation, though. Just a few snippets of sentences about budgets and financial reports.

"—cost overruns for three consecutive quarters." That's Matthew's voice, and it's easy enough to hear, probably because he's clearly irritated. "—reconciliation this quarter."

Whoever is with him responds, but I can't make out his actual words.

"Dammit, Joel, we can't ... women ... lock it down."

I hear the sound of shuffling paper, then another voice, presumably Joel's. "... same page ... international ... channels."

I don't know exactly what they're talking about, but my stomach's starting to twist in response to the very, very scary thoughts that are forming in my mind.

I tell myself this isn't happening. My mind is just spinning off into a bad place. A *very* bad place considering that fears of human trafficking are filling my head.

But there's no way that the Matthew Holt who touched me so gently and made me feel so special could be involved in something as heinous as that.

Then again, I know better than most how someone who seems perfect can turn out to be the worst kind of vile.

Oh god, oh god, oh god...

"... tell Elias the next time I set a meeting, he needs to get his ass to my office," Matthew's voice says, sharp and controlled. "He's ... down ... fucking soon."

Elias Trent. He's the head of Talent Relations, the department that organizes the meet-and-greets. And Joel Carradine is a relatively new hire in that same department, having joined only about three months ago.

My stomach does a clenching number again. I don't want to think about what all this means. I really, really, really don't want to think about it.

But my brain has other ideas, and I stumble away from the door as Bree's voice comes back to me. *"The alien guy said she might be right for some roles they were casting in London."*

The "alien guy" whose initials are E and T.

Elias. Trent.

No. Please, no.

But my mind is already spinning. Misallocated money. Scandal. International stuff. And I'm kicking myself for not thinking of it the first time I heard that name.

Was Elias Trent shipping girls off to London for auditions? Or was that a cover and he was really sending them for something else? Because I've watched enough movies to know that's a recipe for human trafficking. And Liam Neeson is never around when you need him.

Except this can't be right. There's no way the Matthew I know could be involved in something like that.

Except maybe he could. I want to believe that we connected —that I understand who he really is. But maybe I've only seen what he wants me to see.

I've read enough about him to know that he pursued his dream with ruthless intention. Hell, he's said as much in his interviews.

But how ruthless? And why? Money? He's got plenty of money.

"—auction next week. The club ... Maida Vale."

I frown. I went to London with my parents after high school, and our hotel was in Maida Vale.

So there was going to be an auction in London?

"Not like ... clusterfuck." Matthew's voice is as sharp as a knife, and I want to scream with frustration. Just lay it the fuck out for me. Say the words to make me certain that this isn't what it sounds like.

Or—dammit—to make me certain that it is.

"—tomorrow's event," Joel says, and I think he must have turned away because he's much harder to understand. I press my ear to the crack, then snap back when I hear "Jenny." At least I think I do. Maybe it was Minnie. Or even Kenny or Penny.

I'm not sure.

Except in my gut, I know with absolute certainty. They're talking about my friend. My dead friend.

An innocent woman who got caught in a horrible net.

And though it makes me sick to even think it, I'm terrified Matthew was at the heart of whatever horrible scheme reeled her in and got her killed.

So what the hell do I do now?

I spend the rest of the morning in my office, pretending like I'm getting work done. Matthew only pops his head in once to tell me he has to drive out to Redlands to deal with some trouble on a shoot that's currently over-budget, and that he'll be gone the rest of the day.

I nod and smile and tell him to drive safe and I'll see him in the evening. And then—once he's closed the door behind him—I put my head on my desk and tell myself I don't really know anything, and the tears pricking my eyes are for pussies. I'm not allowed to freak out until I'm sure. And I'm not sure yet.

But I will be. I'll do whatever it takes to figure this out, and the first thing I'm going to do is check out Joel Fucking Carradine. From what I know he hasn't been with Hardline that long. But there he was in Matthew's office. If this were a movie, that would be because he's shifting jobs, moving from the outside into the inner circle.

And I figure since this is a company that makes movies, I could do worse than using movie lore to figure out what's going on.

Which is why I end up back in front of the same Human Resources clerk I met on my first day. Only this time, I need the file for Joel Carradine. For my boss, of course.

"Here you go," she says, returning with a thin file. "But didn't he already look at it? The log shows Mr. Holt reviewing the digital file a few weeks ago."

I shake my head, confused. "I'm new. I didn't know personnel files were in the system. He, um, just asked me to get it."

"Well, just take it. He may have a reason for wanting the hard copy. But here," she says, handing me a piece of paper. "That's the instructions on how to access the system. If you're his PA, you may be doing that a lot. And it's easier than popping down here all the time."

I thank her, then take the instructions and the file. Then I hurry back to the office and log onto the system. Sure enough, with the access code I have as Matthew's PA, I have full access to the files of everyone who's ever worked at Hardline. And that includes seeing the electronic trail of everyone who's taken a peek.

Pretty cool.

Even though I have the hard copy, I almost click on Joel Carradines's file, figuring that I can print anything of interest. But I stop myself. If I can see who's accessed it, so can Matthew. And just in case I'm wrong about him—*please, please don't let me be wrong*—I don't want him to know I've been poking around.

And even if he's as pure as Ivory soap, I don't want him to ask me what I've been doing. I want to trust him—but I have to be smart.

And right now, being smart means considering the worst.

I pull out the small notebook I keep in my purse, then label a page with "JC." I've just flipped to Joel's resume when my cell rings. I grab it, see it's Clive, and answer with, "I'm right in the middle of something."

"Meet me for lunch."

I check the clock. It's already twelve-fifteen. "I can't. Seriously, I need to get through this project before—"

"I want to talk to you about the party," he says, his voice oddly stressed. "You know. About why we were there."

"Oh." A chill like cold fingers crawls up my spine. "I'm, uh, working on exactly that right now. And I'm kind of under the gun. Can't you just tell me?"

"Can't. I'm bringing a friend, and he wants to meet in person."

"Clive ..." I'm sure he can hear the irritation in my voice. Why the hell is he telling other people about it?

"Trust me. You need to hear about this now."

I nod, thinking. "Okay. But I don't have much time. I'll call down and leave your name with the gate. Meet me in the tower lobby. Bring some takeout."

"Got it. You'll need to leave Jonah Tucker's name, too."

"Will do," I say, wondering why that name sounds so familiar. "What time?"

"We can be there in fifteen."

"Perfect," I say, thinking that gives me enough time to at least skim Joel's file.

Once Clive's off the line, I turn my attention back to the resume, but I'm having a hard time focusing. My skin feels prickly, and my heart's beating just a little too fast. It's excitement. And it's fear. I'm close to something—I'm certain of it. And Jenny's letter is what started it. "Thanks for kicking my ass into gear," I whisper. "I promise I've got your back now."

I feel a little chill and tell myself it's Jenny giving me a hug from wherever she is now. A thank you for trying. And a promise that she'll help keep me moving in the right direction.

With that thought—and Bree's voice in my head chiding *"way, way, way too woo"*—I turn my attention back to the resume.

Joel Carradine's one smart guy. No doubt about that. Third in his class at Harvard Law, then a cog in some big law firm before moving to the legal department of an international production company with projects at most of the major studios in the US and overseas.

According to his list of skills, he's worked in international talent recruitment, cross-border negotiations, and even crisis management.

Each line seems normal enough, but the more I read, the more things feel slightly off. I can't put my finger on it, but I also can't shake the feeling that the seemingly innocent list of job skills hides something sinister. But I'm not an expert. Not by a long shot.

With a frown, I flip to the next page of the file. He was hired by Elias Trent and interviewed only by Trent. Considering he was hired as Trent's second in command of the Talent Relations department, that doesn't surprise me. I doubt that Matthew even saw the man's resume before pulling it for review.

And why did he pull it in the first place? Hardline has thousands of employees. There's no possible way—and no reason—for Matthew to review every resume. That's why there's a corporate chain of command.

I'm pondering that question when the timer I've set on my phone goes off. I snap photos of the resume, figuring that's safer than making a photocopy.

Then I put the folder together and rush out of the office with a quick wave to Lila and a promise to hurry back after I grab a bite.

I drop the folder back at HR, then continue down to the lobby, just in time to meet Clive and Jonah as they stride into the building.

TWENTY-FOUR

As far as I know, the roof was never intended to be a dining area, but there are several metal tables bolted to the floor and I've come here a few times to sip coffee and clear my head, always upwind from the building's few smokers who come here when they're desperate. It's not well-maintained like the rest of the building, but it's functional, the breeze is nice, and there's a lovely view of the lot and the mountains across the Valley.

Today, it's not crowded at all, which is good because that means that Clive and Jonah and I can grab a table where we're sure not to be overheard.

The guys drove through In-N-Out on their way here, and now we're settled at a table, a spread of cheeseburgers and fries in front of us. I take a sip of Diet Coke, letting the fizz settle my nerves, then look between the two of them. My friend, who I've trusted for years. And Jonah, the guy I've just been introduced to. But who I'll trust since he has the Clive seal of approval.

"So spill it," I say to Clive, unwrapping one of the burgers. "What's so urgent?"

He glances around, then leans in. "Two things," he says, his voice low. "The first is Hardline's Thirsty Thursday meet-and-greet."

I lean forward. "Tonight?"

"Yup. And guess who has a ticket for himself and a plus one?"

"Ryan Gosling?" I quip.

He tilts his head and looks down his nose. "Me. It starts at eight. I'll pick you up at seven-forty-five. We'll be there by eight-fifteen. Never good to seem too eager."

"Yes. Fabulous. Casual? Dressy?"

"Casual, but go with flirty. The more you get noticed the more Hardline folks will talk to you."

"Okay, okay." I nod, mentally inventorying my wardrobe. "This is great. Thank you."

I'm supposed to hang with Matthew later tonight, so I'll tell him that Clive wanted to spend some time, and that I'll head to the treehouse after. Since Matthew didn't say when he'd be back from Redlands, it makes sense that I'd make plans.

"Yeah, this is great," I repeat. "You win the friend of the year award."

"Well, good." He fidgets with his straw. "But after I tell you the rest of it, you may want to take a few points off."

I ease back in my chair, then narrow my eyes at him as I cross my arms. "What did you do?" Surely he didn't tell anyone why I took this job. Panic bubbles inside me as I think about the squinty-eyed stare that Lila's always aiming my direction. If she learns my true motive ...

He glances sideways at Jonah, then winces. "I told him."

I flash a half-smile at Jonah, then speak with clipped precision. "I don't think there's anything wrong with you taking a Hardline employee to one of the parties. I think it's part of my job to understand all facets of the business. I'm sure Jonah doesn't care that I'm really not supposed to be there."

"Yeah, he doesn't care about that," Clive says, as I stare him down with the kind of glance that would kill if this were a superhero movie. "I might have mentioned that you're trying to figure out what happened to Jenny."

"For fuck's sake, Clive. You promised." My stomach twists as I turn to Jonah. "Whatever he told you, please, please don't—"

"It's fine," Clive says, holding his hands up as if I were pointing a gun. "Seriously, it's okay. I've known Jonah forever."

"And I knew Jenny, too," Jonah says. "I liked her."

I take a closer look at Jonah. I hadn't given him much thought at first. All I'd really thought about was how to talk to Clive in a way that didn't give my mission away.

I hadn't expected that Clive had gone and done that already.

Now that I'm sitting here potentially exposed, I take a longer look at the guy whom Clive swears I can trust. He's tall and skinny with wild red hair. Something about him tugs at my memory—a familiar set of freckles, a crooked, endearing smile.

Then it hits me—he looks a bit like the kid from that sitcom everyone watched back in the day, the one who played the wise-cracking, trouble-prone little brother.

"Yeah," he says, apparently realizing where my thoughts have gone. "I used to be on *We're All Family*."

"I remember you. But wow—you're all grown up."

"That's the problem," he says with a sigh, leaning back and giving Clive a quick grin. "Aging out of the cute-kid roles hasn't exactly done me any favors. Transition's been ... let's say 'bumpy.'"

Clive nudges him. "Jonah here's the one who told me he was shocked when he heard about Jenny."

Jonah's easy smile fades. "The Jenny I knew wouldn't kill herself."

"Not my Jenny, either." I blink back tears. "How did you know her?" I dab a fry in ketchup as he answers, but I don't eat it. I'm not hungry anymore.

He shrugs. "Oh, you know. We crossed paths at auditions and at the Hardline parties. Had coffee a few times and bitched about the industry. You know how it is. Banged a couple of times, too," he adds with a blush. "Nothing serious, but I liked her. We had fun together."

I wipe away a tear that's escaped. "She mentioned you," I tell him. "Not by name. She called you her Hardline FWB. Said you were a lot of fun."

He nods, his shoulders hunching. "Thanks. Hearing that ... it helps."

"Is that why you came today? To meet another friend of hers?"

He shakes his head. "Listen, she wanted to make it, no matter what. Like, seriously ambitious. But if Moses appeared in front of her and said it wasn't happening, she'd go off and do something else. Not kill herself over it. That girl had backbone. And she loved her life, her friends, all of it."

"What are you saying?" I ask, though I know exactly what he's saying.

"I'm saying that someone killed her. I'm certain of it."

For a moment, his words sit heavy between us. Then I nod. "That's what I think, too." I consider telling him about the anagram letter, but I don't. Maybe later if I can't figure it out. But I need to stay under the radar, and if too many folks are poking around in Jenny's death ...

I look at Clive, then back to Jonah. "Any idea who?"

He shakes his head. "Not a clue. Except ..." He trails off, looking to Clive, who nods. "Well, when Clive said you were working at Hardline, I thought I should say something."

I look between the two of them. "Why?"

Jonah rubs the back of his neck. "So here's the thing—I've been going to the meet-and-greets at Hardline for years now. Got a few guest spots from them, some decent leads, so they're legit. But ..."

He looks down, biting his lip. "I don't know. Maybe I'm being paranoid."

Clive nudges him. "Just tell her."

Jonah draws a deep breath. "Okay, so ... like, a year ago, this girl I used to see at every event just stopped showing up." He shrugs. "No big deal, right? I figured she'd either booked something or decided to give up acting."

I lean forward. "But that wasn't the case?"

"No idea. But a few months later, another girl stopped showing, too. The last time I saw her, she told me she'd landed a gig in London. She was totally stoked."

"What was the gig?" I ask.

"Don't know. But here's the thing. My uncle's from London, and my cousin was getting married, and I was going to be over in London just a few days after she flew over. So I called Hardline's London office to see if they could get a message to her. Talked to two different folks. Nobody'd heard of her."

I feel cold all over, but I lean back, determined not to assume the worst right off the bat. "And you're sure the gig was with Hardline?"

His brow furrows. "I—well, no. But she did tell me she got the gig through one of the meet-and-greets. So I assumed it was a Hardline job. But maybe she met someone who introduced her to someone and on and on." He looks between me and Clive. "I guess that's possible," he says, but he doesn't sound convinced.

Honestly, neither am I.

"And you couldn't find her at all?"

He shakes his head.

"Did you call the government? Like, whoever keeps track of passports and stuff?"

"I didn't think of it," he says. "I guess someone still could. Her name was Tamra Keane." He spells it out for me, and I type it into my phone. "She lived in Santa Monica and was born in Oklahoma. We had the Okie thing in common."

For a moment, we're all silent. Then he draws a breath and says, "There were others, too. Another girl I knew who stopped coming. And this guy I'd see all the time—Todd—we'd have a beer and shoot the breeze. He—well, he killed himself."

My eyes cut to Clive, whose expression looks as harsh and disturbed as I feel.

"Anything else?" The question comes out in a whisper.

Jonah shakes his head. "I just ... sometimes I think I should have called the police, but I didn't really know anything. Folks give up on acting all the time, you know? Hell, folks give up on LA all the time. It's expensive as shit out here and breaking into acting is hard. So someone not coming to a party? Not really breaking news, right?"

"Guess not," I say. "Who officially sponsors the parties? Hardline, right?"

"Yeah. Well, I guess so. The invites come from the Talent Relations department, and—"

"*Elias Trent,*" I say, thinking about the snippets of conversation I'd overheard between Joel and Matthew.

"Yeah. He didn't come all the time, but I met him once or twice. And his name was always on the Hardline Christmas card."

I nod, feeling a little sick at the thought of Matthew in the midst of all this. "So you met him? Trent?"

"Well, you know. A handshake. Welcome to the party, and all that."

"What's he like?"

"Don Draper type. It's not like I got to know him or anything."

"What about Joel Carradine? Have you heard of him?"

Jonah nods. "Yeah. He's been to several, too. I think he works with Trent."

As I nod, Jonah leans forward. "Listen ..." He trails off, then takes a deep breath. "Whatever you do, can you leave my name out of it? I don't want to get the rep of being a troublemaker or a paranoid freak. Despite appearances, this really is a small town."

"I get it," I say. "And I promise."

He nods. "Okay. Good. And, you know ... about Jenny. I hope you find the fucker who killed her. She was a good egg."

"Yeah," I say. "She really was."

I know I should go back to the office after Clive and Jonah leave, but I can't quite bring myself to head back there yet. Instead I go to my car and just sit. I need to think. To plan.

And the first step of my plan is clearing my schedule for tonight. I pull out my phone, then tap out a quick text:

Clive sucked me into a party tonight. I'll hit ur place after? 12am or so?

I re-read it, add a kiss emoji, then hit send.

His answer comes within seconds. Tell C to be on best behavior.

I tag it with a laugh, then exhale. One problem conquered.

A million problems—aka questions—left to go.

I find Jenny's letter on my phone. I want to look at it with new eyes. Eyes that have heard what Jonah said. Because even though he never used the word "trafficking," the missing girls and the invite to London all sound like something out of the *Taken* franchise.

I AM THESE TORN LINES.
JG
PS: I'm driving on, driving out. Forgive me, this tangled knot.

Torn lines?

I have no idea what that could mean. But the line about driving ...?

That one's poking at my gut.

Driving.

That and another line—*Forgive me.*

Forgive her for what? I have no clue. Maybe she knew something was funky, and she didn't say anything, and the note is all about guilt?

Or maybe it really was suicide, this is her farewell note, and I'm trying too hard.

Maybe not every word in the note has a double meaning.

I don't know. I'm not even sure I *can* know.

But my eye keeps going to the word *tangled.*

Tangled. Driving. Knot.

Tangled knot.

Driving in a tangled knot.

Traffic.

I suck in air as I sit bolt upright. She's describing a snarl of traffic.

The note is more than a clue, the note is an indictment.

Human trafficking.

Elias Trent and Joel Carradine are tied in with human trafficking, and somehow Jenny got sucked into the middle of it.

That's what the note means, I'm certain of it.

What I don't know is Matthew's role. Is he aware? And if so, is he complicit? Or is he trying to shut it down?

Most of all, did he have anything to do with Jenny's death?

The last thought sends a wave of bile up into my throat, and I shake my head, unable to believe it. I know Matthew. It hasn't been long, but I've come to know him intimately. People I respect know him, too. Damien, Nikki, Bree. He's a good man. A talented man who built a business by clawing his way up from nothing.

And yet there was that conversation with Joel Carradine.

I tell myself not to jump to conclusions. I don't have all the facts. The only truly concrete thing I have is Carradine's resume and the strange feeling that there's something funky about it. But what?

I have no idea, and I don't know how to figure it out without going to the FBI or whoever is in charge of shutting down traffickers. But I can't do that without dragging Hardline into all of this ... and I can't drag Hardline in unless I'm one zillion percent sure.

Which means I need to find someone who knows about this stuff. Someone who would recognize the signs of a trafficking operation but isn't part of the government. Someone who—

And then I remember.

Ryan Hunter.

The new dad who was one of the guests of honor at the party where I'd almost drooled over Matthew. He's the head of Stark Security, a private security firm he owns with Damien. He'd been a huge help when Bree was kidnapped. And I know he's done lots of international security work.

Surely he could help me.

And even if he can't, I have no better option. So I do a quick search for the main number, then dial.

"Stark Security. How may I direct your call?"

"Um." It's only as the line is answered that I realize it would have been smarter to ask Nikki for an intro call. Odds are that my cold call isn't going to get me anywhere close to Mr. Hunter himself.

"Hello?"

"Right. Ryan Hunter, please."

"One moment."

There's a brief hold-tone, then a male voice. "Mr. Hunter's office."

"Right. Um, hi. This is Aria Parker. I was at the party for little Maia. I'm Bree Bernstein's old roommate, and, well, I really need to speak to Mr. Hunter."

"Can I tell him what it's regarding?" The voice is sharp. Efficient.

"I'm not sure. That's kind of why I need his help. If I could just explain it to him. I think—well, I think my friend was murdered, and I think—"

"Hold on for one minute." The voice is gentle now, the "busy office" tone traded for one of compassion.

"Um, yes." But by the time I speak, the hold-music is humming again. But only for a moment. Then the line clears and I hear a firm, confident voice saying, "Aria? What's wrong?"

A wave of relief crashes over me with such force I have to shut my eyes. "Mr. Hunter?"

"Call me Ryan. What's wrong?"

"I think—I'm not really sure how to say this, but I think someone may be using Matthew Holt's company as a front for human trafficking. I think my friend Jenny found out. And I think someone killed her."

He's quiet for at least thirty seconds. "All right," he says. "Go on."

"There's a guy who heads up one of the departments at Hardline. I think he's involved. And he has a new guy working under him. I got a hold of the new guy's resume. I—I took a picture of it. On the surface, it looks impressive, but ..."

"But what?"

"This is going to sound stupid, but I read a lot of thrillers and watch way too many movies. Some of the stuff on his resume ... well, it just sounds dicey. I took a picture. I was hoping I could text it to you and you could tell me if I'm being paranoid. Or if I really have stumbled into something bad."

"I see. And have you spoken to Matthew?"

"I—no. Not yet."

The line is silent for a good thirty seconds. "I assume you'd rather not bring him in on this yet? Just in case it turns out to be nothing?"

My entire body sags with relief. "That's it exactly. I feel a little silly worrying as it is, and—"

"What's the employee's name?"

"Joel Carradine."

There's another pause, and I wonder if he's heard the name before. Then he says, "Text me his resume."

He gives me his cell number and I send the image. He's gone for several minutes before returning to the line. "I don't see anything on his resume to be concerned about, but I did have my assistant call two of his references and they checked out. I also did a search with Homeland Security and Europe. Nothing popped there."

"Oh, good. I—I'm glad I didn't bother Matthew. Please don't mention it to him. I feel kind of ridiculous now. Too many movies, I guess."

"Don't give it a second thought. Everything looks fine. Your first time working at an international company?"

"It is."

"It's a much bigger canvas. Sometimes things aren't what they seem."

"I get that," I say, then thank him again before we end the call. I feel better about the human trafficking paranoia, but I'm still troubled about Jenny. And confused by her cryptic note. Because unless I'm misinterpreting it, Jenny did think there was trafficking going on at Hardline.

But I suppose that between Jenny the flighty actress and Ryan the hard-boiled security expert, it's Ryan on whom I should bet.

So I do.

But even having made that decision, I can't shake the feeling that something just isn't right.

TWENTY-FIVE

I'm snuggled into the leather seat as Clive's convertible purrs to a stop in front of the temporary valet stand that Hardline has set up. Tonight's venue is Tacos & Tequila, a Valley favorite known for its variety of tequilas and beers, not to mention its incredible soft shell tacos.

It's a complete dive with a huge patio for outdoor dining, bare lightbulbs strung across the open space for lighting, and mismatched metal chairs and tables, most of which wobble on the uneven stone floor.

I come here all the time for lunch, and I kind of love that this is the place where Hardline is hosting meet-and-greet. I'd assumed all the venues were as fancy as Masque, just with more clothes. The fact that this is so far in the opposite direction completely charms me.

A valet opens the car door for me, and I meet Clive on the sidewalk. He'd warned me the dress code was casual, so I'm in black jeans paired with a black tank under a sheer white blouse. My shoes are boots with two-inch heels that show off my ass. If someone assumes I'm talent, then I look like I've dressed for attention, even while keeping it casual. And if someone recognizes me as Matthew's PA, well, I also look professional. Albeit a little sexy. My plan is to mingle, after all. And the best way to do that is to be seen.

Easy enough to do if I stay on Clive's arm. Seriously, the man is a god. He's also the one who actually picked out my outfit—so I'm in his debt tonight.

"Find me a cute hunk and get me laid," he'd said, "and I'll be Robin to your Batman until we figure out what happened to Jenny."

"Deal," I'd said, even though I knew he'd be my loyal sidekick whether I found him a guy or not. That's just who Clive is.

There's a short line to get in, and I'm deleting spam from my email as we wait. I've just trashed a half-dozen ads for a brand of makeup I never wear when a text alert pops up. I tap it, thinking it might be Matthew, then almost drop my phone.

"What?" Clive says, and I realize that while my phone is still in my hand, I'd both jumped and squeaked.

I step closer so no one can see, then show him the screen, my hand shaking so badly he has to hold it still. It's a photo of me and Jenny, our arms around each other as we strike a goofy pose beside the jaguar statue in front of our high school. I haven't seen that photo in years, and as far as I know, the only place it now exists is in the yearbook from my senior year.

But it's not just the picture. There's a message, too. ***Be careful. He Knows You're Snooping.***

"Shit, girl. Who sent that?"

I can only look up into Clive's eyes and shake my head. "I have no idea."

We've reached the front of the line, and Clive cocks his head. I've known him long enough to translate the gesture: *Going or staying?*

In response, I smile at the woman taking names, though my smile is rather forced and probably looks a bit grim. She checks

Clive off the list, adds my name as his plus-one, and ushers us in.

Easy-squeezy.

Although now that I'm inside, I can't help but wonder if turning around and going back home would have been the better choice. Especially when Clive bends down to whisper in my ear, "What do we do now?"

That, of course, is a very good question. "Drinks," I say. "I think we should get drinks."

"Tacos, too?"

"Why not? Go big or go home, right?"

His grin matches mine, and despite the potential danger, I'm glad he came with me. "You willing to do the food and beverage run?" I ask. "I'm going to mingle."

He frowns. "You think that's safe?"

I shrug. "I don't think we're in an episode of *Sopranos,* if that's what you mean. No one's going to put a bullet in me out on the patio or toss a bag over my head and throw me on a plane to Algiers, wherever the hell that is. But if it makes you feel better, I'll avoid dark corners."

Honestly, it'll make me feel better, too.

He hesitates, going only when I shoo him away and make him promise to bring back a very large margarita along with many, many tacos. Then I look around the patio, hoping to see a familiar face, but knowing it's probably hopeless. I don't know that many aspiring actors. Just a handful I met through Jenny, none of which seem to be here.

I already know Matthew rarely comes to the meet-and-greets since that has the unfortunate side effect of making the already nervous wannabes even more nervous. As for Elias Trent and Joel Carradine, I stupidly didn't think about pulling up their corporate IDs until Clive mentioned it in the car. And Hardline's IT department hasn't yet installed the app on my phone that allows me to access the corporate database remotely.

Which means I'm flying blind.

Very blind since not one single person looks familiar. And even though I don't expect anyone to tackle me here on the patio, I can't deny that my nerves are frayed, and I'm seriously considering finding Clive, blowing off the party, and chilling on the couch with a movie. Preferably something ridiculously stupid and funny, with nary a suspense plot at all.

I'm trying to decide what flick would fit the bill when a camera flash and a woman's giggle catches my attention. I shift toward the light, wondering if an actual celebrity is here, then laugh with delight when I see Wyatt Royce, a photographer I did some freelance work for a few years ago—both modeling and acting as his camera assistant, handing him lenses and all the rest that goes with being a photographer's right hand.

He notices me at the same time that I see him, and his smile soothes my nerves. I head his direction, we meet halfway, and he sweeps me into a hug.

"Aria Parker. Don't tell me you're acting now?"

"Hardly. I told you about the time I was an extra." I shudder. "Not my thing."

"Then what are you—"

"I'm working at Hardline now," I tell him. "I'm Matthew Holt's assistant."

"Yeah? Good for you. Matthew's a solid guy. How long have you been at Hardline?"

I glance at my watch.

He laughs. "That long?"

"A few days, actually. You know Matthew?" I add, circling back to what I consider the most salient point of the conversation.

"Hard not to in my family."

It takes me a second, and then I remember. Wyatt's gained his own fame as a photographer, but he changed his name to do it, not wanting to ride on the coattails of his famous family. His grandmother was Anika Segal, a legend in Hollywood on the same par as Vivien Lorainne.

"So what do you think of him?" I ask.

"He's a great guy," Wyatt says. "Kelsey's worked with Hardline on a few music vids," he adds, referring to his wife, a dancer. "We've gotten to know him pretty well. Why?"

I shrug. "I'm, uh, still new at the job and getting a feel."

His eyes narrow. "Oh, hell no."

I take a step back, unnerved by the cocky grin that lights those golden-brown eyes. "What?"

"You. Oh, this is truly rich."

"Dammit, Wyatt," I say. "What are you talking about?"

Clive walks up with food, which he plunks down on a nearby table. Then he passes me a margarita. "Well, hello," he says, clearly interested. I'm not surprised. With his gorgeous face and long, lean body, Wyatt is definitely Clive's type. Just not his *type*.

"Down, boy," I say, and Wyatt laughs.

"I'm flattered," Wyatt says, "but the wife keeps me all to herself."

"Pity," Clive says, then extends his hand. "Clive Sterling. Undercover hetero and this one's fake date," he adds, tossing a nod my way.

"And a conversation hog." I point at Wyatt. "You. Back on topic. What were you about to say?"

"I really shouldn't."

I cross my arms and stare him down. "You know I have Kelsey on speed dial."

"Fine." He holds his hands up in surrender. "It's just that I was talking to Matthew this morning. He was driving to San

Bernardino County, and we were just shooting the breeze. He might have mentioned he was seeing someone. Sounded pretty happy about it, too."

"Oh." Despite the smile that immediately attacks my face, I regret saying anything about Matthew. Plus, I have to fight the very teenage-ish urge to beg Wyatt to tell me Every Single Thing including tone of voice. And bummer about the phone call, because facial expressions would have been nice, too.

"Too early for congrats?"

"I really like him," I admit, in what I have to confess is an understatement. "It's just—no one at work knows, and I'm here, and—"

He nods, then presses a finger to his lips. "Your secret is safe with me. And good luck. Kelsey calls him a complicated guy, but I'd say he's worth it." He holds up his camera. "Technically, I'm on duty."

"Right. Tell Kelsey we need to have lunch. It was great bumping into you."

"You, too," he says, then motions for me to stand next to Clive. We do, and he clicks off a few frames before raising the camera again in a wave.

"Wait," I call.

He turns back, brows raised in question.

"Do you trust him?"

"Matthew?" He looks at me as if I asked if the moon is up in the sky. "Honestly, Ari? I'd trust him with my life. More important, I'd trust him with Kelsey's."

I nod, relief flooding my body. Because that's an assessment that means a hell of a lot.

I take Clive's arm and turn, intending to tug him into the crowd and let the mingling begin. But all I manage is the turn, because my path is blocked by a tall man with broad shoulders, honey-blond hair, and an expression on his chiseled face that makes perfectly clear he's a man who expects to be both listened to and obeyed.

"Ariadne Parker," he says, his green eyes hard on me. "I'm Joel Carradine. I think we need to talk."

"I—" I try to get an actual word out, but my mouth has gone completely dry. I take a quick sip of my margarita, then try again. "Mr. Carradine. It's a pleasure to meet you. Please call me Ari. I'm Mr. Holt's new PA."

The words come out steady and firm, and I haven't bolted in terror. After a sketchy start, I consider this a total victory.

He glances down, then slowly skims his gaze up until he's looking straight into my eyes. "His PA? I think you're more than that. And," he adds, gesturing toward an exit off the patio that presumably leads to an alley, "I think we ought to have a chat."

I glance toward Clive, who's not only moved closer, but has hooked his arm around my waist. He tightens it now, and I take some comfort in the fact that he has my back.

Carradine takes a single step toward the exit, his focus still on me. "Shall we?" When I don't move, he turns his attention to Clive. "Don't worry. I'll bring her right back."

"I really shouldn't," I say. "I made plans to meet Mr. Trent tonight, and I need to find him before—"

"No."

I lift my chin, giving him my most bitchy glare. "Excuse me?"

"No, you didn't make plans." His mouth curves into the tightest of smiles. "I'm Mr. Trent's right hand. Managing his calendar is the least of my duties."

I clear my throat. "I meant that I planned to introduce myself."

"I see." He slips his hands into his jacket pockets, and I can't help but wonder what might be in there. A knife? A small gun? A miniature nuclear weapon?

I squeeze Clive's hand hard, trying to ward off hysteria. "So, if you'll just excuse me, I'm going to go find him." I start to turn away, but Joel takes two long steps and parks himself right in front of me. "That's not happening."

Beside me, Clive stiffens, but I squeeze his hand and try to telepathically order him to just stay chill. Surely this scary badass won't pull anything here. The place is overrun with potential witnesses. Granted, no one seems to be paying any attention to us at the moment, but surely if he slit my throat, someone would notice. Wouldn't they?

I lift my chin. "Look, I get that you're Trent's guard dog, but I *am* going to go find him. So deal with it." I start to walk away, but he grabs my elbow. "Hey!"

"Mr. Trent isn't here."

"Oh." I frown. "I was under the impression he always attended these events."

Once again, he points to the exit. "We should talk in private."

"I'd rather talk here."

That smile is back. "I'm afraid I have to insist."

I glance at Clive, who shakes his head.

"Please, Ms. Parker."

I look at Clive. The truth is, I doubt the guy's going to kill me in an alley. I open my phone, then text Carradine's resume to Clive. "That's got this freak's name, address, all that info. If anything happens to me..."

"I'm not going to kill you in a back alley," Carradine says. "No matter how tempting the thought might be."

He sounds so exasperated that I actually have to fight a grin.

So, okay. Maybe this isn't the scene in the movie where the girl does a stupid thing and gets her throat slit.

I draw a breath, meet Clive's eyes, then nod at Carradine. "Let's go."

I'm right about the gate leading to an alley, but what I didn't expect was the sleek, black limo idling in the trash-strewn road. I whip around to face Carradine. "There is no way in hell I'm getting into that car with you."

"Just a short ride and an informative talk." He reaches for my arm. I knee him in the balls. Or I try. Apparently, the moves from the self-defense class I took in college haven't stuck with me.

I start to run, managing to pull my arm out of Carradine's grip. I'm just about to yank open the gate when a familiar voice calls my name.

"Aria! Stop!"

I whirl around to see the back window of the limo descending to reveal Matthew's face even as the door is pushed open. He extends a hand, his eyes hard on mine. "Get in."

TWENTY-SIX

I stand there, frozen. Not sure if I'm shocked or confused or terrified or what.

"Matthew?"

His name comes out a question, but the truth is I don't even know what I'm asking. *What the fuck?* more or less sums it up, but I can't seem to push that question past my reality-muddled lips.

"Aria, baby, do you trust me?"

Slowly, I lift my chin. "I—I thought I did," I whisper. *I thought I loved you.*

"Well, I trust you," he says. "Enough to tell you everything now. But you have to get in the car."

I don't move.

I hear his sigh of exasperation, and it almost makes me smile. But nothing's funny right now. I feel like that little girl all over again. That same young Ariadne when she learned that the Stair Man who'd rescued and protected her was really The Cat. And he hadn't come to help her at all. He'd only come to steal the diadem her parents loved. To steal it ... and to shatter every good thing in her family for years and years and years.

"Aria? Baby, are you listening?"

I shake myself, lifting my head again to face him.

"I won't hurt you. No one's going to hurt you. I love you," he adds, the words coming so casually that it makes my heart ache. As if he says them every day. As if this isn't the very first time I've heard him say that.

"I love you," he repeats. "But you opened a door, and now the clock's ticking."

I blink. "Clock?"

"Department heads can see when a personnel file is accessed. And who accessed it."

I shake my head, still confused.

"Dammit, Ari. You pulled Joel's file. Elias would have been notified. And he would have assumed that you pulled it for me. He may not have figured out the truth about Joel yet, but he would at least know that we've been watching."

It's as if he's speaking Latin. "I don't know what you're talking about."

"Get in the damn car. You, too, Joel."

"But if she—"

"If we have to leave her behind, we do. But we're under the gun here."

They're still speaking Latin, but I'm starting to catch the gist. Especially when Joel circles the limo and climbs in from the other side.

"Thirty more seconds," Matthew says. "Then explanations will have to wait."

I look around, trying to decide what to do. That's when Matthew extends his hand. "Do you trust me?" he asks again.

And, dammit, I do. I have no idea what the fuck is going on, but I know with absolute certainty that Matthew won't hurt me. Not physically, anyway. But I'm starting to fear that he's going to break my heart.

"I trust you," I say, climbing in beside him and pulling the door shut. "But Clive doesn't. If I don't come back soon, he's probably going to call the police."

Matthew shakes his head. "Don't worry. Wyatt will explain everything to him."

"Wyatt? He's in all of this?" Whatever the hell *this* is.

"He's a good friend. He knows almost all my secrets. Including how I feel about you."

Hot tears stream down my cheeks. "Matthew, don't toy with me. Please. I want to believe there's nothing bad going on, but—"

"Oh, there's bad shit going on. But it's going on despite me, not because of me. And you deciding to play detective on the night that I'd arranged to finally take Elias Trent down ... well, I won't say you gummed up the works. But I will say you've made things a hell of a lot more interesting."

The words are harsh, but he squeezes my hand, a tiny smile touching his lips.

"I'd apologize," I say. "But since I still don't know what's going on, I think maybe I want to wait on that."

He chuckles. "Fair enough," he says, as the limo reaches the end of the alley. The glass between us and the driver lowers, and I can see more clearly through the front windshield.

Ryan Hunter is there, standing with six other men, all wearing dark clothes. Another man stands with them, his hands behind his back. Cuffed, I realize when he turns and takes a step toward the limo before being yanked back by one of the men in black.

"That's my cue," Joel says, then slides out of the limo, leaving the door wide open.

I look between the sight in front of us and Matthew. "I'm sorry," I say. I'm not even sure what I'm apologizing for, but I know enough to recognize the man in cuffs. Because even though I've only seen his photo once in a company newsletter, I'm one-hundred percent confident that he's Elias Trent.

"Stark Security took him down?" I ask.

Matthew nods. "With some help from Homeland Security and the FBI," he adds, pointing to a few of the men in the group.

"So I was right? Jenny got caught up in a trafficking scheme?"

"I'm afraid so." His words are heavy, and though he takes my hand, he doesn't quite meet my eyes. "I'm so sorry. We're still trying to work out all the details, but from what we know, she made the mistake of going to Trent with her concerns."

"And then she realized her mistake," I say, with sudden clarity. I grab my phone from my back pocket, then find the photo of the letter. "I should have unscrambled it sooner," I say, showing the image to Matthew. "I am these torn lines," I read. "It's an anagram for *Elias Trent*, with just a few extra letters." I look up at him. "I think she was in a hurry to mail this to me. And I figured out the last part about driving, too," I begin, but Matthew's already got it.

"Trafficking." He exhales. "Damn, I wish she'd come to me."

I blink back tears. "Maybe she was going to. Maybe that's why he got her. He must have forced her to the bridge. Jenny was smart. She wouldn't have just gotten in a car with him."

"I never met her personally," Matthew says, his own eyes misty. "I never met any of the women they got their claws into." He squeezes my hand. "You'll have to tell me about her. We'll have to learn what we can about all of them. They deserve to be seen."

"How long have you known?"

He shakes his head. "Not long enough. Trent was smart. He used the Hardline meet-and-greets, but that's all. Everything else was done through shell companies he created with an overseas group. The women thought they were going over for Hard-line. But they weren't."

He drags his fingers through his hair. "I got wind of it about two months ago, then pulled Ryan in. He's coordinated with teams in Europe. With luck, we'll rescue most of the women who got filtered through the meet-and-greets. And any other women who got caught in those bastards' nets."

I hear the fury in his voice and nod, my throat too clogged with tears to speak.

"You poked your nose in a little too close. I was afraid Elias or his people were going to notice you."

"I think he did. Matthew," I say urgently, "I think there may be more of his team inside. Someone sent me this." I show him the text from my yearbook with the warning.

"Ah, yeah." He clears his throat. "Actually, that was me."

"You?" I gape at him. "What the hell?"

"I found out you were coming, and I thought it would scare you off. Send you running back home. I didn't want you here, Ari." His voice is hard. Stern. "Don't you get it? If Elias or one of his flunkies got their mitts on you, this operation would be all over. They'd be out of this country in a heartbeat, and the odds of us recapturing them would slip down to nil."

"What? Why?"

"Because I'd let them go," he says, his voice as gentle as a caress. "If that was the price to get you back and keep you safe, I'd accept whatever conditions they named."

"Matthew." I search for more words, but find none.

"I've wanted you for a long time, Ari. I won't risk losing you now."

"Oh." It's the only word I can get out past my tears. He bends forward and gently kisses me. "I love you, Ariadne Parker."

"I love you, too," I whisper, my heart so full right now I fear it might explode.

I snuggle closer, watching as someone shoves Trent into the back of what I think must be a government car. Joel stands with Ryan Hunter, deep in conversation.

I close my eyes, feeling suddenly queasy. "I'm sorry," I whisper.

"Hush. It's over now. Soon enough Elias's whole network is going to fall. This is a good night, baby. A good night for Jenny, and for all of the others."

"I know. That's not what I'm sorry for." I shift so that I can see his face. "I'm sorry that I doubted you. I didn't want to believe you were involved, but when I heard you and Joel talking ... I couldn't hear all the words, but what I did hear ... well, it sounded like you two were talking about trafficking, and—

"We were," he says. "Just from the good guy side of the equation."

"Did you know I was there?"

He shakes his head. "But later I noticed that the door was ajar." He offers a wry smile. "I hoped you hadn't overheard. Then later, when I learned that Clive and Jonah had signed onto the lot, I was afraid you might be playing detective."

"And sure enough ..."

Our eyes meet.

"You picked a bad night," he says, then kisses my forehead.

"Maybe I picked a good one," I counter. "After all, I got to see you and Joel take him down." I frown. "Who does Joel work for, anyway? Hardline security? FBI?"

Matthew shakes his head. "Stark Security. One of their newer agents." He tilts his head, smiling as he studies me.

"What?" I narrow my eyes. "Are you about to chew me out for something stupid I did?"

"I'm not," he says, his voice soft. "I was just thinking that tonight was a twofer. We got the bad guy. And I got you."

"Yup," I say. "No more secrets. I like it."

"So do I," he says. But I can't help but notice that he doesn't quite look me in the eye before he bends over to kiss me.

TWENTY-SEVEN

My head practically spins from how quickly things move in the next days and weeks. Joel acts as a liaison between Hardline, Stark Security, the FBI, Homeland, and Interpol. His daily reports are detailed and thorough, and Matthew and I go over them line by line the minute each report arrives.

Trent and his cohorts—all now in custody—used the sterling infrastructure of the business that Matthew had worked so hard to build, to hide the rot they were growing underneath.

And dozens of women paid the price for that.

Jenny had paid the price.

I hate Trent. I hate everyone in his operation. I despise every last one of them. And I wish I could stand in front of them and scream. Scream for Jenny. For the girls they trafficked. For every victim now struggling to get her life back together.

I wish I could scream—and I wish I could deliver a killing blow, because those people shouldn't even exist on this earth.

Lila, of course, is a wreck. I don't like the woman, but I can see the pain on her face. The horror that she'd actually dated a man like Elias Trent. The fury that he'd fooled her. And she's promised Matthew she'll do whatever it takes to make sure that

Elias hadn't somehow used his connection to her as a means to infiltrate Matthew's private files.

As for Matthew, his anger is twisted up with guilt. He blames himself, and no matter how much I try to soothe him and absolve him, he's having none of it.

"I should have seen it sooner," he tells me. "I should have stopped it faster." And though I tell him that he did his best—more, he shut it down—that's not enough for him.

But he's not shirking away. No matter how much this whole debacle has crushed his heart, he's stepped up and faced down the media that can so often be damn brutal.

He's gone on every major news network, owning up to the fact that Hardline was exploited. Standing firm, he's told the world that they caught it as soon as they could, that the perpetrators would be brought to justice, and that Hardline was implementing safeguards to ensure nothing like this could ever happen again. And that Matthew himself was overseeing that initiative.

On screen, he looks calm and composed in his suit and tie, the armor of a man in control. But when he's not in front of the cameras, that armor slips, and the man I hold in my arms isn't a god or an emperor or even a hardened businessman.

He's just a good man, hurt by reality and by circumstances that he can't go back and change.

"You've been a rock through all of this," I tell him one evening as we're snuggled together on the sofa in the treehouse. The video screen is down, and we've paused *The Thomas Crown Affair*, a movie we both love, so that we can read the latest report from Homeland on Matthew's phone.

He looks at me. "A rock? No, baby, you've been *my* rock. My strength. My port in a storm. Call it whatever you like, but I couldn't have gotten through this without you."

He presses his lips to my forehead. "I love you," he whispers, and I sigh with pleasure. He's told me that so often since that night in the limo, but hearing it tonight brings tears to my eyes.

My smile is watery as I say, "It sounds silly because you're only doing what should be done, but I'm so proud of how you've handled all this. I mean, you've stepped up so much more than so many people would."

"No, I—"

I press a finger to his lips. "Yes. You've helped the authorities, you haven't spouted bullshit to the public, and you've put money and your own time into helping. What Elias Trent did wasn't your fault."

I squeeze his hand and keep my finger on those gorgeous lips. "But the way you handled it *was* your choice. And the fact that you're the kind of man who would make those choices is one of the reasons I love you, too."

"I've made a lot of choices in my life," he says, his voice tinged with something dark. "Trust me when I say that not all of them would win your approval."

I shrug. "Not the point," I say, though the truth is I'm curious about that past that he holds in such disdain.

As if he's read my mind, his mouth quirks into a half smile, and he offers a tiny shrug. "But no matter what I've done before, I do think I've taken the right path on this."

"You did," I say. "You helped so much. From funding rescue operations to rehab centers and all the rest."

"It was the right thing to do," he says. "And the good karma can't hurt, either, right? Balancing the scale. Making up for my checkered past."

He says it as a joke, but I can't shake the feeling that he means it. That he truly believes there's something horrible he has to make up for.

"Like what?" Bree asks the next morning as we're sipping

our Sunday lattes at Blue Bottle—a tradition we used to share with Jenny. I tear off a piece of chocolate chip cookie and munch on it. It may only be ten, but it's never too early for cookies.

"I'm not sure," I admit.

"Maybe he feels guilty. Hardline's his baby, and that monster Trent was operating right under his nose."

"I don't think that's it," I tell her. "He's done so much and been so open with the media. I think it's something far removed from the trafficking."

"Hmm." She sips her coffee. "Well, this is just gossip, but there's always been a lot of buzz about the way he built Hardline. Shady deals. Less than conventional financing. Some folks say that his start-up capital was dicey, and that's why he's never gone public. Doesn't want anyone looking too closely." She shrugs. "I don't know if anything was illegal per se. More likely he managed to cut through the usual paperwork and just bull-dozed his way onto the scene."

"But that's ambition, isn't it? I mean, unless you're saying he stole money or committed fraud or something."

She just shrugs. "I'm not saying anything. Rumors are rumors and the ones I've heard are so vague I can't remember the details. But maybe this whole thing has made him think about how Hardline came into being." She shrugs. "Although it hardly matters now. Hardline's been a hit-making machine for years. Any funny business about financing would have taken place long ago."

We share a glance. We both know that *long ago* doesn't make anything okay.

I eat the last bite of cookie, then wash it down with my latte. "You might be right. He's in the spotlight now for owning what Trent was doing at Hardline and using all his resources to try and make it right for the victims. So maybe he's feeling guilty about whatever he did—or didn't do—back when he was getting his start." I shrug. "You think?"

She cocks her head. "You want to know what I really think?"

"Duh. Yes."

"I think the only way you'll know is to ask him."

"Well, fuck," I say, then sit back in my chair. "If he did do dicey stuff back in the day, he's not going to want to tell me."

"Yeah, but if it's eating him up, he needs to get it out of his system. Be his sounding board. Remind him that you love him. Maybe wait a few days to ask. In the meantime, touch him a lot. And sex," she adds with a mischievous smile. "Lots and lots of sex."

I laugh. "That's why we're friends. I like the way you think." She lifts her hand for a high five, and I give it a nice smack before saying, "There's something else I need to talk to you about."

"Yeah?" She glances up, frowns, then shifts her chair, trying to get back in the shade of the umbrella as the sun continues to move across the sky. "I'm all ears."

"It's about the house."

Her shoulders sag, and she groans. "Dammit, Ari. Not again. I know you're spending a lot of nights at Matthew's, but you can't go away and forget—"

"What? No! That was one time. One. Time." I'd left for a long weekend of skiing at Mammoth, and I'd stupidly left behind two open cartons of fresh donuts. Which, apparently, is like making everything for free at Ikea. The latter would get swarms of college kids. The house got swarms of ants.

"No ants? No bugs? Please tell me it isn't mice."

"Jeez. Your house is pristine, okay? And it will stay that way until you find another renter." I buff my nails on my shirt. "I'm moving into this very cool treehouse property in the hills. It comes with a roommate, but the terms are pretty sweet."

I'm still talking when she leaps from her chair, and by the time I'm finished, she's on my side of the table giving me a massive hug. "That's awesome. My little girl is all grown up and living the good life."

"I am," I say. But I don't tell her the rest of it. That part of me is afraid that the reason he wants me to move in is more about masking his feelings of guilt over the trafficking scheme than it is about the two of us.

Matthew finishes taping the last of the boxes, then straightens, rubbing his back as his gaze flicks around my bedroom. Not that it feels like mine anymore, what with my life packed up in eleven boxes and a bevy of suitcases.

"You meant it when you said you don't have much stuff." He folds the last empty box and leans it against the wall.

"Easier that way." I shrug, taking a seat on the edge of the stripped bed, then scooting over so he can sit beside me. "Did I mention that I've moved apartments almost as often as I've changed jobs?"

"And why do you do that? Rent issues?"

"No. Not like you mean. But my dad pretty much sold his soul so that we wouldn't lose the house after the diadem was stolen."

A shadow crosses his face, and I squeeze his hand, touched by how deeply he empathizes with the pain in my past.

"Dad worked crazy hours and borrowed from people he shouldn't have, just so he could pay the mortgage."

Matthew frowns. "He told you that?"

"Well, not me. I was a kid. But I'd overhear things. Made me scared, you know?"

He frowns, his brow furrowing into a crease as he nods. "That must have been hard."

I lean across him for the Diet Coke I'd left on the bedside table. "I swore I'd never be in that position even if that meant living in tiny efficiencies and always chasing the lowest rent."

Matthew's brow furrows, his expression so sad it almost breaks my heart the way he's feeling my pain.

He tightens his arm around my waist, pulling me closer as he brushes my hair off my forehead. "But that ends now. You have a home with me."

"I do," I say, tilting my head up and smiling at him and hoping he can't see how nervous I am. It's not a side of me I want him—or anyone—to see. That hidden part of me that knows not to put my trust in anyone or anything because it always falls apart. The Stair Man. The Cat.

Nothing lasts. Not really. And wishing won't change that at all.

Except you trust Matthew ...

The thought pings at my mind, undeniably true, and while I wouldn't change anything between Matthew and me, some part of me wonders when and how exactly he managed to squeeze through my defenses.

I don't know, but he did. And for that, I will always be grateful. Because not only do I want him desperately, but the fact that I let him in gives me hope that I'm not irredeemably fucked up.

"—the job?"

I shake my head, realizing I'd zoned out. "Sorry. What?"

"I said that I get the frequent moves. What's the backstory for your job shifts?"

I grin. "Boredom."

He chuckles. "Fair enough."

"But also my dad again," I admit. "He held the same job his entire life. Different titles over the years, but the same treadmill. He never said as much, but I knew he hated it. He was never eager to go to the office. Never excited by the possibilities in a new day. It was just a slog."

I shrug dramatically. "I don't want my life to be a slog."

He squeezes my hand. "Does that mean you'll be bailing on me and Hardline soon?"

I laugh. "Dunno. Lots of different jobs at a studio. Maybe I'll go from being a PA to being a stunt double."

He laughs, the sound rich and warm. "Yeah? I'd pay good money to see that."

"Considering it's your studio, I guess it would be on your dime."

He glances pointedly at the bed, then back at me in that way he has, where it feels like he's peeling back all my layers. Exposing me. "Instead of a stunt double, you could be a body double."

I feign shock, my skin warm and tingly. "Mr. Holt, are you suggesting I get naked with other actors?"

He grimaces, making me laugh. "Clearly I hadn't thought that through."

"Well, I'm a bit intrigued now."

"Are you?" His voice drops lower, a velvety rumble that does things to me that are usually only featured in my late-night fantasies.

"Mmm." I pat the bed behind us. "It's still mine for now."

His lips curve into a devastating smile. "Why, Ms. Parker. Are you suggesting that you'd sleep with the boss?"

"Hell, yes."

He chuckles. "I do like the way you think."

In one quick move, he cups the back of my head, tugging me

toward him until his mouth claims mine. Soft at first, but when I fist my hand in his shirt and groan with need, I feel the change throughout his body. His mouth going harder, more demanding. No longer teasing but craving.

His fingers twine in my hair, keeping me where he wants me, so close I can smell the lingering hint of cedar from his closet, along with the intoxicating scent of his cologne.

His lips are hard. The kiss wild. As hot and intimate as fucking, and I relish it, craving nothing more, and at the same time craving everything.

Craving him. Starved for him.

I shift on the mattress, moving to straddle his lap, my hands on his shoulders as I grind against him, his cock hard beneath me, his tongue fucking my mouth as my body cries out in desperate, sweet longing.

Without warning, he flips us, and I gasp as I find myself on my back, his knees on either side of my hips as he looms above me. His lips curve into a sensual grin that sends heat racing through my veins. "I think," he murmurs, his voice low and rough, "that you're wearing too many clothes."

"Mmm. You should probably do something about that."

His brow lifts, but he says nothing. Just reaches for the hem of my tank top. His knuckles brush my skin, sending a ripple of heat through me, and I raise my arms as he pulls the tank over my head, his gaze never leaving mine as he tosses it aside.

The tank has a shelf bra, and now I'm naked from the waist up, my hard nipples acting as indisputable witnesses of what I want.

"You're stunning." His words are reverent, almost a whisper, but it's the way he looks at me—like I'm something precious—that makes me shiver ... and the touch of his hands cupping my breasts that makes me moan.

I close my eyes as he cradles my tits, his thumbs teasing both my nipples and sending sparkling, golden threads of heat racing through my body to gather at my core. "Matthew," I whisper, "please."

"Please what?" His voice at my ear is low, barely a whisper, and his sultry tone coupled with the tickle of his breath sends shivers of longing through me.

"Just ... just *please*."

I hear the low rumble of his laughter, a sound of pure pleasure mixed with vibrant heat. And before I have a chance to beg again, his lips find mine in a kiss so wild and deep I feel it all the way to my core.

His hands slide down my sides, setting my body on fire. He's holding me. Possessing me.

I arch back, wanting what he's giving—and what he's taking. Wanting to be possessed.

To be *his*.

His mouth claims mine again. Wilder this time, and I moan as our tongues and lips dance and tease. I spread my legs, my hips arching up, craving the press of his body against mine. And craving more the feel of him deep inside me.

"Please," I murmur, so drunk with lust I'm not even sure I said the word aloud.

I groan when his lips leave mine, then tremble when he trails a line of kisses down my throat. Over my collarbone.

I cry out when his mouth closes over my nipple. The sensation is exquisite, sharp and sweet and I feel it all the way down to my core. My clit throbbing. My body craving. He isn't even touching me there, and I'm right at the precipice, every cell humming as I teeter on the edge.

"Matthew." His name is little more than a gasp.

He lifts his head, his eyes locking on mine as his hand slides down my body, slipping just beneath the waistband of my leggings, then stopping. The corner of his mouth quirks up. "Beg me," he whispers. "Tell me what you want."

"You." No single word has ever held that much truth, but he just shakes his head.

"Right now, baby. Tell me. I want to hear you tell me."

"Touch me." I beg. "Fuck me."

His smile is sensual sunshine. "Whatever the lady wants," he murmurs as his clever fingers dip lower into my leggings, brushing over my slick heat.

"Yes. Please." My eyes are closed, my head back, my hands on my own breasts as my body strives to reach that singular place that is clear, pure pleasure. "Don't stop," I murmur. "Please, don't stop."

"Not a chance," he says, his voice a promise that sends another wave of heat coursing through me. He shifts, his free hand catching the edge of my leggings and tugging them down in one smooth motion, leaving me naked before him, every inch of me exposed. But I don't feel vulnerable. Quite the opposite. I feel strong. Powerful.

And loved.

"Christ, you're beautiful."

I feel the heat of a full-body blush in response to his words. I know I'm attractive, but the way he says it is unlike anything anyone has ever said to me. As if he doesn't mean the way I look, but the way I *am*. Like he sees me in a way no one else ever has.

"Oh, yes," I whisper as his hands slide up my thighs, his touch igniting every cell in my body as he moves higher and higher until he finally reaches my core.

He settles between my legs, his fingers brushing over my center, teasing me until I'm squirming beneath him, desperate for more.

"Matthew, please," I whisper, my voice breaking on the word.

He doesn't make me wait. Slowly, deliberately, he slides a finger inside me, then another, his touch both gentle and commanding. My hips move instinctively, seeking him, my body desperate for the rhythm he's setting.

"You're so ready for me," he murmurs, his voice thick with desire. "Do you know how hot that makes me?"

I can only whimper in response.

He flashes that cocky grin, then quickly sheds his clothes. And though I mourn the loss of contact, I can't deny that I enjoy the show.

I enjoy it much more when he returns, his thumb brushing over my clit, sending sparks shooting through me. "Tell me, sweetheart. Tell me what you want."

"You," I gasp, barely able to form the word as his touch sends me spiraling higher and higher. "I want you."

His eyes hold mine, and with a groan, he leans forward, his hand replaced by the hard, unrelenting press of his cock against my core. He pauses, his gaze searching mine, giving me the chance to stop this, to stop him.

But stopping is the last thing I want.

"Please," I whisper, my voice steady despite the wild beat of my heart. "Don't you even think about stopping."

His groan is low and guttural and wildly sexy as he thrusts into me, filling me completely, and I gasp, my hands clutching at his tight ass as my body adjusts to the feel of him. He pauses, giving me a moment, and then he begins to move, slow and deliberate, each thrust sending a new wave of pleasure rippling through me, taking me just that much higher with every motion, every sensation.

"Baby," he murmurs, his voice raw, that single word holding a world's worth of emotion.

I cling to him, lost in pleasure, as he drives me closer and closer to the edge, his pace quickening, his movements more urgent as his own control begins to unravel. I claw at his back as those glorious, wild sensations build inside me. Wilder and wilder until I can't contain myself anymore and I shatter, my orgasm ripping through me in waves. I cry out his name even as he cries out mine, his own release exploding on the tail of mine, so that our bodies tremble together and all I can hear is the low, guttural murmur of my name on his lips, and all I can feel is the soft glow of heaven.

For a moment, neither of us moves, the only sound in the room the mingled cadence of our ragged breaths. Then, slowly, he lifts his head, his lips curving into a lazy, satisfied smile that makes my heart skip a beat.

"So," he says matter-of-factly, "you looking forward to moving in with me?"

I laugh. "You know, I think it's going to work out just fine."

TWENTY-EIGHT

Matthew strolled through the cavernous halls of MOCA, his footsteps echoing on the polished floors. The Museum of Contemporary Art's unique architecture served to keep the guests moving through the skylit galleries, past the dramatic art that kept patrons coming again and again.

He'd gone to the office first, to do what he had to do. But he couldn't stay. He'd had to get out. Get air.

Get sanctuary. And somehow fill his head with beauty instead of betrayal.

Lila had been at her desk, of course. Just as she always was. Just as she'd always been beside him since they were teens. They'd been friends. Colleagues. She'd been his confidante and his right hand, but she'd always wanted more.

Was that why she'd betrayed him? Why she'd helped Trent, and, in helping, tarnished Hardline?

He hadn't wanted to believe it. Even with all the evidence he'd gathered, he hadn't wanted to face that horrible truth.

At first, her story had seemed so plausible. She'd known nothing of Trent's dealings. She'd been used, just as Matthew had been. Just as the company had been.

But over the last few weeks, the truth had come out, along with the evidence to back it up. She'd betrayed him. The woman who'd once watched his back just as he'd watched hers. And she'd tossed it all away.

At first, he'd told himself that it was only about Elias. That she was lonely, and it was an affair. Just sex. That she knew nothing about the horrible enterprise Trent was running, using his position at Hardline as camouflage.

But he'd only been fooling himself. The bond between him and Lila that he'd once believed was so strong had been slashed long ago. She'd stayed because of what he could offer—a salary, a position, the cache of being at his right hand.

But she'd checked out of their friendship long ago. She'd wanted more than he could give, and—unwilling to settle for less—she'd gotten her own kind of payback by aligning herself with Trent, a reality for which he finally had enough evidence to assure himself that her treachery was real and not his imagination.

And that morning he'd left the bed he shared with Aria to meet with Roger Tate, the Chief of Security for the Hardline Lot.

Together they'd gone to his office where, of course, Lila was waiting behind her desk, her chin high as if daring him to punish her for all the ways she'd wronged him.

She hadn't caused a scene, thank goodness. She'd simply asked for time to pack her things. That's when he'd left, leaving this woman he'd once called his friend in Tate's charge. Tate would radio the waiting Federal agents to come up, then they'd escort Lila downstairs.

He knew what would happen after that, too. The Feds would cut her a deal. The Special Agent in charge had already told him that she'd be offered a reduced sentence in exchange for her testimony, and Matthew knew her well enough to know she'd agree.

He could live with that.

Anything to have her out of his life.

Anything to have a fresh start with Ari.

He'd kissed her cheek before leaving, half-hoping that she would wake up, but mostly relieved that she stayed lost in slumber.

He knew that he'd need this time away from the office. The space to clear his head in one of his favorite Los Angeles locations.

How often did he come here, just enjoying the energy of the place? The precision and imagination of the artists, so often unappreciated by those who considered only earlier, more realistic periods to be "real" art.

But that was the thing about art, be it plays or films or paintings or sculpture: it was always evolving.

And, he supposed, that was the thing with people, too.

God knew he wasn't the same man he'd been at nineteen when he and Lila were doing whatever it took to find food. And he wasn't the same man he'd been at twenty-nine, when he was scrambling to launch the nascent Hardline Entertainment into a studio that could hold its own against the established Hollywood monoliths.

In fact, the only constant for him across those years had been Aria. First as his touchstone—the pure and innocent representation of what he had to live up to. Then as something he cherished. Something magnificent and innocent that he needed to protect.

And then—though when the change had come, he couldn't say—as someone he craved. A woman who fired his senses, fueled his imagination, and gave wing to his imagination.

And the miracle of his life was that after years of fantasy, she was his now. Truly his. Her touch both aroused him and soothed him. Her kisses tempted him. Her skin fascinated him.

He had never felt more himself than in the moments he was with her, and every time they made love it seemed as if his entire soul had gone supernova.

But it was all a lie.

Because she wasn't his. She belonged to the man he pretended to be, not the man he was.

And if he introduced her to that man, he feared that he would lose her forever.

He wasn't as vile as Trent or as duplicitous as Lila. But he wasn't a good man. He knew it. And soon Aria would know it. She'd have to, if there was ever going to be anything real between them.

But once she knew, would they even have a chance?

With a sigh, he kept walking, letting the brushstrokes reach out to him, the sculptures entice him. This was his favorite place in the city. The quiet. The weight of the space. The way the art connected to the world and to him. Often raw and strange, but always filling his soul.

He stopped in front of a Rothko, the bold blocks of color blurring into each other as he let his mind drift. The horror that Elias Trent's damage would never be over, and the investigation would surely go on for years.

With misty eyes, he thought of the half-dozen dead girls, each of whom weighed on his soul, a dark and heavy nugget of guilt. But more living victims had been located, too, and he took comfort in knowing they were now safe and getting the help they needed.

More than that, Trent and his cohorts were in custody, and soon they'd be in prison. Just like they deserved.

Matthew would never forget, but things were going back to normal, whatever the hell that was. And he was even optimistic that the scandal wouldn't hurt Hardline's reputation too deeply. A reputation he'd worked to build for over twenty years, clawing his way into the industry, making a name for himself, building a brand and then a studio with enough gravitas to contain it.

Hardline was profitable. It was respected. And Matthew was the man who'd built it all.

But he wasn't a man who deserved it.

He'd spent his whole life working to build his dream. To become the man he'd wanted to be. The kind of man she believed him to be.

Aria.

She'd been his rock through all of this, grounding him when he felt untethered. Her belief in him, her ability to cut through his guilt with a single look or touch—had kept him going when the weight of it all threatened to pull him under.

But she didn't know the full truth. She thought he was a good man. An honorable man. But he wasn't that man, not really. And once she knew the truth, he would lose her.

So that was the dilemma. Keep her close with a lie or lose her with the truth. The man he used to be would lie to keep her. The man she deserved and wanted would tell the truth.

He loved her, so how the hell could he walk away? But at the same time, he loved her, so how the hell could he let her live a lie?

It was a dilemma he didn't want to face. And so he was here, losing himself in beauty, hoping a solution would show itself. And knowing that sooner or later he'd have to leave this sanctuary, go home, and make the hardest damn choice of his life.

He was such a fucking hypocrite, wasn't he? Standing in front of cameras while he was praised for bringing down the trafficking ring, all the while keeping secrets that could destroy the fragile trust he and Aria had built.

He should have told her already. The rational part of him

knew that. But every time he thought about it, fear clawed its way up his throat. She'd look at him differently, wouldn't she? And she'd walk away.

He'd survived plenty of losses in his life, but he couldn't bear the thought of losing her. There was more than just lust or attraction between them. What he felt was deep and raw, and it humbled him as much as it anchored him.

With a sigh, he moved to a bench in the center of the gallery, letting himself sink onto the cool metal. His elbows rested on his knees, his hands clasped as he stared at the floor.

What was he so afraid of? She already knew he wasn't perfect. But this wasn't just about bad choices or moral gray areas. This was about betrayal. About the line he'd crossed, even if it was years ago. Even if he'd told himself it was necessary to survive, to build something that would be his. That would last.

Hardline.

His betrayal tainted the whole damn company.

She deserved to know. And every second that ticked by without telling her was another moment of betrayal.

Every time she looked at him with trust in her eyes, every time she defended him or reminded him that he wasn't the villain, it chipped away at him. Because he wasn't the man she thought he was. Not entirely.

He'd built an empire, clawed his way to the top, and done things most men couldn't even imagine. And yet, the hardest thing he'd ever have to do was to simply tell the truth.

But he had to do it.

He couldn't keep lying to her, couldn't keep pretending he was something he wasn't. Not if he wanted a future with her. And he did—dear God, he did.

It had to end now.

Tonight, he would tell her everything. Despite his terror

that she might turn her back and walk away, tonight he would do what he had to do.

He drew in a breath, the decision settling heavy on his shoulders. He didn't know what words he'd use or how he'd even start the conversation, but he'd tell her everything.

Because if the truth was what it took to keep her—really keep her—then he'd risk it.

He just had to find the words.

I wake to find myself bathed in the sunlight streaming in through the bedroom skylight. Groggy, I roll over, my hand searching for Matthew, but all I find are cool sheets. With a frown, I push myself up on my elbow so that I can see the clock —*past ten!*

Immediately, I leap naked out of bed. "Matthew?"

I grab my robe off the back of a chair and shove my arms into it as I head into the living area, expecting to find him working on his laptop. But there's no Matthew.

I start to head back to the bedroom to grab my phone off the bedside table, but the smell of coffee captures me and I divert to the kitchen. Both for coffee, and because the fact that it's brewing is at least evidence that Matthew's up and awake ... and therefore must be somewhere.

The note sitting by the coffee maker under my favorite mug fills in the rest of the puzzle.

LOVELY, ARIA—

YOU LOOK SO BEAUTIFUL ASLEEP I COULDN'T BEAR TO WAKE YOU. AND YOU KNOW WHAT DAY IT IS. I THOUGHT YOU WOULD PREFER TO SPEND THE MORNING IN BED.

> *I WILL EITHER SEE YOU AT THE OFFICE LATER OR AT HOME.*
>
> *AND JUST IN CASE YOU'RE WONDERING, I DID KISS YOU GOODBYE. I'LL KISS YOU HELLO WHEN I SEE YOU.*
>
> *LOVE YOU—*
>
> *M*

I grin and hug the letter, then take one of the pens from a nearby canister, write Love You Back beneath his signature, and stick the note on the refrigerator door with a magnet.

Then I take my coffee and head to the shower. I'm half considering spending the day shopping, but I decide against it. As sweet as Matthew's offer is, I don't want anyone to think I don't deserve my job or that I'm only doing it half-assed. And right now, I'm doing important work—exploring the creation of a charity that focuses on stopping trafficking and helping the victims. I'm eager to get that launched, especially since I know the guilt Matthew carries is heavy, though not deserved.

He's trying to soothe his soul by creating something meaningful to help the victims and keep potential victims safe.

It's important to him, and that's one of reasons I love him.

Once I'm clean and dressed, I gather my purse and phone, then check my watch. It's already past eleven, and I breathe a sigh of relief, knowing that Lila should be out of the building by now. This time, for good.

I say a silent thank you to Matthew for letting me sleep in. I really wasn't looking forward to witnessing her walk of shame.

I'm humming a little tune under my breath as I walk into the Hardline office, but the sight of the security guard and two men who are clearly Federal agents stops me cold.

Lila is still there, standing behind her cluttered, box-covered desk as she packs up her things. Her movements are methodical, and though her face is set in a mask of icy detachment, I see the fire in her eyes when she turns and looks at me.

I consider turning around and going down to the employee restaurant, but before I can slip back out, she says, "Ariadne Parker. Come to gloat?"

"I—no." I want to kick myself for being tongue-tied. She's the bitch who got involved with Trent. Who knew about the trafficking. And who said absolutely nothing.

She sniffs, as haughty as ever. "At least one of us got what we wanted."

"Excuse me?"

"Don't play dumb. You wanted him, didn't you? Well, congratulations. He's yours—for now."

"Matthew? You're jealous that I'm with Matthew? You were sleeping with that snake who kidnapped women!"

"I'm taking a deal, sweetie. Nobody's putting me on trial."

I glance toward the guard, who looks as disgusted as I feel. She's getting off by agreeing to testify. On the one hand, I want every iota of evidence piled up against Trent and his flunkies. On the other hand, I want her behind bars, too.

But I don't say any of that. I'm not going to talk to her. I'm just going to go to my office and wait out her departure.

I've almost reached my door when she says, "Joke's on you, Aria. You're so proud of getting your hooks into Matthew, but you won't want him once you learn the truth."

I stiffen, but I tell myself to go into my office, shut the door, and not take the bait.

Unfortunately, I'm terrible at taking my own advice. I cross my arms and turn to her. "What truth?"

She shakes her head, like a frustrated guardian bemoaning the foolish antics of a toddler. "You're just a girl chasing a fantasy. Like a teenager swooning over the bad boy, completely oblivious to how truly bad he is."

"Oh, cut the bullshit, Lila. I am not doing the Mean Girl Dance with you. Be jealous on your own time."

Her chin lifts. "Oh, I am jealous. He was mine before he was yours, remember? And I know where all the bodies are buried."

I say nothing. But I also don't leave. Which, I guess, is the equivalent of saying something.

"You're just dying to know what I'm talking about, aren't you?"

I say nothing.

Her smile is thin. "Too bad I can't tell you where to find all the dirt on our perfect little Matthew. That would be breaking an oath to never reveal that he keeps a safe behind the Vivien Lorainne photo." She puts a hand over her mouth, her eyes Betty Boop wide. "Oopsie."

My heart skips a beat. I know the photo well—Matthew had told me it was the first thing he ever bought with the profit from his first film.

"The code is his birthday," she continues. "And I'm sure you can figure out the year. So cliche, don't you think? The powerful older man and his sweet, young fuck toy."

I stand there, silent but seething as she grabs her box of belongings and stands, her next words slicing through me like a blade. "Maybe there aren't any secrets in that safe. I'm not actually saying there's anything in there that would tear you two apart. Doesn't matter, though. Even if he has no secrets—you two won't last. You're this month's eye candy. Next time, I bet she's a redhead."

She walks out without another word, the agents by her side, and I'm left standing there, trembling, as her words echo in my head, a toxic mixture of jealousy and bitterness.

I know she said those things only to hurt me. She wanted to get a reaction. Wanted to piss me off.

And it worked.

But that doesn't mean that what she said's not true.

The photo hangs on an interior half-wall that visually divides the living and dining areas. It sits above a small bookcase devoted to books about Hollywood's Golden Age.

I stand staring at it, my purse dropped carelessly at my feet. I'd come in, then crossed to this spot, not even bothering to pull the front door closed behind me.

I've been standing for what feels like an eternity, but has probably only been a minute. Outside, I can hear the rustle of leaves and the low hum of traffic in the distance.

I shouldn't do this.

It's vile to poke into someone's private things, and if Matthew were to start rummaging through the box that contains my childhood diaries, I would be livid.

And yet here I stand, staring at a photo that may hide a dark secret.

No—that *does* hide a dark secret. I'm certain of it, because I'm certain Lila wants me to open it. That should be enough to have me backing away. At the very least, I should tell Matthew what she said and let him show me.

But he could refuse, and I think that would be worse, because surely my imagination can spin a tail more horrible than the truth.

I take a step forward, then stop, my internal debate still raging.

Move, dammit. Just make a damn decision and move.

Right.

With that pathetic pep talk, I inch even closer to the photo, then reach out, figuring that before I get too into my head over this, I should at least confirm that there's a safe back there.

At first, I can't find it, and a wave of disappointment mixed with relief washes over me. But since I'm not sure whether I'm bummed or gleeful, I keep trying even though the photo seems glued to the wall.

Then my fingers find a tiny latch on the right side of the frame, I press it, and that side of the frame pops off the wall with a sharp little *click*.

It's on a hinge, and I take the popped side and push it to the left, as if I were opening a book.

And there it is. A small safe with an electronic keypad.

Which means I have to stand there and debate the ethics all over again.

Fuck it.

I'm doing this. I got this far, and yes, I could argue with myself forever, but I've stuck my big toe into the pool now, and I know I'm diving in.

And maybe Matthew doesn't even need to know. Maybe I can see what's in there, deal with it, process it, maybe have a good cry ... and then I'll be done with it.

Maybe ...

I shouldn't do it. I know that. Just like I know that I'm going to feel guilty as hell for doing it.

But, yeah. I'm doing it.

Before I can talk myself out of it, I punch in the six digits of Matthew's birthday. I hear the click of release. I turn the handle, and the safe opens smoothly on its well-oiled hinges.

Oh. My. God.

My knees go weak, and a wave of nausea crests over me, so intense that I have to reach out and grip the safe's door to keep from sagging to the floor.

This can't be real. How the hell can this be real?

But there it is, diamonds gleaming in the light from the living room lamps, the beautiful, dancing sparkles almost too much to bear. Only one diamond is missing—the large yellow diamond that should be at the point. The diamond that is worth an absolute fortune. That spot is empty, like an eye that can see nothing.

Vivien Lorainne's diadem.

My family's heirloom. The near-magical headpiece that had been the glue of my family. The glue that The Cat had stolen. A fiend who I had once called the Stair Man. Who I had once believed was my protector. My friend.

But who turned out to be nothing more than a thieving alley cat.

A con man.

A man who would steal and scrape and scam to build his empire.

Matthew.

Matthew stole the diadem.

Matthew is The Cat.

TWENTY-NINE

"I didn't want you to learn about it like this."

I almost jump out of my skin at his voice, and I whip around to find Matthew standing in the open doorway, his gorgeous face reflecting the shock that I feel. *Thief. Cat. Stair Man.*

Matthew.

"It was you." I want to say more, but I was barely able to choke out those words. And, honestly, no more words are necessary.

"I've been trying to figure out how to tell—"

"Oh, the hell you have." My voice is like acid. "Maybe when I told you about how *someone* stole it. That seems like it would have been the perfect entree into the *I'm a thieving prick* conversation."

He slides his hands into his pockets. "It would have. Yes."

I point behind me to the safe.

"You stole it. My family's diadem. The one that was the anchor for our home, our life. I told you what happened when —" My voice breaks, and I take a step back, rapidly blinking away tears. "You stole it," I repeat, but this time my voice is barely a whisper.

"Yes."

It's one word, but it is heavy with pain and guilt. Right now, I really don't care about his pain. And I want him to wallow in guilt.

I cross my arms and glare. "So why the fuck didn't you say anything?"

He takes a step toward me, moving slowly with one hand extended, as if he's trying to befriend a stray kitten. "That's easy to say, but harder to do."

"Why?" I snap the word out.

"Why do you think?" I hear the edge of frustration in his voice. "And how would that conversation even go?"

"Maybe it would start with, 'Aria, I have something to tell you.' And, oh, maybe we'd have that conversation before you got me into bed."

He drags his fingers through his hair. "Do you think I don't regret what I did? Don't regret staying silent?"

"I haven't got a clue what you regret, Matthew." My voice is so brittle it's a wonder it doesn't shatter like glass. "I don't think I know you at all."

He takes a step toward me, his long stride closing the distance between us. The air seems to shimmer with his proximity, his nearness making it hard for me to think. And harder to revel in my fury.

"Why?" I demand. "Why the fuck did you steal it? Just so you could put it in a safe? So you could own something pretty and keep it hidden in the dark?"

He closes his eyes. When he opens them again, all I see is the calm businessman. This is the Matthew Holt who negotiated himself into the entertainment biz, then pulled himself to the top by his fingernails.

A career that was launched, I realize, by a dangerous leap

off a diamond. "Hardline." My voice is low and heavy with understanding. "You used the diadem to launch Hardline."

His hands slide back into his pockets, and he moves even closer. He must see the way my eyes narrow, though, because he stops, then leans back against the couch. "The yellow diamond, yes. The diadem I sold to finance my first couple of indie films before I formed the company."

I stew on that, because something's not right. "You, what? Pawned them?"

"Sold," he says, his voice toneless. "Outright. You get a better price that way. The yellow diamond by itself. The diadem with the smaller diamonds intact."

"You bastard." My throat feels dry. Cracked. Hell, my entire body feels cracked. As if just the slightest gust of air could shatter me completely. "That diadem is a treasure. A Hollywood legacy. And Vivien Lorainne gave it to my family. To *us*. You destroyed us," I shout. "You ripped my family to shreds. We almost had to live on the streets because of you." The words are pouring out of me, hard and painful. But not one word reflects what's truly eating me up. Not a single syllable even suggests the true depth of my pain.

"Aria, please. I—"

"I trusted you," I whisper, my heart turning to stone. "Back then. You saved me. That monster was going to—" I cut myself off with a shudder, unable to even whisper the vile ways that fucking babysitter's evil boyfriend would have touched me. Used me. Because hadn't he been leading up to that every time he came into the house?

I shudder, pushing that from my mind. Thinking only of Matthew. "I trusted you," I snap. "I trusted you, and you betrayed me."

My tears are flowing freely now, and I hug myself. I see the pain all over his face, but I don't care. Hell, I celebrate it. Let him be tortured, too.

"Aria, I didn't mean to ...." He trails off, his voice thin. Broken. As if I've shattered something in him.

Good.

He takes a step forward, but I hold up my hand, allowing him only that one. "I told you about my father," he begins, speaking softly. "I couldn't live like that. Small-time thefts and con jobs. I knew what I wanted. And the only useful thing my father ever did for me was give me a solid skillset."

"Stealing," I say, scoffing.

He shrugs. "I'm not that man anymore. But the man I was twenty years ago had dreams. You know that. And I made those dreams into reality."

"That *reality*—the films, the studio, the backlots, the record labels—it was all built on the broken back of my family's legacy. So fuck you, Matthew," I snap. "Fuck. You."

I snatch up my purse and hurry toward the door, knocking his outstretched arm out of my way. "I'll come by tomorrow for my stuff. Don't be here," I say, then burst out the door and run up the steps to where my car's parked on the narrow road.

I throw the door open, slide inside, then slam it shut and lock it, just in case he's coming after me. But he doesn't. After a moment, he even turns off the porch light.

For some reason, that's what does me in, and I clench my fists around the steering wheel and sob for what seems like hours. He doesn't check on me, and I tell myself I'm glad. Nice to know that even after breaking up with the man who may have been the love of my life, I still rank above average at lying to myself.

"*Fuck it,*" I say. "And fuck you, Matthew."

Then I start the car and head down the hill toward the Valley. It's only when I reach Studio City that the question occurs to me: If he sold the diadem for seed money for his entertainment dynasty, then how can that same diadem be sitting in a safe in his living room?

I groan, realizing the answer.

He stole it back.

The cemetery is quiet, the gravestones lit only by the glow of a full moon that hangs eerily over Los Angeles.

I'd intended to drive to my old house to crash for the night, since I know Bree hasn't found a new renter. Then tomorrow I'd head back to the treehouse for my stuff once I'm sure he's at Hardline.

After that … well, maybe I can be Bree's tenant again.

But I never made it to the house. Instead, my car seemed to magically steer itself toward the cemetery.

Now I kneel on the grave of my friend, my eyes leaky with tears as I trace my fingertip over the words carved deep into the marble stone.

Jennifer Garland.

Beloved Daughter.

Loving Friend.

The air is damp, carrying the faint scent of earth and grass, and a chill seeps into my skin despite my hoodie.

"I miss you," I whisper. "I'm sorry I haven't been here in a while. Things have been crazy, you know?" I look up to the heavens, wondering if she does know, and certain that somehow she does. That she's still with me. Still Jenny, but at the same time something more.

"I know it doesn't change anything. We always knew—Bree and me, I mean. We knew you didn't kill yourself. But it's official now. One of the pricks that Trent hired cut a deal, and he told the cops all about how Trent told him to make it look like suicide."

I sigh. I'd been so happy when Joel had told me and Matthew that truth. But it was a hollow victory, because Jenny's still dead.

"Your note helped," I tell her. "Sorry I didn't open it right away. I was—well, I was crushing on my boss. On Matthew. And not just crushing. I think—I *know*—I was in love. But he fucked it all up.

"That's why I'm here tonight," I admit. "Because I'm so angry with him, but at the same time, I want him back. And I don't have anyone to talk to about it, and I miss you so much, and—"

I break off because the tears are coming with a vengeance now. Tears for Jenny. For all the girls. For me and Matthew, and everything we lost. Everything he destroyed by stealing that damn diadem.

"But I guess he helped you," I say aloud. "Matthew fucked up big-time with me, but he's gone all in about the trafficking. He totally owned what Elias Trent did. Didn't try to sweep it under the rug so that he could save the business."

I sniffle. "That was really cool of him, you know? I mean, it worked out fine—in fact, the public seems to have really given him kudos. But man ... it could have gone the other way. It could have destroyed him."

My heart squeezes, and I have to press my lips together to hold back more tears. I know how deeply he put Hardline into the line of fire, but I never really understood just how much Hardline was at risk until right now, as I lay it all out for Jenny.

"I miss him already," I whisper. "Dammit, Jenny. I don't know what to do. He did this stupid, horrible thing, and I want to hate him for it, but—*fuck*."

I slam a fist into the grass. "I want you here. I want to be able to talk to you."

"You can talk to me."

I almost scream. Then I realize the soft voice is coming from behind me, and it's familiar.

I wipe my cheeks, then turn around, and before I know it, I'm on my feet and launching myself into Bree's outstretched arms.

"How are you here?"

She shrugs. "You need me, I'm there. That's our deal, right?"

"Okay, but how did you know?"

She taps her head then points to mine. I cross my arms and stare her down.

"You have got to be kidding me," she says. "You're the one who's all with the karmic energy. Okay, *fine*," she adds when I just keep staring. "Matthew called. He tracked your phone here, and thought it was better if I came than him." She bites her lower lip, then adds, "He sounds in pretty bad shape."

"Good." I sit back on the grass. "Considering what he did, he ought to be." Except the sting has gone out of my voice. And from the look on Bree's face, she knows it, too.

She makes a face at the damn grass, then joins me on the ground. "If I have grass stains on my ass, you owe me a new pair of jeans."

I laugh, and it feels good. "That seems fair. But if I have to buy you a pair of jeans, you have to get dinner."

She extends her hand. "Deal." I take it, we shake, and then we burst into laughter.

And, yeah, it feels *really* good.

She cocks her head. "You hear that?"

"What?"

"Jenny."

I stay quiet, listening to the rustle in the trees. "She's laughing with us," I say.

Bree just snorts. "The hell she is. She's laughing *at* us. She's always thought we were nuts."

"And she was right." I reach for her hand. "I love you."

"I know. Now tell me the rest of it."

"He stole it," I say. "Matthew's The Cat."

She draws in a deep breath. "I know. He told me."

I gape at her. "What? When?"

"Just now. I think he figured I needed to know everything. And I really am sorry. But, sweetie, that was a long time ago."

"Doesn't feel like it."

"Well, that's because you only learned about it five minutes ago. But that doesn't change the fact. It's been twenty years. Close to that, anyway. And yeah, he stole it. But he also protected you. He's the reason those fucking monsters never came near you again."

I don't say a word. She's right.

"And the truth is, I don't think it was as bad as you thought. The financial stuff, I mean."

"What are you talking about?"

"Just that we were kids. Neither one of us understood about mortgages and stuff. And it's not like your dad would have really discussed mortgages and interest rates and stuff with you. You just overheard things. Put your own spin on them."

"So?"

"So, you never lost the house. We grew up right next door to each other, and you were always there. My parents never worried that you might move. You always had food. Your family took some knock-out vacations, too." She shrugs. "I'm just saying that when your little, a bulldog looks like an elephant, you know?"

I shrug, but I don't say anything. Because, well, maybe she's right.

"He still stole it—then sold it. And then he stole it again."

Her eyes go wide. "Really?"

"Well, he has it now, doesn't he?"

She shrugs. "Did he tell you that he stole it back?"

I shake my head. She tilts hers.

"So what is the lesson here?"

I scowl because she's right. I need to talk to him.

I lick my lips, then pull up my knees and hug them. "The thing is ... well, the thing is that I want him. I do. I just don't know how to forgive him."

"Forgiveness doesn't mean forgetting," Bree says gently. "It doesn't mean pretending it didn't happen. It just means you're willing to let go of the hurt and move forward. And think about it. He used it to get his career started, sure. But then he got it back—stole it or bought it, he got the diadem back and kept it intact. Mostly, anyway. He said he couldn't track down the yellow diamond. But that's not the point," she continues. "The question is *why*. Why did he go to all the trouble to get it back?"

"Because it's one of his treasures," I say. "Because of Vivien Lorainne."

"Oh, fuck that. Because of *you*."

I know I should argue, but I don't. Because I want that to be true. I want it so damn bad. But I'm not ready to admit it. Not to Bree. I can barely admit it to myself.

"Hear me out, okay? The man risked everything to find out what happened to Jenny and the others, and when he learned the truth, he didn't try to cover it up because it would embarrass his company. He got it back, then kept that diadem like it's sacred—and that's because of you, and not some movie star. And," she adds with a triumphant lilt in her voice, "let's not forget the night he protected you as a kid. He didn't have to do that, either, but he did."

"I know, but ..."

"Stop arguing with me. Listen," she says, "Ash isn't perfect. Hell, the man's done things that would make your toes curl— and not in the fun way. But he's a good man. And a damn good husband. People aren't one-dimensional. We have flaws, and those flaws don't erase the good."

I stare at her, my chest tight with emotion. "You really think Matthew's a good man?"

She smiles, brushing a stray tear from my cheek. "I do. More important, you think so, too."

She's right, and a fresh wave of tears spills down my cheeks. Bree pulls me close again, holding me tight. "Take your time," she whispers. "But then go talk with him. Don't let the past rob you of your future."

We sit there beneath the stars, and I try to dig deep. I try to forgive. But he lied to me from day one. Lied by staying quiet. For not telling me who he was or what he did or even hinting that our lives had intersected.

How do I forgive that?

And even if I find the way, how can I ever trust him again?

THIRTY

Matthew paced the living room, the shadows of twilight lengthening across the polished wood floors. He'd built this place himself. Knew every inch of it, every nail, every fixture.

She'd only left two days ago, but already the treehouse felt unfamiliar. Foreign, even.

He missed the stack of books she'd kept on one of the side tables. The soft throw she'd use to cover her feet as they snuggled together on the couch.

And now—oh, God—the faint trace of her perfume had almost faded away.

She was gone. And his home was now nothing more than a mausoleum of memories.

The lonely silence pressed in on him, suffocating and absolute. He grabbed his phone and scrolled through his contacts without thinking. Joel's name caught his eye, and before he could talk himself out of it, he tapped the screen.

"Hey," Joel answered after the second ring. "Don't tell me there's trouble with the case?"

"Nothing like that."

"So this is a social call. What's up?"

"I need a drink."

A pause. Then, "You all right?"

"Not even close."

"I'll meet you. Where?"

Matthew rattled off the address of a bar just off Ventura Boulevard that he'd noticed a few times. He wasn't sure why he'd picked it—maybe because it was unassuming, the kind of place where no one would recognize him or care who he was. Joel agreed without hesitation, and Matthew hung up, grabbing his keys before he could change his mind.

The bar was even darker inside than it had seemed from the street. Faint strains of classic rock hummed from an old jukebox in the corner, and the low murmur of conversation filled the air. It wasn't crowded, but it wasn't empty either—a handful of patrons nursed drinks at the bar or slouched in vinyl booths.

Matthew chose a stool at the far end of the bar, away from the others. He ordered a scotch, neat, and watched the bartender pour it with practiced efficiency. The first sip burned all the way down, but it didn't dull the ache in his chest.

He was halfway through his drink when Joel appeared, his broad shoulders filling the doorway as he scanned the room. Spotting Matthew, he crossed the floor with easy strides, sliding onto the stool beside him.

"You look like hell," Joel said, flagging down the bartender. "Bad day?"

Matthew huffed a humorless laugh. "You could say that."

Joel ordered a bourbon, neat, then tilted his head to study Matthew. "This is your party. What's going on?"

Matthew swirled the amber liquid in his glass, watching the way the light fractured through it. He wasn't sure what he wanted to say. Hell, he wasn't sure he could say anything at all.

"It's a woman," he admitted finally, keeping his tone neutral. "I screwed up. She found out, and now she's gone."

"Screwed up how?"

"Old sins," he said quietly. "Things I did a long time ago. Before Hardline. Well, things I did to finance Hardline."

Joel eyed him, nodding slowly.

"She thought she knew me, but this—this changed everything."

Joel leaned back, his expression thoughtful. "And now she's seeing an asshole version of you instead of the guy she fell for."

Matthew nodded. "Pretty much."

Joel's fingers tapped absently on the bar. "That's rough."

"It's eating me up," he admitted. "I can't change who I was. And I thought she knew I wasn't that man anymore."

Joel nodded slowly. "Not really my area of expertise," he said. "You know my track record with women."

Matthew nodded. In truth, he didn't know the details. All he knew was that Joel's wife had left him over three years ago, and he had backed off of relationships altogether, though that didn't stop the flow of women in his bed.

"Listen," Joel finally said. "If this stuff about you was a punch in the gut, you can't blame her for needing time."

"I know," Matthew dragged his fingers through his hair. "But it's still fucking brutal."

"Yeah, well, love hurts." Joel sighed, then took another sip of his drink, then set the glass down with a deliberate motion. "You've changed, though. You know that, right?"

Matthew shot him a sideways glance. "Have I?"

Joel smirked faintly. "Okay, we haven't known each other that long, but if this goes back decades, then yeah. I mean, you've built an empire, Matthew. You've taken care of people. You've done a hell of a lot of good. Don't let one mistake define you."

Matthew let out a slow breath, the tension in his shoulders easing slightly. "I'm not. She is."

Joel chuckled. "Bullshit."

One word, but pretty fucking perceptive.

"Listen, I've been there. Made my share of mistakes, too. Some worse than you can probably imagine."

That caught Matthew's attention. He turned to look at Joel fully, his curiosity piqued.

But Joel didn't elaborate, just lifted his glass in a silent toast. "We've all got skeletons, buddy. You need to remember that they're dead and gone. The trick is to keep the skeletons buried without letting them drag the man you are now down into the grave, too."

"And how the hell do I do that?"

Joel shrugged. "Show her, man. Show her that you've changed."

The drive back to the treehouse felt endless, the city lights blurring together as he replayed Joel's words in his mind. *Show her that you've changed.*

Had he?

By the time he pulled into the driveway, he still didn't have an answer. The house loomed in the darkness, a shadow of the sanctuary it had once been.

He stepped inside, but the space that had once been as comforting as a cocoon now felt hollow. Empty.

He went to the window and looked out over the Valley below. Was she out there, perhaps in her old rental? Or had she gone to stay with Bree and Ash? Or maybe to a hotel.

Hell, maybe she was sitting in a hotel bar right now, sipping a martini and laughing with some man who didn't really want her—just wanted to get her into bed.

But Matthew wanted her. Christ, how he wanted her.

With a sigh, he headed for the kitchen, another scotch calling his name. But he paused on the way, a DVD case catching his eye. *The Thomas Crowne Affair*. Pierce Brosnan, Rene Russo, and that sheer black dress.

They'd watched it together, and he'd deferred to her insistence that the remake was better. He wasn't sure he agreed, but he had to concede that it was definitely hotter.

So hot they'd paused the movie after that scene, their own lovemaking making the dance that had steamed up the screen seem tame by comparison.

They'd watched the rest of the movie naked, curled up next to each other on the sofa, and despite the very energetic sex and their nakedness and the way his cock refused to chill, it was one of the sweetest moments of his life. A moment that showed him how a life with her could be. Fun. Sensual. Surprising. Tender.

Loving.

He closed his eyes, saying a silent prayer to Saint Dismas, the patron saint of thieves. And to Saint Peter, the patron saint of repentance. He wasn't Catholic. Hell, he hadn't stepped foot in a church in years. But right then, he needed all the help he could get. And with luck, one of the two would help him figure out what to do next.

Show her that you've changed.

With a sigh, he moved to the console and took out the DVD. He put it back into its case, then returned it to its place in the bookcase.

That was when he saw her collection of poems. She'd left it sitting on the shelf in front of the videos. She'd probably put it down for a moment as she chose a flick, then forgot to pick it back up again.

It was one of her favorite books. They'd sit in the evening, and she'd flip through the pages, reading him snippets that moved her.

With a sigh, he closed his eyes. This walk down memory lane was eating at his gut, but he couldn't keep himself from twisting the knife a little bit more by flipping through the pages himself. But as he opened the book, a piece of paper fell to the floor. He bent to pick it up, realizing it had been a bookmark, and he'd just lost her place.

Then he saw the words on the page, and they hit him like a punch to the gut—

Read this to Matthew someday. It's the way I feel about him.

He sank onto the couch, the paper tight in his hand.

He'd spent years trying to atone for his past, to build something good and true. And for a while, he'd believed he'd succeeded.

Now, without Aria, it all felt hollow.

The trick is not letting them bury you.

He didn't know if he could win her back. Didn't know if she would ever trust him again—or if she'd even want him once she knew the full truth. But he had to try. Because if he didn't, then everything he'd built, everything he'd become, would mean nothing.

He stood up, and for the first time since she'd walked out, he felt the faintest flicker of hope.

THIRTY-ONE

The envelope is plain, tucked under the windshield wiper of my car, the creamy paper catching the glow of the streetlights. I notice it as I'm leaving Clive's house—and his couch that I'm currently calling home. My plan is to drown my sorrow in a dark theater, fortified by a too-big bucket of popcorn and an unhealthy amount of Diet Coke, and I'm hurrying to catch the nine o'clock show.

At first, I think the envelope is an advertisement. But when I pull it free, I see my name written in a bold, elegant hand. No logo, no return address. Just the faint, familiar scent of Acqua di Parma Colonia clinging to it.

Matthew.

I glance around, scanning the street as if he might be lurking in the shadows. But it's quiet—just a couple of kids skateboarding on the sidewalk and an elderly man walking his tiny dog.

With my heart thudding, I tear the envelope open and pull out a single piece of sky-blue cardstock. The words are simple, just a few lines stenciled neatly across the page:

Tonight. 9 p.m. Work. The rooftop.

That's all it says. No explanation. No apology. Just an invitation—if it even qualifies as that. It feels more like a dare.

Fuck that.

He probably thinks this fixes everything. That I'll walk into whatever he's planned, and we'll tie a neat little bow on this mess.

Anger burns through me, hot and sharp.

And yet ...

I sigh, because despite the burst of anger, there's something else burning inside me. Something light. Something more sunshine than fire.

I don't let myself name it. Instead, I climb into the car and toss the card onto the passenger seat as I start the engine then head for the theater. I try not to think about it—that one stupid piece of paper. But at every light and stop sign, I glance over, as if it's a living thing, demanding my attention.

The rooftop. Tonight.

I grimace and try to push that thought out of my brain.

When I'm finally parked, I shove the invitation into my purse, then open the glove compartment where I keep an extra deck of Tarot cards. Because sometimes you just need to do a quick check, regroup, and gather yourself.

I cut the deck four times, then spread the cards on the passenger seat, just where the invitation had been moments before. Then I close my eyes and draw one from the spread.

The Two of Cups.

My heart squeezes a little, and I hold the card with one hand, then trace over the intricate artwork with my fingertip. Two figures stand together, offering their cups to one another, their connection undeniable. It's about partnership. Love built on mutual trust and understanding. At least, that's what my Tarot book says.

I sigh. *Trust and understanding.* That pretty much sums it up. How can I trust him when he's kept so much of himself hidden from me?

But is it himself?

I'm not sure if the little voice comes from the two on the card, my own mind, or if I'm channeling Bree. But I know I can't ignore the question. He has the diadem, yes. But he got it twenty years ago when he was The Cat.

He's not a thief anymore. If anything, he's the epitome of a businessman, with fingers in all sorts of corporate pies.

Am I the same person I was twenty years ago? Ten? Even five?

I'm not—I know that.

But at the same time, I wasn't ever a thief.

So everyone deserves a second chance except him?

I mentally glare at the errant thought. My mind is going in circles, but somewhere in those spinning thoughts is the flicker of something I've been missing for days. Not certainty—God knows I'm nowhere near that—but something softer, gentler. A little bit of hope. Maybe enough to make me brave.

Forgiveness doesn't mean forgetting.

I exhale slowly, then, tuck the card into my purse. It's a sign, and I'm going to hold it close.

The elevator hums as it rises, and I swear I can feel every vibration as it ascends. I'm the only one in the car—possibly the only one in the building—and the numbers above the door tick by at an infuriatingly steady pace.

Nine.

Ten.

I watch, not sure if I want to will the thing to go faster or slower.

Eleven.

Twelve.

And then the car glides to a stop, and I realize with a sudden jolt of terror that the doors are going to open onto the rooftop— and there's no going back from here.

I half-consider jamming the button for the lobby, then hiding in the corner, but that's only nerves. I want to be here.

More than that, I think I have to be here.

Then the doors slide open with a quiet ding. Cool air rushes in, carrying the faint scent of wood smoke.

I hesitate, the threshold feeling like the edge of a cliff.

My stomach twists. What if I'm just setting myself up to be hurt all over again? What if I step out there and it all falls apart?

The possibility terrifies me, but I also know that if I step off this car and onto the roof, then I've created a future where Matthew and I at least have a chance. That chance might evaporate ten minutes from now, but at least it will have existed.

I think about Bree's words About forgiveness not meaning forgetting. I think about how Matthew risked everything to find the truth about Jenny and the others. And about how I still miss him so much it feels like a physical ache.

But what if it's not enough?

It will be. It has to be.

But what if it's not?

I can't answer that question. All I can do is remind myself that it's Matthew. And at the very least, he's worth the chance.

I draw in a breath, then step out of the car into the cool night air. Behind me, the elevator doors close softly, cutting off any chance of retreat.

There is a small brick wall that separates the elevator bank from the rest of the roof, so I can see nothing except the dimly lit emergency exit instructions on the brick and the golden glow that seems to be rising from behind the wall. I should be grateful the wall is there; it gives me another moment in which to gather myself.

But I'm not. I'm ready to be all-in. Ready enough that I hurry to my right, arching around the edge of the wall and then stopping short and gasping when I see the fairyland spread out in front of me.

It's beautiful. Magical.

And nothing at all like the dingy rooftop littered with cigarette butts and decorated with slightly rusty furniture.

It's the same place, and yet *this* place is utterly enchanting, completely transformed into something magical. String lights stretch across the rooftop, forming a ceiling grid that casts a warm, golden glow. At the center, flames flicker out of a tall barrel, dancing and shimmering, their glow competing with the Valley lights spread out beneath us like a glittering sea that feels both infinite and intimate.

And there, by the fire, is Matthew.

He's standing tall, not moving, yet somehow seeming to grow larger than life from nothing more than the fact of his existence. There's a heat in his eyes that's not from the fire, and though I'd told myself to take this slowly, I can't deny that his gaze and this magical fairyland are both making me melt in the sweetest of ways.

He's wearing dark jeans and a navy sweater that clings to his frame, the sleeves pushed up to his elbows in that way he always does when he's thinking, planning. His hands are tucked into his pockets, but even from here, I can see the tension in his posture. The way his shoulders are just slightly hunched, like he's bracing for a storm.

For me.

I lift my chin and take a step toward him, noticing only then that although he's standing tall and straight, his face looks worn. As if he hasn't slept in days.

I wonder if he sees the same in my face.

As if we're both thinking that same thing, our eyes meet and hold. Then I look away, afraid of what I'm feeling. Afraid that I want him too much, and because I do, I'm not thinking about this right.

"You came." His voice is soft, but it carries over the rooftop, over the crackle of the fire.

I shrug. "I'm just here for a party on a roof. Had no idea who left me that invitation."

The corner of his mouth twitches. He takes a step toward me. "I wouldn't have blamed you if you stayed away."

"I probably should have." I take a step toward him.

"So why didn't you?"

I shrug, then sweep my hand to indicate the roof. "And miss all this?"

"Window dressing," he says. "The only thing I care about is you. Not the fire or the lights. Not the roof or the elevator or the building or the whole damn Valley below us. Just you, Aria. Put me to the test. Throw the labors of Hercules at me. Anything. Just give me the chance to prove that I'm not The Cat. I'm not the man you hate. Not anymore."

For a moment, I just look at him, because the truth is that he's right and he's wrong.

And maybe that's okay.

"Aria?"

"You are The Cat," I say, my voice little more than a whisper.

"Aria, no, I—"

"No. Wait." I swipe a finger under my eye to wipe away a

tear. "I never hated The Cat," I tell him. "I hated the Stair Man because he made me love him. And then he turned out not to be who I thought he was. But he's you, Matthew. You're The Cat. And you're the Stair Man. And you're Matthew."

"Please, Aria. Let me—"

"The Stair Man left," I say firmly cutting him off. "The Cat betrayed my family. But Matthew Holt ..." I trail off, my throat clogged with tears. "Matthew Holt never hurt me. He wouldn't hurt me."

His brow furrows. "No," he whispers. "I wouldn't."

He takes a step closer. "I can't change the past. But I love you, Aria. I love you, and I'll spend the rest of my life proving it to you if you'll let me."

I glance around at the rooftop. "It's beautiful," I say, "but I didn't need the grand gesture. I just needed ..." I trail off with a shrug. Because there's only one thing I need. The only thing I think I'll ever truly need. "I just need you," I say, my throat clogging with tears.

He hurries to me, then pulls me into his arms, and before I know it, I'm lost in a kiss, soft at first, then deeper as he pulls me closer, his arms wrapping around me like he never wants to let go.

Honestly, I know the feeling.

When we finally break apart, both of us breathless, he reaches out and strokes my hair. "Aria, baby, I wish you'd told me you didn't need grand gestures earlier." His face is alight with humor. "I went to all this trouble."

I laugh as I take another look around the roof. "You did a damn good job." I brush my fingertip over his jaw, enjoying the feel of his beard stubble on my skin. "If you have a blanket, maybe we could christen the roof before heading back down."

His mouth twitches. "I think we can add that to the agenda. But that wasn't the grand gesture I was talking about."

I shake my head, confused. Then even more confused when he slips into the shadows and then returns with something that looks like a hatbox.

"For you," he says.

I take it, both curious and delighted. I set it on one of the nearby tables, then untie the bow that's holding the box closed.

Slowly, I take off the lid, then gasp when I see what's inside. *The diadem.*

My family's diadem.

Carefully, I lift it from the box. Its diamonds catch the firelight, scattering it in a million directions. And there, at the point, is the priceless yellow diamond.

"Oh, God, Matthew. Tell me you didn't steal it back. I don't think I can—"

"*No.*" The word is hard. Firm. "It had been sold five times in private sales. It took a hell of a lot of doing, but I tracked it down. I bought it, baby. Free and clear."

I gape at him. "It must have cost a fortune." It was already priceless when Vivien Lorainne owned it, and over time the diamond would only become more valuable. Add in the history —the Hollywood connection, the theft—and the price would have increased simply because of the story behind the stone.

He shrugs. "I had to give you back the diadem your family lost. That diamond was my rock that launched all of this." He gestures to the building below us and the studio backlot below. "And that diadem is the start of a path that led me to you. I owe your family everything that means anything to me. Especially you. So nothing less than returning it would do."

"I—" I shake my head. It's the only thing I'm capable of, as words have completely abandoned me.

"After that night—after I got you away from those monsters —I couldn't stop thinking about you. You were so strong, so resilient. You fascinated me."

"Matthew …"

"Wait. Let me finish." He looks down, his shoulders rising and falling with a heavy breath before he lifts his head and meets my eyes.

"I watched you grow up, Aria. At first, I'd just check in every few months to make sure you were okay. I felt a responsibility—not because I'd got you away from those prick babysitters, and not because I'd stolen the diadem. Just … I don't know. Just to make sure you were safe. And you were. You're gentle and vulnerable and quirky, Aria. But you're so damn strong, too."

He draws a breath. "But then years passed and you moved to Los Angeles, right into my backyard. I started watching more closely. I knew you didn't have a steady job, and I thought I might help, but then I realized that was part of who you were. Part of that fire you have inside you. And somewhere along the way, I fell in love with you, even though I had no right to."

The words hang in the air between us, heavy and raw. Tears spill down my cheeks, and I don't bother wiping them away.

"I can't change the past. But I love you, Aria. I love you, and I will spend the rest of my life proving it to you if you'll let me."

For a long moment, I can't speak. I can't even breathe. The diadem trembles in my hands, and I set it down on the table before I drop it. Then I take a step toward him.

And another.

Then I'm in his arms, his warmth wrapping around me like a shield against the cold night air as tears of relief and joy spill down my cheeks. His hold is tight, almost desperate, like he's afraid I might slip away. And for the first time in days, I feel whole again.

"I love you," I whisper, my voice muffled against his chest. "God help me, I love you, too."

He tilts my chin up with his finger, and his dark eyes search mine. Then he kisses me, slow and tender, his lips warm against mine. A kiss of hope. Of promises.

And of a future I'm finally ready to believe in.

And as the city sparkles around us, I know that somehow, someway, we'll find our way forward.

Together.

EPILOGUE

"Don't be nervous," Aria whispered, as Matthew adjusted his tie for the third time in as many minutes.

"I'm not," he lied. "Why would I be?" Just because he was about to meet her parents. The parents from whom he'd taken the thing they loved most in the world.

Not to mention that he'd stolen the diadem.

The Manhattan restaurant was small and quiet, and Aria had assured him that it was a favorite in their family. It wasn't too fancy, but it wasn't casual, either. It was the kind of place for family celebrations. Birthdays, anniversaries, prom night.

For meeting the parents.

Beside him, she squeezed his hand as they moved through the small, dim space to the table in the rear where Gregory and Elaine Parker were pushing back their chairs and standing, both smiling and eager to see their little girl—and to meet the man who had claimed her.

"So you're Matthew," her father said, extending a hand. He was tall, his hair mostly gray, his eyes both direct and welcoming. "Aria's told us so much about you."

He felt a quick kick of fear, but then he saw the humor in

her face and knew that she hadn't told her parents everything. "All good, I hope."

"Let's just say I've not seen her so smitten since that horse she fell in love with the summer she went away to camp."

Matthew laughed at the twinkle in Gregory's eyes, and knew that no matter what else happened tonight, he liked the man. "That's going to be tough competition," he said. "I hope I can rise to the challenge."

Her mother laughed. "Don't tease him, Greg. It's been a lifetime, and you still tell the story about how intimidated you were when you met my parents."

Gregory shrugged. "Tradition. What can I say?"

Her mother extended her hand, and he took it, gently kissing her fingers with a courtly air. He saw so much of Aria in her, that he would have recognized her as Aria's mother even without the introduction.

"I'm Elaine," she said. "But call me Ellie."

"It's wonderful to meet you," he said, meaning it. Not only were her parents not remotely intimidated by him, as were so many folks who worshiped either money or celebrity, but they were utterly charming.

And that wasn't just a first impression, he realized, as the meal went on, with the four of them laughing and talking in an easy flow of conversation.

"It must be fascinating working in Hollywood," Ellie said at one point. "Was that always a dream of yours?"

He almost thanked her for asking the question. It was a natural segue to where he needed this night to go.

"I grew up poor, but I wanted to make something of myself. I didn't know how at first, but I'd always entertained myself by making up stories. And whenever I needed to escape, I'd sneak into a movie theater."

"Sneak?" Greg asked.

He shrugged. "Like I said, I grew up poor."

Ellie nodded. "You've done very well for yourself."

"Yes, ma'am," he said, as Aria squeezed his hand under the table. "I owe a lot of that to those days in a theater. I became fascinated, especially with older movies. The Golden Age." He shrugged. "I started collecting memorabilia. Especially related to actors I particularly loved."

He lifted a hand, signaling a waiter before continuing. "Vivien Lorainne is at the top of my list."

Ellie reached out and took her husband's hand. "We actually have a family connection to her. Did Aria tell you?"

"The diadem," he said. "Her great-grandfather?"

Greg nodded. "My grandfather, yes. He created it. And before she was murdered, Vivien gave it to him. It was ... special to our family."

"I know," he said. "Ari told me the story."

With perfect timing, the waiter brought over the silver-wrapped box that Matthew had entrusted him with earlier. He indicated Greg, and the waiter handed him the box, then slipped away.

"I don't—what is this?"

"A small present," Matthew said, holding tight to Aria's hand.

"What are you—" she began with a whisper, but he cut her off with a small shake of his head.

Greg untied the bow, then lifted the lid off the box. His hand flew to his mouth and Ellie leaned over, peered in, and then gaped at Matthew.

"This can't be—" Ellie's voice faltered as she looked from the diadem to Matthew, then back again. "Where did—how did you find this?"

"I acquired it years ago. After I met Aria, I learned its history. And I knew that it had to be returned to its family."

Aria's hand brushed his beneath the table. He turned slightly, meeting her eyes, then melted a bit at the love he saw shining there.

"Matthew, we couldn't," Greg said. "It's wonderful knowing that it wasn't stripped of its stones and sold piecemeal, but it must have cost you a fortune. We can't possibly accept it."

"I thought you might say that, sir. Which is why I have another proposal."

Greg's brow furrowed. "I'm not sure I'm following."

"What if you were to keep it, but to give me one of the diamonds?"

"Give you—" Greg shook his head, looking perplexed. But beside him, Elaine's eyes shone, and Matthew could see the smile tugging at her mouth.

"One of the diamonds?" Aria said. "Matthew, what are you—"

"It's just that I need one," he said, reaching into his pocket and pulling out a second box, this one black and velvet. He turned to Aria, then opened the box, revealing a white gold ring with an empty setting. "An engagement ring needs a diamond."

Aria stared at him, her eyes wide, and in that moment, her parents and the restaurant disappeared. It was just them. Then she broke into a radiant smile, her laughter bubbling up like champagne. "Yes," she whispered. "Oh, yes."

Across the table, Greg laughed. "Well, hell, yes, son. You'll have that diamond."

His heart swelled as Aria kissed him, her lips soft and sure. When they pulled apart, her eyes sparkled with love. And with the promise of a future. He drew her close, his hand closing around hers as she rested her head on his shoulder.

For the first time in days—hell, maybe years—he felt completely at peace. And no matter what challenges lay ahead, he knew they'd face them together.

. . .

AUTHOR'S NOTE:

I hope you enjoyed Matthew and Aria's story! If you're curious about Bree and Ash, you can learn more in WICKED HEAT. A few other characters have stories as well. Learn more about Wyatt in WICKED GRIND, and about Ryan Hunter in TAME ME. And if you like things on the spooky side, don't miss POSSESS ME, a Nikki & Damien novella that features Vivien Lorainne ... and a spook-size serving of the occult.

Finally, I think Joel is perfect hero material. Be sure to subscribe to my newsletter so you'll know when he gets a book!

XXOO

JK

AUTHOR'S NOTE

I hope you enjoyed Matthew and Aria's story! If you're curious about Bree and Ash, you can learn more in WICKED HEAT. A few other characters have stories as well. Learn more about Wyatt in WICKED GRIND, and about Ryan Hunter in TAME ME. And if you like things on the spooky side, don't miss POSSESS ME, a Nikki & Damien novella that features Vivien Lorainne ... and a spook-size serving of the occult.

Finally, I think Joel is perfect hero material. Be sure to subscribe to my newsletter so you'll know when he gets a book!

XXOO
JK

EXCERPT: RELEASE ME

The first book in the sexy, emotionally charged Stark Saga—a romance between a powerful man who's never heard "no" and a fiery woman who says "yes" on her own terms...

ONE

A cool ocean breeze caresses my bare shoulders, and I shiver, wishing I'd taken my roommate's advice and brought a shawl with me tonight. I arrived in Los Angeles only four days ago, and I haven't yet adjusted to the concept of summer temperatures changing with the setting of the sun. In Dallas, June is hot, July is hotter, and August is hell.

Not so in California, at least not by the beach. LA Lesson Number One: Always carry a sweater if you'll be out after dark.

Of course, I could leave the balcony and go back inside to the party. Mingle with the millionaires. Chat up the celebrities. Gaze dutifully at the paintings. It is a gala art opening, after all, and my boss brought me here to meet and greet and charm and chat. Not to lust over the panorama that is coming alive in front of me. Bloodred clouds bursting against the pale orange sky. Blue-gray waves shimmering with dappled gold.

I press my hands against the balcony rail and lean forward, drawn to the intense, unreachable beauty of the setting sun. I regret that I didn't bring the battered Nikon I've had since high school. Not that it would have fit in my itty-bitty beaded purse.

And a bulky camera bag paired with a little black dress is a big, fat fashion no-no.

But this is my very first Pacific Ocean sunset, and I'm determined to document the moment. I pull out my iPhone and snap a picture.

"Almost makes the paintings inside seem redundant, doesn't it?" I recognize the throaty, feminine voice and turn to face Evelyn Dodge, retired actress turned agent turned patron of the arts—and my hostess for the evening.

"I'm so sorry. I know I must look like a giddy tourist, but we don't have sunsets like this in Dallas."

"Don't apologize," she says. "I pay for that view every month when I write the mortgage check. It damn well better be spectacular."

I laugh, immediately more at ease.

"Hiding out?"

"Excuse me?"

"You're Carl's new assistant, right?" she asks, referring to my boss of three days.

"Nikki Fairchild."

"I remember now. Nikki from Texas." She looks me up and down, and I wonder if she's disappointed that I don't have big hair and cowboy boots. "So who does he want you to charm?"

"Charm?" I repeat, as if I don't know exactly what she means.

She cocks a single brow. "Honey, the man would rather walk on burning coals than come to an art show. He's fishing for investors and you're the bait." She makes a rough noise in the back of her throat. "Don't worry. I won't press you to tell me who. And I don't blame you for hiding out. Carl's brilliant, but he's a bit of a prick."

"It's the brilliant part I signed on for," I say, and she barks out a laugh.

The truth is that she's right about me being the bait. "Wear a cocktail dress," Carl had said. "Something flirty."

Seriously? I mean, Seriously?

I should have told him to wear his own damn cocktail dress. But I didn't. Because I want this job. I fought to get this job. Carl's company, C-Squared Technologies, successfully launched three web-based products in the last eighteen months. That track record had caught the industry's eye, and Carl had been hailed as a man to watch.

More important from my perspective, that meant he was a man to learn from, and I'd prepared for the job interview with an intensity bordering on obsession. Landing the position had been a huge coup for me. So what if he wanted me to wear something flirty? It was a small price to pay.

Shit.

"I need to get back to being the bait," I say.

"Oh, hell. Now I've gone and made you feel either guilty or self-conscious. Don't be. Let them get liquored up in there first. You catch more flies with alcohol anyway. Trust me. I know."

She's holding a pack of cigarettes, and now she taps one out, then extends the pack to me. I shake my head. I love the smell of tobacco—it reminds me of my grandfather—but actually inhaling the smoke does nothing for me.

"I'm too old and set in my ways to quit," she says. "But God forbid I smoke in my own damn house. I swear, the mob would burn me in effigy. You're not going to start lecturing me on the dangers of secondhand smoke, are you?"

"No," I promise.

"Then how about a light?"

I hold up the itty-bitty purse. "One lipstick, a credit card, my driver's license, and my phone."

"No condom?"

"I didn't think it was that kind of party," I say dryly.

"I knew I liked you." She glances around the balcony. "What the hell kind of party am I throwing if I don't even have one goddamn candle on one goddamn table? Well, fuck it." She puts the unlit cigarette to her mouth and inhales, her eyes closed and her expression rapturous. I can't help but like her. She wears hardly any makeup, in stark contrast to all the other women here tonight, myself included, and her dress is more of a caftan, the batik pattern as interesting as the woman herself.

She's what my mother would call a brassy broad—loud, large, opinionated, and self-confident. My mother would hate her. I think she's awesome.

She drops the unlit cigarette onto the tile and grinds it with the toe of her shoe. Then she signals to one of the catering staff, a girl dressed all in black and carrying a tray of champagne glasses.

The girl fumbles for a minute with the sliding door that opens onto the balcony, and I imagine those flutes tumbling off, breaking against the hard tile, the scattered shards glittering like a wash of diamonds.

I picture myself bending to snatch up a broken stem. I see the raw edge cutting into the soft flesh at the base of my thumb as I squeeze. I watch myself clutching it tighter, drawing strength from the pain, the way some people might try to extract luck from a rabbit's foot.

The fantasy blurs with memory, jarring me with its potency. It's fast and powerful, and a little disturbing because I haven't needed the pain in a long time, and I don't understand why I'm thinking about it now, when I feel steady and in control.

I am fine, I think. *I am fine, I am fine, I am fine.*

"Take one, honey," Evelyn says easily, holding a flute out to me.

I hesitate, searching her face for signs that my mask has

slipped and she's caught a glimpse of my rawness. But her face is clear and genial.

"No, don't you argue," she adds, misinterpreting my hesitation. "I bought a dozen cases and I hate to see good alcohol go to waste. Hell no," she adds when the girl tries to hand her a flute. "I hate the stuff. Get me a vodka. Straight up. Chilled. Four olives. Hurry up, now. Do you want me to dry up like a leaf and float away?"

The girl shakes her head, looking a bit like a twitchy, frightened rabbit. Possibly one that had sacrificed his foot for someone else's good luck.

Evelyn's attention returns to me. "So how do you like LA? What have you seen? Where have you been? Have you bought a map of the stars yet? Dear God, tell me you're not getting sucked into all that tourist bullshit."

"Mostly I've seen miles of freeway and the inside of my apartment."

"Well, that's just sad. Makes me even more glad that Carl dragged your skinny ass all the way out here tonight."

I've put on fifteen welcome pounds since the years when my mother monitored every tiny thing that went in my mouth, and while I'm perfectly happy with my size-eight ass, I wouldn't describe it as skinny. I know Evelyn means it as a compliment, though, and so I smile. "I'm glad he brought me, too. The paintings really are amazing."

"Now don't do that—don't you go sliding into the polite-conversation routine. No, no," she says before I can protest. "I'm sure you mean it. Hell, the paintings are wonderful. But you're getting the flat-eyed look of a girl on her best behavior, and we can't have that. Not when I was getting to know the real you."

"Sorry," I say. "I swear I'm not fading away on you."

Because I genuinely like her, I don't tell her that she's wrong —she hasn't met the real Nikki Fairchild. She's met Social Nikki who, much like Malibu Barbie, comes with a complete set of accessories. In my case, it's not a bikini and a convertible. Instead, I have the Elizabeth Fairchild Guide for Social Gatherings.

My mother's big on rules. She claims it's her Southern upbringing. In my weaker moments, I agree. Mostly, I just think she's a controlling bitch. Since the first time she took me for tea at the Mansion at Turtle Creek in Dallas at age three, I have had the rules drilled into my head. How to walk, how to talk, how to dress. What to eat, how much to drink, what kinds of jokes to tell.

I have it all down, every trick, every nuance, and I wear my practiced pageant smile like armor against the world. The result being that I don't think I could truly be myself at a party even if my life depended on it.

This, however, is not something Evelyn needs to know.

"Where exactly are you living?" she asks.

"Studio City. I'm sharing a condo with my best friend from high school."

"Straight down the 101 for work and then back home again. No wonder you've only seen concrete. Didn't anyone tell you that you should have taken an apartment on the Westside?"

"Too pricey to go it alone," I admit, and I can tell that my admission surprises her. When I make the effort—like when I'm Social Nikki—I can't help but look like I come from money. Probably because I do. Come from it, that is. But that doesn't mean I brought it with me.

"How old are you?"

"Twenty-four."

Evelyn nods sagely, as if my age reveals some secret about me. "You'll be wanting a place of your own soon enough. You call me when you do and we'll find you someplace with a view.

Not as good as this one, of course, but we can manage something better than a freeway on-ramp."

"It's not that bad, I promise."

"Of course it's not," she says in a tone that says the exact opposite. "As for views," she continues, gesturing toward the now-dark ocean and the sky that's starting to bloom with stars, "you're welcome to come back anytime and share mine."

"I might take you up on that," I admit. "I'd love to bring a decent camera back here and take a shot or two."

"It's an open invitation. I'll provide the wine and you can provide the entertainment. A young woman loose in the city. Will it be a drama? A rom-com? Not a tragedy, I hope. I love a good cry as much as the next woman, but I like you. You need a happy ending."

I tense, but Evelyn doesn't know she's hit a nerve. That's why I moved to LA, after all. New life. New story. New Nikki.

I ramp up the Social Nikki smile and lift my champagne flute. "To happy endings. And to this amazing party. I think I've kept you from it long enough."

"Bullshit," she says. "I'm the one monopolizing you, and we both know it."

We slip back inside, the buzz of alcohol-fueled conversation replacing the soft calm of the ocean.

"The truth is, I'm a terrible hostess. I do what I want, talk to whoever I want, and if my guests feel slighted they can damn well deal with it."

I gape. I can almost hear my mother's cries of horror all the way from Dallas.

"Besides," she continues, "this party isn't supposed to be about me. I put together this little shindig to introduce Blaine and his art to the community. He's the one who should be doing the mingling, not me. I may be fucking him, but I'm not going to baby him."

Evelyn has completely destroyed my image of how a hostess for the not-to-be-missed social event of the weekend is supposed to behave, and I think I'm a little in love with her for that.

"I haven't met Blaine yet. That's him, right?" I point to a tall reed of a man. He is bald, but sports a red goatee. I'm pretty sure it's not his natural color. A small crowd hums around him, like bees drawing nectar from a flower. His outfit is certainly as bright as one.

"That's my little center of attention, all right," Evelyn says. "The man of the hour. Talented, isn't he?" Her hand sweeps out to indicate her massive living room. Every wall is covered with paintings. Except for a few benches, whatever furniture was once in the room has been removed and replaced with easels on which more paintings stand.

I suppose technically they are portraits. The models are nudes, but these aren't like anything you would see in a classical art book. There's something edgy about them. Something provocative and raw. I can tell that they are expertly conceived and carried out, and yet they disturb me, as if they reveal more about the person viewing the portrait than about the painter or the model.

As far as I can tell, I'm the only one with that reaction. Certainly the crowd around Blaine is glowing. I can hear the gushing praise from here.

"I picked a winner with that one," Evelyn says. "But let's see. Who do you want to meet? Rip Carrington and Lyle Tarpin? Those two are guaranteed drama, that's for damn sure, and your roommate will be jealous as hell if you chat them up."

"She will?"

Evelyn's brows arch up. "Rip and Lyle? They've been feuding for weeks." She narrows her eyes at me. "The fiasco about the new season of their sitcom? It's all over the Internet? You really don't know them?"

"Sorry," I say, feeling the need to apologize. "My school schedule was pretty intense. And I'm sure you can imagine what working for Carl is like."

Speaking of...

I glance around, but I don't see my boss anywhere.

"That is one serious gap in your education," Evelyn says. "Culture—and yes, pop culture counts—is just as important as—what did you say you studied?"

"I don't think I mentioned it. But I have a double major in electrical engineering and computer science."

"So you've got brains and beauty. See? That's something else we have in common. Gotta say, though, with an education like that, I don't see why you signed up to be Carl's secretary."

I laugh. "I'm not, I swear. Carl was looking for someone with tech experience to work with him on the business side of things, and I was looking for a job where I could learn the business side. Get my feet wet. I think he was a little hesitant to hire me at first—my skills definitely lean toward tech—but I convinced him I'm a fast learner."

She peers at me. "I smell ambition."

I lift a shoulder in a casual shrug. "It's Los Angeles. Isn't that what this town is all about?"

"Ha! Carl's lucky he's got you. It'll be interesting to see how long he keeps you. But let's see... who here would intrigue you...?"

She casts about the room, finally pointing to a fifty-something man holding court in a corner. "That's Charles Maynard," she says. "I've known Charlie for years. Intimidating as hell until you get to know him. But it's worth it. His clients are either celebrities with name recognition or power brokers with more money than God. Either way, he's got all the best stories."

"He's a lawyer?"

"With Bender, Twain & McGuire. Very prestigious firm."

"I know," I say, happy to show that I'm not entirely ignorant, despite not knowing Rip or Lyle. "One of my closest friends works for the firm. He started here but he's in their New York office now."

"Well, come on, then, Texas. I'll introduce you." We take one step in that direction, but then Evelyn stops me. Maynard has pulled out his phone, and is shouting instructions at someone. I catch a few well-placed curses and eye Evelyn sideways. She looks unconcerned "He's a pussycat at heart. Trust me, I've worked with him before. Back in my agenting days, we put together more celebrity biopic deals for our clients than I can count. And we fought to keep a few tell-alls off the screen, too." She shakes her head, as if reliving those glory days, then pats my arm. "Still, we'll wait 'til he calms down a bit. In the meantime, though..."

She trails off, and the corners of her mouth turn down in a frown as she scans the room again. "I don't think he's here yet, but—oh! Yes! Now there's someone you should meet. And if you want to talk views, the house he's building has one that makes my view look like, well, like yours." She points toward the entrance hall, but all I see are bobbing heads and haute couture. "He hardly ever accepts invitations, but we go way back," she says.

I still can't see who she's talking about, but then the crowd parts and I see the man in profile. Goose bumps rise on my arms, but I'm not cold. In fact, I'm suddenly very, very warm.

He's tall and so handsome that the word is almost an insult. But it's more than that. It's not his looks, it's his presence. He commands the room simply by being in it, and I realize that Evelyn and I aren't the only ones looking at him. The entire crowd has noticed his arrival. He must feel the weight of all those eyes, and yet the attention doesn't faze him at all. He smiles at the girl with the champagne, takes a glass, and begins to chat casually with a woman who approaches him, a simpering smile stretched across her face.

"Damn that girl," Evelyn says. "She never did bring me my vodka."

But I barely hear her. "Damien Stark," I say. My voice surprises me. It's little more than breath.

Evelyn's brows rise so high I notice the movement in my peripheral vision. "Well, how about that?" she says knowingly. "Looks like I guessed right."

"You did," I admit. "Mr. Stark is just the man I want to see."

TWO

"Damien Stark is the holy grail." That's what Carl told me earlier that evening. Right after "Damn, Nikki. You look hot."

I think he was expecting me to blush and smile and thank him for his kind words. When I didn't, he cleared his throat and got down to business. "You know who Stark is, right?"

"You saw my resume," I reminded him. "The fellowship?" I'd been the recipient of the Stark International Science Fellowship for four of my five years at the University of Texas, and those extra dollars every semester had made all the difference in the world to me. Of course, even without a fellowship, you'd have to be from Mars not to know about the man. Only thirty years old, the reclusive former tennis star had taken the millions he'd earned in prizes and endorsements and reinvented himself. His tennis days had been overshadowed by his new identity as an entrepreneur, and Stark's massive empire raked in billions every year.

"Right, right," Carl said, distracted. "Team April is presenting at Stark Applied Technology on Tuesday." At C-Squared, every product team is named after a month. With only twenty-three employees, though, the company has yet to tap into autumn or winter.

"That's fabulous," I said, and I meant it. Inventors, software developers, and eager new business owners practically wet themselves to get an interview with Damien Stark. That Carl had snagged just such an appointment was proof that my hoop-jumping to get this job had been worth it.

"Damn straight," Carl said. "We're showing off the beta version of the 3-D training software. Brian and Dave are on point with me," he added, referring to the two software developers who'd written most of the code for the product. Considering its applications in athletics and Stark Applied Technology's focus on athletic medicine and training, I had to guess that Carl was about to pitch another winner. "I want you at the meeting with us," he added, and I managed not to embarrass myself by doing a fist-pump in the air. "Right now, we're scheduled to meet with Preston Rhodes. Do you know who he is?"

"No."

"Nobody does. Because Rhodes is a nobody."

So Carl didn't have a meeting with Stark, after all. I, however, had a feeling I knew where this conversation was going.

"Pop quiz, Nikki. How does an up-and-coming genius like me get an in-person meeting with a powerhouse like Damien Stark?"

"Networking," I said. I wasn't an A-student for nothing.

"And that's why I hired you." He tapped his temple, even as his eyes roamed over my dress and lingered at my cleavage. At least he wasn't so gauche as to actually articulate the basic fact that he was hoping that my tits—rather than his product—would intrigue Stark enough that he'd attend the meeting personally. But honestly, I wasn't sure my girls were up to the task. I'm easy on the eyes, but I'm more the girl-next-door, America's-sweet-heart type. And I happen to know that Stark goes for the runway supermodel type.

I learned that six years ago when he was still playing tennis and I was still chasing tiaras. He'd been the token celebrity judge at the Miss Tri-County Texas pageant, and though we'd barely exchanged a dozen words at the mid-pageant reception, the encounter was burned into my memory.

I'd parked myself near the buffet and was contemplating the tiny squares of cheesecake, wondering if my mother would smell it on my breath if I ate just one, when he walked up with the kind of bold self-assurance that can seem like arrogance on some men, but on Damien Stark it just seemed sexy as hell. He eyed me first, then the cheesecakes. Then he took two and popped them both in his mouth. He chewed, swallowed, then grinned at me. His unusual eyes, one amber and one almost completely black, seemed to dance with mirth.

I tried to come up with something clever to say and failed miserably. So I just stood there, my polite smile plastered across my face as I wondered if his kiss would give me all the taste and none of the calories.

Then he leaned closer, and my breath hitched as his proximity increased. "I think we're kindred spirits, Miss Fairchild."

"I'm sorry?" Was he talking about the cheesecake? Good God, I hadn't actually looked jealous when he'd eaten them, had I? The idea was appalling.

"Neither of us wants to be here," he explained. He tilted his head slightly toward a nearby emergency exit, and I was overcome by the sudden image of him grabbing my hand and taking off running. The clarity of the thought alarmed me. But the certainty that I'd go with him didn't scare me at all.

"I—oh," I mumbled.

His eyes crinkled with his smile, and he opened his mouth

to speak. I didn't learn what he had to say, though, because Carmela D'Amato swept over to join us, then linked her arm with his. "Damie, darling." Her Italian accent was as thick as her dark wavy hair. "Come. We should go, yes?" I've never been a big tabloid reader, but it's hard to avoid celebrity gossip when you're doing the pageant thing. So I'd seen the headlines and articles that paired the big-shot tennis star with the Italian supermodel.

"Miss Fairchild," he said with a parting nod, then turned to escort Carmela into the crowd and out of the building. I watched them leave, consoling myself with the thought that there was regret in his eyes as we parted ways. Regret and resignation.

There wasn't, of course. Why would there be? But that nice little fantasy got me through the rest of the pageant.

And I didn't say one word about the encounter to Carl. Some things are best played close to the vest. Including how much I'm looking forward to meeting Damien Stark again.

"Come on, Texas," Evelyn says, pulling me from my thoughts. "Let's go say howdy."

I feel a tap on my shoulder and turn to find Carl behind me. He sports the kind of grin that suggests he just got laid. I know better. He's just giddy with the anticipation of getting close to Damien Stark.

Well, me, too.

The crowd has shifted again, blocking my view of the man. I still haven't seen his face, just his profile, and now I can't even see that. Evelyn's leading the way, making forward progress through the crowd despite a few stops and starts to chat with her guests. We're on the move again when a barrel-chested man in a plaid sport coat shifts to the left, once again revealing Damien Stark.

He is even more magnificent now than he was six years ago.

The brashness of youth has been replaced by a mature confidence. He is Jason and Hercules and Perseus—a figure so strong and beautiful and heroic that the blood of the gods must flow through him, because how else could a being so fine exist in this world? His face consists of hard lines and angles that seem sculpted by light and shadows, making him appear both classically gorgeous and undeniably unique. His dark hair absorbs the light as completely as a raven's wing, but it is not nearly as smooth. Instead, it looks wind-tossed, as if he's spent the day at sea.

That hair in contrast with his black tailored trousers and starched white shirt give him a casual elegance, and it's easy to believe that this man is just as comfortable on a tennis court as he is in a boardroom.

His famous eyes capture my attention. They seem edgy and dangerous and full of dark promises. More important, they are watching me. Following me as I move toward him.

I feel an odd sense of déjà vu as I move steadily across the floor, hyperaware of my body, my posture, the placement of my feet. Foolishly, I feel as if I'm a contestant all over again.

I keep my eyes forward, not looking at his face. I don't like the nervousness that has crept into my manner. The sense that he can see beneath the armor I wear along with my little black dress.

One step, then another.

I can't help it; I look straight at him. Our eyes lock, and I swear all the air is sucked from the room. It is my old fantasy come to life, and I am completely lost. The sense of déjà vu vanishes and there's nothing but this moment, electric and powerful. Sensual.

For all I know, I've gone spinning off into space. But no, I'm right there, floor beneath me, walls around me, and Damien Stark's eyes on mine. I see heat and purpose. And then I see nothing but raw, primal desire so intense I fear that I'll shatter under the force of it.

Carl takes my elbow, steadying me, and only then do I realize I'd started to stumble. "Are you okay?"

"New shoes. Thanks." I glance back at Stark, but his eyes have gone flat. His mouth is a thin line. Whatever that was—and what the hell was it?—the moment has passed.

By the time we reach Stark, I've almost convinced myself it was my imagination.

I barely process the words as Evelyn introduces Carl. My turn is next, and Carl presses his hand to my shoulder, pushing me subtly forward. His palm is sweating, and it feels clammy against my bare skin. I force myself not to shrug it off.

"Nikki is Carl's new assistant," Evelyn says.

I extend my hand. "Nikki Fairchild. It's a pleasure." I don't mention that we've met before. Now hardly seems the time to remind him that I once paraded before him in a bathing suit.

"Ms. Fairchild," he says, ignoring my hand. My stomach twists, but I'm not sure if it's from nerves, disappointment, or anger. He looks from Carl to Evelyn, pointedly avoiding my eyes. "You'll have to excuse me. There's something I need to attend to right away." And then he's gone, swallowed up into the crowd as effectively as a magician disappearing in a puff of smoke.

"What the fuck?" Carl says, summing up my sentiments exactly.

Uncharacteristically quiet, Evelyn simply gapes at me, her expressive mouth turned down into a frown.

But I don't need words to know what she's thinking. I can easily see that she's wondering the same thing I am: What just happened?

More important, what the hell did I do wrong?

THREE

My moment of mortification hangs over the three of us for what feels like an eternity. Then Carl takes my arm and begins to steer me away from Evelyn.

"Nikki?" Concern blooms in her eyes.

"I—it's okay," I say. I feel strangely numb and very confused. This is what I'd been looking forward to?

"I mean it, Nikki," Carl says, as soon as he's put some distance between us and our hostess. "What the fuck was that?"

"I don't know."

"Bullshit," he snaps. "Have you met before? Did you piss him off? Did you apply for a job with him before me? What the hell did you do, Nichole?"

I cringe against the use of my given name. "It's not me," I say, because I want that to be the truth. "He's famous. He's eccentric. He was rude, but it wasn't personal. How the hell could it have been?" I can hear my voice rising, and I force myself to tamp it down. To breathe.

I squeeze my left hand into a fist so tight my fingernails cut into my palm. I focus on the pain, on the simple process of breathing. I need to be cool. I need to be calm. I can't let the Social Nikki facade slip away.

Beside me, Carl runs his fingers through his hair and sucks in a noisy breath. "I need a drink. Come on."

"I'm fine, thanks." I am a long way from fine, but what I want right then is to be alone. Or as alone as I can be in a room full of people.

I can see that he wants to argue. I can also see that he hasn't yet decided what he's going to do. Approach Stark again? Leave the party and pretend it never happened? "Fine," he growls. He stalks off, and I can hear his muttered "Shit," as he disappears into the crowd.

I exhale, the tension in my shoulders slipping away. I head toward the balcony, but stop once I see that my private spot has been discovered. At least eight people mingle there, chatting and smiling. I am not in a chatty, smiley mood.

I veer toward one of the freestanding easels and stare blankly at the painting. It depicts a nude woman kneeling on a hard tile floor. Her arms are raised above her head, her wrists bound by a red ribbon.

The ribbon is attached to a chain that rises vertically out of the painting, and there is tension in her arms, as if she's tugging downward, trying to get free. Her stomach is smooth, her back arched so that the lines of her rib cage show. Her breasts are small, and the erect nipples and tight brown areolae glow under the artist's skill.

Her face is not so prominent. It's tilted away, shrouded in gray. I'm left with the impression that the model is ashamed of her arousal. That she would break free if she could. But she can't.

She's trapped there, her pleasure and her shame on display for all the world.

My own skin prickles and I realize that this girl and I have something in common. I'd felt a sensual power crash over me, and I'd reveled in it.

Then Stark had shut it off, as quickly as if he'd flipped a switch. And like that model I was left feeling awkward and ashamed.

Well, fuck him. That twit on the canvas might be embarrassed, but I wasn't going to be. I'd seen the heat in his eyes, and it had turned me on. Period. End of story. Time to move on.

I look hard at the woman on the canvas. She's weak. I don't like her, and I don't like the painting.

I start to move away, my own confidence restored—and I collide with none other than Damien Stark himself.

Well, shit.

His hand slides against my waist in an effort to steady me. I back away quickly, but not before my mind processes the feel of him. He's lean and hard, and I'm uncomfortably aware of the places where my body collided with his. My palm. My breasts. The curve of my waist tingles from the lingering shock of his touch.

"Ms. Fairchild." He's looking straight at me, his eyes neither flat nor cold. I realize that I have stopped breathing.

I clear my throat and flash a polite smile. The kind that quietly says "Fuck off."

"I owe you an apology."

Oh.

"Yes," I say, surprised. "You do."

I wait, but he says nothing else. Instead, he turns his attention to the painting. "It's an interesting image. But you would have made a much better model."

What the...?

"That's the worst apology I've ever heard."

He indicates the model's face. "She's weak," he says, and I forget all about the apology. I'm too intrigued by the way his words echo my earlier thoughts. "I suppose some people might be drawn to the contrast. Desire and shame. But I prefer something bolder. A more confident sensuality."

He looks at me as he says this last, and I'm not sure if he's finally apologizing for snubbing me, complimenting my composure, or being completely inappropriate. I decide to consider his words a compliment and go from there. It may not be the safest approach, but it's the most flattering.

"I'm delighted you think so," I say. "But I'm not the model type."

He takes a step back and with slow deliberation looks me up and down. His inspection seems to last for hours, though it must take only seconds. The air between us crackles, and I want to move toward him, to close the gap between us again. But I stay rooted to the spot.

He lingers for a moment on my lips before finally lifting his head to meet my eyes, and that is when I move. I can't help it. I'm drawn in by the force and pressure of the tempest building in those damnable eyes.

"No," he says simply.

At first I'm confused, thinking that he's protesting my proximity. Then I realize he's responding to my comment about not being the model type.

"You are," he continues. "But not like this—splashed across a canvas for all the world to see, belonging to no one and everyone." His head tilts slightly to the left, as if he's trying out a new perspective on me. "No," he murmurs again, but this time he doesn't elaborate.

I am not prone to blushing, and I'm mortified to realize that my cheeks are burning. For someone who just a few moments ago mentally told this man to fuck off, I am doing a piss-poor job of keeping the upper hand. "I was hoping to have the chance to talk to you this evening," I say.

His brow lifts ever so slightly, giving him an expression of polite amusement. "Oh?"

"I'm one of your fellowship recipients. I wanted to say thank you."

He doesn't say a word.

I soldier on. "I worked my way through college, so the fellowship helped tremendously. I don't think I could have graduated with two degrees if it hadn't been for the financial help. So thank you." I still don't mention the pageant. As far as I'm concerned, Damien Stark and I are deep in the land of the do-over.

"And what are you doing now that you've left the hallowed halls of academia?"

He speaks so formally that I know he's teasing me. I ignore it and answer the question seriously. "I joined the team at C-Squared," I say. "I'm Carl Rosenfeld's new assistant." Evelyn already told him this, but I assume he hadn't been paying attention.

"I see."

The way he says it suggests he doesn't see at all. "Is that a problem?"

"Two degrees. A straight-A average. Glowing recommendations from all your professors. Acceptance to Ph.D. programs at both MIT and Cal Tech."

I stare at him, baffled. The Stark International Fellowship Committee awards thirty fellowships each year. How the hell can he possibly know so much about my academic career?

"I merely find it interesting that you ended up not leading a product development team but doing gruntwork as the owner's assistant."

"I—" I don't know what to say. I'm still spinning from the surreal nature of this inquisition.

"Are you sleeping with your boss, Ms. Fairchild?"

"What?"

"I'm sorry. Was the question unclear? I asked if you were fucking Carl Rosenfeld."

"I—no." I blurt the answer out, because I can't let that image linger for longer than a second. Immediately, though, I regret speaking. What I should have done was slap his face. What the hell kind of question is that?

"Good," he says, so crisply and firmly and with such intensity that any thought I have of verbally bitch-slapping him vanishes completely. My thoughts, in fact, have taken a sharp left turn and I am undeniably, unwelcomely turned on. I glare at the woman in the portrait, hating her even more, and not particularly pleased with Damien Stark or myself. I suppose we have something in common, though. At the moment, we're both picturing me out of my little black dress.

Shit.

He doesn't even try to hide his amusement. "I believe I've shocked you, Ms. Fairchild."

"Hell yes, you've shocked me. What did you expect?"

He doesn't answer, just tilts his head back and laughs. It's as if a mask has slipped away, allowing me a glimpse of the real man hidden beneath. I smile, liking that we have this one small thing in common.

"Can anyone join this party?" It's Carl, and I want desperately to say no.

"How nice to see you again, Mr. Rosenfeld," Stark says. The mask is firmly back in place.

Carl glances at me, and I can see the question in his eyes. "Excuse me," I say. "I need to run to the ladies' room."

I escape to the cool elegance of Evelyn's powder room. She's thoughtfully provided mouthwash and hairspray and even disposable mascara wands. There is a lavender-scented salt scrub on the stone vanity, and I put a spoonful in my hands, then close my eyes and rub, imagining that I'm sloughing off the shell of myself to reveal something bright and shiny and new.

I rinse my hands in warm water, then caress my skin with my fingertips. My hands are soft now. Slick and sensual.

I meet my eyes in the mirror. "No," I whisper, but my hand slides down to brush the hem of my dress just below my knee. It's fitted at the bodice and waist, but the skirt is flared, designed to present an enticing little swish when you move.

My fingers dance across my knee, then trail lazily up my inner thigh. I meet my gaze in the mirror, then close my eyes. It's Stark's face I want to see. His eyes I imagine watching me from that mirror.

There's a sensuality in the way my fingers slowly graze my own skin. A lazy eroticism that some other time could build to something hot and explosive. But that's not where I'm going— that's what I'm destroying.

I stop when I feel it—the jagged, raised tissue of the five-year-old scar that mars the once-perfect flesh of my inner thigh. I press my fingertips to it, remembering the pain that punctuated that particular wound. That had been the weekend that my sister, Ashley, had died, and I'd just about crumbled under the weight of my grief.

But that's the past, and I close my eyes tight, my body hot, the scar throbbing beneath my hand.

This time when I open my eyes, all I see is myself. Nikki Fairchild, back in control.

I wrap my restored confidence around me like a blanket and return to the party. Both men look at me as I approach. Stark's face is unreadable, but Carl isn't even trying to hide his joy. He looks like a six-year-old on Christmas morning. "Say your good-byes, Nikki. We're heading out. Lots to do. Lots to do."

"What? Now?" I don't bother to hide my confusion.

"Turns out Mr. Stark's going to be out of town on Tuesday, so we're pushing the meeting to tomorrow."

"Saturday?"

"Is that a problem?" Stark asks me.

"No, of course not, but—"

"He's attending personally," Carl says. "Personally," he repeats, as if I could have missed it the first time.

"Right. I'll just find Evelyn and say goodnight." I start to move away, but Stark's voice draws me back.

"I'd like Ms. Fairchild to stay."

"What?" Carl speaks, expressing my thought.

"The house I'm building is almost complete. I came here to find a painting for a particular room. I'd like a feminine perspective. I'll see her home safely, of course."

"Oh." Carl looks like he's going to protest, then thinks better of it. "She'll be happy to help."

The hell she will. It's one thing to wear the dress. It's another to completely skip the presentation rehearsal because a self-absorbed bazillionaire snaps his fingers and says jump. No matter how hot said bazillionaire might be.

But Carl cuts me off before I can form a coherent reply. "We'll speak tomorrow morning," he tells me. "The meeting's at two."

And then he's gone and I'm left seething beside a very smug Damien Stark.

"Who the hell do you think you are?"

"I know exactly who I am, Ms. Fairchild. Do you?"

"Maybe the better question is, who the hell do you think I am?"

"Are you attracted to me?"

"I—what?" I say, verbally stumbling. His words have knocked me off center, and I struggle to regain my balance. "That is so not the issue."

The corner of his mouth twitches, and I realize I've revealed too much.

"I'm Carl's assistant," I say firmly and slowly. "Not yours. And my job description does not include decorating your goddamn house." I'm not shouting, but my voice is as taut as a wire and my body even more so.

Stark, damn him, appears not only perfectly at ease, but also completely amused. "If your job duties include helping your boss find capital, then you may want to reconsider how you play the game. Insulting potential investors is probably not the best approach."

A cold stab of fear that I've screwed this up cuts through me. "Maybe not," I say. "But if you're going to withhold your money because I didn't roll over and flounce my skirts for you, then you're not the man the press makes you out to be. The Damien Stark I've read about invests in quality. Not in friendships or relationships or because he thinks some poor little inventor needs the deal. The Damien Stark I admire focuses on talent and talent alone. Or is that just public relations?"

I stand straight, ready to endure whatever verbal lashes he'll whip back at me. I'm not prepared for the response I get.

Stark laughs.

"You're right," he says. "I'm not going to invest in C-Squared because I met Carl at a party any more than I'd invest in it because you're in my bed."

"Oh." Once again, my cheeks heat. Once again, he's knocked me off balance.

"I do, however, want you."

My mouth is dry. I have to swallow before I can speak. "To help you pick a painting?"

"Yes," he confirms. "For now."

I force myself not to wonder about later. "Why?"

"Because I need an honest opinion. Most women on my arm

say what they think will make me happy, not what they actually mean."

"But I'm not on your arm, Mr. Stark." I let the words hang for a moment. Then I deliberately turn my back and walk away. I can feel him watching me, but I neither stop nor turn around. Slowly, I smile. I even add a little swing to my step. This is my moment of triumph and I intend to savor it.

Except victory isn't as delicious as I expected. In fact, it's a little bitter. Because secretly—oh, so secretly—I can't help but wonder what it would be like to be the girl on Damien Stark's arm.

FOUR

I cross the entire room before I pause, my heart pounding wildly in my chest. Fifty-five steps. I counted every one of them, and now that there's no place left to go I am simply standing still, staring at one of Blaine's paintings. Another nude, this one lying on her side across a stark white bed, only the foreground in focus. The rest of the room—walls, furniture—are nothing more than the blurred gray suggestions of shapes.

The woman's skin is pale, as if she's never seen the sun. But her face suggests otherwise. It reflects so much ecstasy that it seems to glow.

There is only one splash of color on the entire canvas—a long red ribbon. It is tied loosely around the woman's neck, then extends between her heavy breasts to trail down even farther. It slides between her legs, then continues, the image fading into the background before meeting the edge of the canvas. There's a tautness to the ribbon, though, and it's clear what story the artist is telling; her lover is there, just off the canvas, and he's holding the ribbon, making it slide over her, making her writhe against it in a desperate need to find the pleasure that he's teasing her with.

I swallow, imagining the sensation of that cool, smooth satin stroking me between my legs. Making me hot, making me come...

And in my fantasy, it's Damien Stark who is holding that ribbon.

This is not good.

I ease away from the painting toward the bar, which is the only place in the entire room where I'm not bombarded by erotic imagery. Honestly, I need the break. Erotic art doesn't usually make me melt. Except, of course, it's not the art that's making me hot.

I do, however, want you.

What had he meant by that?

More to the point, what do I want him to mean by that? Which, of course, is a bullshit question. I know what I want. The same thing I wanted six years ago. I also know it will never happen. And even the fantasy is a very bad idea.

I scan the room, telling myself I'm only looking over the art. Apparently this is my night for self-deception. I'm looking for Stark, but when I find him, I wish that I hadn't bothered. He's standing next to a tall, lithe woman with short dark hair. She looks like Audrey Hepburn in Sabrina, vibrant and beautiful. Her small features are alight with pleasure, and as she laughs she reaches out and touches him in a casual, intimate gesture. My stomach hurts just watching them. Good God, I don't even know this man. Can I really be jealous?

I consider the possibility, and in the spirit of tonight's theme, I deceive myself once more. Not jealousy—anger. I'm pissed that Stark could so cavalierly flirt with me even though he's obviously enthralled by another woman—a beautiful, charming, radiant woman.

"More champagne?" The bartender holds out a flute.

Tempting. Very tempting, but I shake my head. I don't need to get drunk. I need to get out of here.

More guests arrive, and the room overflows with people. I look for Stark again, but he has disappeared into the crowd. Audrey Hepburn is nowhere in sight, either. I'm sure wherever they are, they're having a dandy time.

I sandwich myself between a wall and a hallway cordoned off with a velvet rope. Presumably it leads to the rest of Evelyn's house. Right now, it's the closest thing to privacy I have.

I take out my phone, hit speed dial, and wait for Jamie to answer.

"You will so not believe this," she says, skipping all the preliminaries. "I just did the nasty with Douglas."

"Oh my God, Jamie. Why?" Okay, that came out before I had the chance to think about it, and while this revelation about Douglas is not good news, I'm grateful to be dragged so forcefully into Jamie's problems. Mine can wait.

Douglas is our next-door neighbor, and his bedroom shares a wall with mine. Even though it's only been four days, I have a pretty good idea of how often he gets laid. The idea that my best friend is another ticky mark on his bedpost does not thrill me.

Of course, from Jamie's perspective, he's a mark on her bedpost.

"We were by the pool drinking wine, and then we got in the hot tub and then..." She trails off, leaving "and then" to my imagination.

"He's still there? Or are you at his place?"

"God, no. I sent him home an hour ago."

"Jamie..."

"What? I just needed to burn some energy. Trust me, it's good. I'm so mellow now you wouldn't even believe."

I frown. Like a girl who collects stray puppies, Jamie brings home a lot of men. She doesn't, however, keep them around.

Not even until morning. As her roommate, I find that conve-
nient. There's nothing quite like meeting an unshaved, unshow-
ered, half-naked man staring into your refrigerator at three in
the morning. As her friend, however, I worry.

She, in turn, worries about me for precisely the opposite
reason. I've never brought a man home, much less kicked him
out. As far as Jamie is concerned, that makes me subnormal.

This, however, isn't the time to get into it with my best
friend. But Douglas? She had to go and pick Douglas? "Am I
going to have to avert my eyes every time I see him in the
complex?"

"He's cool," she says. "No big deal."

I close my eyes and shake my head. The mere thought of
being naked like that—emotionally and physically—overwhelms
me. Not a big deal? The hell it's not.

"How about you? Did you actually manage to form words
this time?"

I scowl. As my best friend since forever, Jamie knows a few
too many of my secrets. I'd told her all about my ambiguous
encounter with uber-hottie Damien Stark at the pageant reception. Her reaction had been typical Jamie—if I'd just opened my
mouth and formed actual words, he would have ditched
Carmela and had his way with me. I'd told her she was insane,
but her words had been like tinder to my smoldering fantasy.

"I talked to him," I admit now.

"Oh, really?" Her voice rises with interest.

"And he's coming to the presentation."

"And...?"

I have to laugh. "That's it, Jamie. That was the point."

"Oh. Well, okay, then. No, seriously, that's fabulous, Nik.
You totally rocked it."

When she puts it that way, I have to agree.

"So what's he like now?"

I consider the question. It's not an easy one to answer. "He's... intense." Hot. Sexy. Surprising. Disturbing. No, it's not Stark that's disturbing—it's my reaction to him.

"Intense?" Jamie parrots. "Like that's a revelation? I mean, the guy owns half the known universe. I hardly think he'd be all warm and fuzzy. More like dark and dangerous."

I frown. Somehow, Jamie has summed up Damien Stark perfectly.

"Anything else to report? How are the paintings? I won't ask if you've seen any celebrities. Any celebrity younger than Cary Grant, and you're clueless. I mean, you could probably trip over Bradley Cooper and not even know it."

"Actually, Rip and Lyle are here, and they're being civil to each other despite their feud. It'll be interesting to see if the show gets picked up for another season."

The silence at the other end of the line tells me I have scored big with that one, and I make a mental note to thank Evelyn. It's not easy to surprise my roommate.

"You bitch," she finally says. "If you don't come back with Rip Carrington's autograph, I am so finding a new best friend."

"I'll try," I promise. "Actually, you could come here. I kind of need a ride."

"Because Carl keeled over and died from surprise when Stark said he'd do the meeting?"

"Sort of. He left to go prep. The meeting's been bumped to tomorrow."

"And you're still at the party, why?"

"Stark wanted me to stay."

"Oh, did he?"

"It's not like that. He's looking to buy a painting. He wanted a female perspective."

"And since you're the only female at the party..."

I remember Audrey Hepburn and feel confused. I'm most

definitely not the only female at the party. So what is Stark's game?

"I just need a ride," I snap, unfairly taking my irritation out on Jamie. "Can you come get me?"

"You're serious? Carl left you stranded in Malibu? That's like an hour away. He didn't even offer to reimburse cab fare?"

I hesitate a fraction of a second too long.

"What?" she demands.

"It's just that—well, Stark said he'd make sure I got home."

"And what? His Ferrari's not good enough for you? You'd rather ride in my ten-year-old Corolla?"

She has a point. It's Stark's fault I'm still here. Why should I inconvenience one of my friends—or fork over a buttload of money for cab fare—when he already said he'd get me home? Am I really that nervous about being alone with him?

Yes, actually, I am. Which is ridiculous. Elizabeth Fairchild's daughter does not get nervous around men. Elizabeth Fairchild's daughter wraps men around her little finger. I may have spent my whole life trying to escape from under my mother's thumb, but that doesn't mean she didn't manage to drill her lessons in deep.

"You're right," I say, even though the idea of Damien Stark wrapped around any woman's finger remains a little fuzzy. "I'll see you at home."

"If I'm asleep, wake me up. I want to hear everything."

"There's nothing to tell," I say.

"Liar," she chides, then clicks off.

I slide my phone into my purse and head back to the bar—now I want that champagne. I stand there holding my glass as I glance around the room. This time, I see Stark right away. Him and Audrey Hepburn. He's smiling, she's laughing, and I'm working myself up into quite a temper. I mean, he's the reason I'm stranded here, and yet he hasn't made any effort to speak to me again, to apologize for the whole "be my decorating wench" fiasco, or to arrange a ride for me. If I have to call a cab I am absolutely going to send a bill to Stark International.

Evelyn passes by, arm in arm with a man with hair so white he reminds me of Colonel Sanders. She pats him on the arm, murmurs something, then disengages herself. The colonel marches on as Evelyn eases up next to me. "Having a nice time?"

"Of course," I say.

She snorts.

"I know," I say. "I'm a terrible liar."

"Hell, honey, you weren't even putting any effort into that one."

"I'm sorry. I'm just..." I trail off and tuck a loose strand of hair behind my ear. I'd curled it and pinned it up in a chignon. A few loose curls are supposed to hang free and frame my face. Right now, the damn thing is just annoying me.

"He's inscrutable," Evelyn says.

"Who?"

She nods toward Damien, and I look in that direction. He's still talking with Audrey Hepburn, but I'm struck by the certainty that he had been watching me only moments earlier. I have nothing to base that on, though, and I'm frustrated, not knowing if the thought is wishful thinking or paranoia.

"Inscrutable?" I repeat.

"He's a hard man to figure out," Evelyn says. "I've known him since he was a boy—his father signed me to represent him when some damn breakfast cereal wanted his face on their television spots. As if Damien Stark with a sugar high was the way we wanted to go. No, I landed the boy some damn good endorsements, helped make him a goddamned household name. But most days I don't think I know him at all."

"Why not?"

"I told you, Texas. Inscrutable." She draws out each syllable, then punctuates the word with a shake of her head. " 'Course I don't fault him, not with the shit that was piled onto that poor kid. Who wouldn't end up a little bit damaged?"

"You mean the fame? That must have been hard. He was so young." Stark won the Junior Grand Slam at fifteen, and that had pushed him into the stratosphere. But the press had latched onto him long before that. With his good looks and working-class background, he'd been plucked out of the flurry of hope-fuls as the tennis circuit's golden boy.

"No, no." Evelyn waves her hand as if dismissing the thought. "Damien knows how to handle the press. He's damn good at protecting his secrets, always has been." She eyes me, then laughs, as if to suggest she was only joking. But I don't think so. "Oh, honey, listen to me ramble. No, Damien Stark is just one of those dark, quiet types. He's like an iceberg, Texas. The deep parts are well hidden and what you do see is hard and a little bit cold."

She chuckles, amused at her own joke, then waves at someone who's caught her attention. I glance toward Damien, looking for evidence of the wounded child that Evelyn has recalled, but all I see is unerring strength and self-confidence. Am I seeing a mask? Or am I really looking at the man?

"What I'm trying to say," Evelyn continues, "is that you shouldn't take it personally. The way he acted, I mean. I doubt he meant to be rude. He was probably just off in his head and didn't even realize what he was doing."

I, of course, have moved past the snub at our meeting, but Evelyn doesn't realize that. My current issues with Damien Stark are wide and varied—ranging from the simple problem of a ride home to more complicated emotions that I'm not inclined to analyze.

"You were right about Rip and Lyle," I say, because she

keeps looking in Stark's direction, and I want to head off any suggestion that we edge our way into that conversation. "My roommate is in awe that I'm in the same room with them."

"Well, come on, then. I'll introduce you."

The two stars—both polished and shined within an inch of their lives—are perfectly polite and perfectly dull. I have nothing to say to them. I don't even know what their show is about. Evelyn can't seem to wrap her head around the possibility that anyone could either not care or not know about all things Hollywood. She seems to think I'm merely being coy and is about to leave me alone with these two.

Social Nikki would smile and make polite small talk. But Social Nikki is getting a bit frayed around the edges, and instead, I reach out, snagging a bit of Evelyn's sleeve before she escapes too far. She looks back at me, her brows raised in question. I have nothing to say. Panic bubbles in me; Social Nikki has completely left the building.

And then I see it—my excuse. My salvation. It's so unexpected—so completely out of place—that I half wonder if I'm not hallucinating. "That man," I say, pointing to a skinny twenty-something with long, wavy hair and wire-framed glasses. He looks like he belongs at Woodstock, not an art show, and I hold my breath, expecting the apparition to vanish. "Is that Orlando McKee?"

"You know Orlando?" she asks, then answers her own question. "Of course. The friend who works for Charles. But where did you two meet?" She nods goodbye to Lyle and Rip, who could care less about our departure; they're back to arguing between themselves and smiling brightly at the women who sidle in close for a snapshot.

"We grew up together," I explain as Evelyn steers me through the throng.

The truth is our families lived next door to each other until

Ollie went off to college, and even though he's two years older than me, we were inseparable until Ollie turned twelve and was shipped off to boarding school in Austin. I had been beside myself with envy.

I haven't seen Ollie for years, but he's the kind of friend that you don't need to talk to every day. Months can go by, and then he'll call me out of the blue, and we pick up the conversation like it had never stopped. He and Jamie are my closest friends in the world and I am beyond giddy that he's here, right when I need him so desperately.

We're close now, but he hasn't noticed us. He's talking about some television show with another guy, this one in jeans and a sport coat over a pale pink button-down. Very California. Ollie's hands are moving, because that's the way he talks, and when he flails one hand my direction, he glances that way out of reflex. I see the moment that realization hits him. He freezes, his hand drops, and he turns to face me, his arms going out wide.

"Nikki? My God, you look amazing." He pulls me into a tight Ollie hug, then pushes me back, his hands on my shoulders as he looks me up and down.

"Do I pass inspection?"

"When have you not?"

"Why aren't you in New York?"

"The firm transferred me back last week. I was going to call you this weekend. I couldn't remember when you were moving out here." He pulls me into another spontaneous hug, and I'm grinning so wide my mouth is starting to hurt. "Damn, it's good to see you."

"I take it you two know each other," the guy in jeans says drolly.

"Sorry," Ollie says. "Nikki, this is Jeff. We work together at Bender, Twain & McGuire."

"What he means is that I work for him," Jeff says. "I'm a

summer associate. Orlando is a third year now, and they love him there. I think Maynard's about ready to make him a partner."

"Very funny," Ollie says, but he looks pleased.

"Look at you," I say. "My little guppy's grown into a full-fledged shark."

"Ah-ah. You know the rules. For every lawyer joke you make, I get to make two dumb blonde jokes."

"I take it back."

"Come on, Jeff," Evelyn says. "Let's let these two catch up. We'll go find our own trouble to get into."

It would be polite to tell them not to bother, but neither one of us does. We're too wrapped up in reminiscing, and I'm too happy to have Ollie beside me.

We talk about everything and nothing as we head for the door, taking our conversation outside by silent agreement. I'm completely absorbed, warmed by memories and Ollie's familiar face. But as we reach the door, I turn back and look at the room. I'm not sure why I do. Maybe it's just a reflex, but I think it's something more. I think I'm looking for someone. For him.

Sure enough, my eyes find Damien Stark right away. He's no longer with Audrey Hepburn. Now he's talking with a short, balding man. He's focused and attentive. But his head lifts and his eyes find me.

And in that singular moment, I know that if he asked me to blow off my friend and stay in the room with him, I would do it.

Damn him, and damn me, but I would stay with Damien Stark.

Grab Your Copy Now
books2read.com/JK-RM

ALSO BY J. KENNER

For all of JK's Stark World and other titles,
please visit www.jkenner.com

The Stark Saga

He'd pay any price to have her...

release me

claim me

complete me

take me (novella)

have me (novella)

play my game (novella)

seduce me (novella)

unwrap me (novella)

deepest kiss (novella)

entice me (novella)

anchor me

hold me (novella)

please me (novella)

lost with me

damien

indulge me (novella)

delight me (novella & bonus content)

cherish me (novella)

embrace me (novella)

enchant me

interview with the billionaire

The Fallen Saint Series

His touch is her sin. Her love is his salvation

My Fallen Saint

My Beautiful Sin

My Cruel Salvation

Sinner's Game

Charismatic. Dangerous. Sexy as hell.
Meet the elite team of Stark Security.

Shattered With You

Shadows Of You

(free prequel to Broken With You)

Broken With You

Ruined With You

Wrecked With You

Destroyed With You

Memories of You

Ravaged With You

Hidden With You

Charmed By You

Tangled With You

Entwined With You

Craved By You

The Steele Books/Stark International:

He was the only man who made her feel alive.

Say My Name

On My Knees

Under My Skin

Take My Dare (includes short story Steal My Heart)

Stark International Novellas:

Meet Jamie & Ryan-so hot it sizzles.

Tame Me

Tempt Me

Tease Me

Touch Me

S.I.N. Trilogy:

It was wrong for them to be together...

...but harder to stay apart.

Dirtiest Secret

Hottest Mess

Sweetest Taboo

Most Wanted:

Three powerful, dangerous men.

Three sensual, seductive women.

Wanted

Heated

Ignited

Man of the Month

Who's your man of the month...?

Down On Me

Hold On Tight

Need You Now

Start Me Up

Get It On

In Your Eyes

Turn Me On

Shake It Up

All Night Long

In Too Deep

Light My Fire

Walk The Line

Royal Cocktail (bonus book)

*Bar Bites: A Man of the Month Cookbook(by J. Kenner & Suzanne M. Johnson)

Blackwell-Lyon:

Heat, humor & a hint of danger

Lovely Little Liar

Pretty Little Player

Sexy Little Sinner

Tempting Little Tease

Rising Storm:

Writing as Julie Kenner

Small town drama

Rising Storm: Tempest Rising

Rising Storm: Quiet Storm

PARANORMAL

Demon Hunting Soccer Mom

Like Buffy... grown up!

Paranormal women's fiction

Carpe Demon

California Demon

Demons Are Forever

Deja Demon

The Demon You Know (short story)

Demon Ex Machina

Pax Demonica

Day of the Demon

How To Train Your Demon

The Dark Pleasures Series:

Billionaire immortal romance

Caress of Darkness

Find Me In Darkness

Find Me In Pleasure

Find Me In Passion

Caress of Pleasure

ABOUT THE AUTHOR

J. Kenner (aka Julie Kenner) is the *New York Times, USA Today, Publishers Weekly, Wall Street Journal* and #1 International bestselling author of over one hundred novels, novellas and short stories in a variety of genres.

JK has been praised by *Publishers Weekly* as an author with a "flair for dialogue and eccentric characterizations" and by *RT Bookclub* for having "cornered the market on sinfully attractive, dominant antiheroes and the women who swoon for them." A five-time finalist for Romance Writers of America's prestigious RITA award, JK took home the first RITA trophy awarded in the category of erotic romance in 2014 for her novel, *Claim Me* (book 2 of her Stark Trilogy) and the RITA trophy for *Wicked Dirty* in the same category in 2017.

In her previous career as an attorney, JK worked as a lawyer in Southern California and Texas. She currently lives in Central Texas, with her husband, two daughters, and two rather spastic cats.

Stay in touch! Text JKenner to 21000 to subscribe to JK's text alerts.

www.jkenner.com

www.ingramcontent.com/pod-product-compliance
Lightning Source LLC
Chambersburg PA
CBHW050514110726
47899CB00005B/1449